SWEET
MAGIC

Connie Shelton

Books by Connie Shelton
THE CHARLIE PARKER MYSTERY SERIES
Deadly Gamble
Vacations Can Be Murder
Partnerships Can Be Murder
Small Towns Can Be Murder
Memories Can Be Murder
Honeymoons Can Be Murder
Reunions Can Be Murder
Competition Can Be Murder
Balloons Can Be Murder
Obsessions Can Be Murder
Gossip Can Be Murder
Stardom Can Be Murder
Phantoms Can Be Murder
Buried Secrets Can Be Murder
Legends Can Be Murder
Weddings Can Be Murder
Alibis Can Be Murder
Escapes Can Be Murder
Holidays Can Be Murder - a Christmas novella

THE SAMANTHA SWEET SERIES

Sweet Masterpiece   *Sweets Begorra*
Sweet's Sweets   *Sweet Payback*
Sweet Holidays   *Sweet Somethings*
Sweet Hearts   *Sweets Forgotten*
Bitter Sweet   *Spooky Sweet*
Sweets Galore   *Sticky Sweet*
            Sweet Magic

Spellbound Sweets - a Halloween novella
The Woodcarver's Secret

THE HEIST LADIES SERIES
Diamonds Aren't Forever
The Trophy Wife Exchange
Movie Mogul Mama

CHILDREN'S BOOKS
Daisy and Maisie and the Great Lizard Hunt
Daisy and Maisie and the Lost Kitten

SWEET MAGIC

Samantha Sweet Mysteries, Book 13

Connie Shelton

Secret Staircase Books

Sweet Magic
Published by Secret Staircase Books, an imprint of
Columbine Publishing Group, LLC
PO Box 416, Angel Fire, NM 87710

Book layout and design by Secret Staircase Books
Cover images © Makeitdoubleplz, Unholyvault, RKasprzak, and
Andrey Anischenko

First trade paperback edition: September, 2019
First e-book edition: September, 2019

* * *
Publisher's Cataloging-in-Publication Data

Shelton, Connie
Sweet Magic / by Connie Shelton.
p. cm.
ISBN 978-1945422751 (paperback)
ISBN 978-1945422768 (e-book)

1. Samantha Sweet (Fictitious character)—Fiction. 2. Taos, New
Mexico—Fiction. 3. Paranormal artifacts—Fiction. 4. Bakery—Fiction. 5.
Women sleuths—Fiction. 6. Chocolate making—Fiction. I. Title

Samantha Sweet Mystery Series : Book 13.
Shelton, Connie, Samantha Sweet mysteries.

BISAC : FICTION / Mystery & Detective.
813/.54

For Dan, Daisy and Missy—my pack

My fantastic editing team—Susan Slater, Shirley Shaw, and Stephanie Dewey—each of you has suggested things that help me see something new in my writing. Beta readers Christine, Judi, Sandra—you ladies are so good at this!

And especially to you, my readers—I cherish our connection through these stories.
Thank you, everyone!

"The world is full of magic things,
patiently waiting for our senses to grow sharper."
—W. B. Yeats

Chapter 1

The bride looked lovely in her white gown, a simple sheath which barely touched the toes of her hiking boots. Kelly Sweet lifted her skirt thigh high to keep it from grazing the carpet of pine needles on the pathway.

"Mom, do you have the day pack with my sandals and makeup?"

Samantha puffed a little at the 9,000-foot altitude, taking an extra deep breath before she answered. "Don't worry about it. Zoë has it and she's five minutes behind us."

"Did I remember to put my hair clips in it?"

"I'm sure you did, Kel. Got my hands a little full at the moment." Sam instantly regretted her abrupt tone, even though toting a two-tier cake up a trail frazzled her nerves a bit. She felt sure this wasn't what the Forest Service had in mind when they rated this trail 'easy.'

With the wedding taking place at a lovely but remote mountain clearing, her bakery sales off the charts this month, and her biggest client showing up yesterday with a complicated new contract she'd not had a moment to study, she'd awakened this morning with a somewhat short fuse. Her husband, Sheriff Beau Cardwell, had, of course, received an emergency call at five a.m. but he'd assured Sam he would be at Pine Ridge Point in plenty of time for the noon ceremony.

Kelly and Scott had reserved the picnic area weeks ago and even persuaded a couple of their friends to spend the night up here to be sure no one else encroached. Kelly wanted to arrive early to ensure her veil was in place, her makeup perfect, and her wild cinnamon-colored curls somewhat tamed. Her large cast of friends was here to be sure the flower-covered arch was in place, the cake and serving pieces set up, and the clearing was reasonably free of elk droppings. This last request was never a certainty anywhere in the forest.

The walk from the parking area wasn't long, scarcely over a quarter mile, but the idyllic setting would make people believe they were miles from any form of civilization. Guests had been charged with bringing their own folding chairs, and an assortment of small tables had been carted up the day before. Attire was informal for everyone but the bride and groom—Kelly had insisted they go traditional white for her and a tux for Scott. Her professor fiancé normally sported jeans, a turtleneck, and blazer but he was so obviously head-over-heels for Kelly that he willingly went along with all her suggestions for the wedding ceremony and reception.

Sam spotted the scenic clearing ahead and breathed a sigh of relief. The young couple's friends had been hard at work, and the setting was gorgeous. Tall, fragrant Ponderosa pines and a scattering of white-trunked aspens ringed a grassy clearing (mercifully free of animal evidence). The willow arch had been placed where the couple would stand and was now intertwined with bold yellow and purple wildflowers. A table was ready for the cake and Sam headed there immediately.

Riki Davis-Jones, Kelly's best friend and her employer, was waiting to lend a hand and together they removed the cake from its protective box.

"Funny, they don't seem to weigh this much when I carry them from the bakery kitchen out to my delivery van," Sam said with a chuckle.

"You should have asked Evan or one of the others to carry it," Riki said. "You *know* anyone would have been happy to assist."

"Evan and Beau both offered but I wasn't sure how soon they'd get here," Sam told her. "I'm such a mother hen about my cakes, especially the one for my own daughter's wedding. Can you imagine if it had gotten messed up?"

Riki rolled her eyes. "Oh—hell to pay, pure hell."

"As it is, I brought my emergency kit." Sam slipped the small pack off her shoulders and unzipped it to reveal an ice pack, a plastic box with several extra buttercream flowers, and a pastry bag filled with icing to match the cake's soft ivory coating. She automatically went into critique mode, checking the cake from all angles, piping a couple of the tiny frosting pin-dots that had been smashed.

Riki spotted her fiancé, Deputy Evan Richards, coming up the trail along with Beau and two others from their office, and headed toward them. The morning's emergency must have been resolved, Sam thought with delight. No matter how strongly a law enforcement man assures you he'll be there, she'd learned not to count on it until she actually saw him. She stowed her decorating supplies and set the pack in a cool spot under the table.

Behind a temporary canvas screen—partially a place to hide the park's latrines, and today a spot from which the bride could make her entrance—Sam saw Kelly fidgeting. She had spread a blanket to stand on after removing her hiking boots, and now she was nervously glancing toward the trail.

Luckily, Sam's best friend Zoë appeared nearly at the same moment. She had slung the bag of accessories and beauty products Kelly wanted over her shoulder, freeing her hands to grip a plastic crate of catering supplies. Weighing in at a solid one-hundred pounds, Zoë never asked her recruits—in this case her husband Darryl, plus Beau and all his deputies—to carry anything she wouldn't tackle herself. Bless her, Sam thought, coming all the way up here to do the reception food. She would have never let Kelly ask it of her friend; the reception could have taken place back in town at Zoë and Darryl's B&B. But Zoë had volunteered and, in fact, seemed excited about the beautiful setting and the gathering of close friends. Even now, under a load, a bright smile lit her face when she spotted Sam and Kelly.

Zoë handed off the plastic crate and shed the tote bag so Kelly could finish getting ready. Sam was amazed to see how, with a few quick orders, Zoë quickly had the covered trays of hot barbequed beef, corn on the cob, potato salad, and coleslaw delivered and arranged on the serving table. A massive plastic container of watermelon wedges sat at the end and, of course, there would be wedding cake for dessert.

The minister from Zoë's church, a rather informal

group of hippies and mountain men who espoused a curious mixture of the Ten Commandments, Eastern philosophy and flower-child worship practices, arrived right on time. Her long hair sported many rows of tiny braids with flower stems interwoven. She raised her face to the sky and declared this to be the perfect day for a wedding.

At that, everyone began to notice the groom didn't seem to be anywhere in sight. From her makeshift 'dressing room' Kelly peered around the corner. About the time Sam began to feel a flutter of anxiety, she heard voices from below. Coming up the trail was her client, Stan Bookman, owner of Book It Travel, accompanied by Scott Porter.

How those two had timed it to arrive together, Sam had no idea—probably coincidence. Scott's gaze darted around, looking for Kelly, while Bookman headed straight for Sam.

"Any chance to look at the new contract yet?" he asked, after the merest of greetings.

"It's been a little busy, Stan," she said, really trying not to let her feelings of impatience creep into her voice. "I'm taking tomorrow to stay home and catch up on things, once the kids are away on their honeymoon."

"Oh? Where are they going?" he asked. "Someplace exciting? I hear Scott's a history professor. Not taking her off to an archaeological dig or anything is he?"

Sam laughed. "Oh, no. Nothing like that. They're going very informal with it—as you can tell by the wedding, it's their style. Just a drive up through the Rockies—Colorado, Wyoming. He's got several weeks off from the university so they'll take their time."

A thoughtful look crossed Stan's face and it seemed

he was about to say something, but the minister—Lily Fairchild was her name—called them all to take their seats. One of Scott's students, an accomplished guitarist, struck the opening chords of Pachelbel's *Canon in D major*, and the group quickly settled and became quiet. Sam immediately looked for Beau and steered him to the only two empty seats near the front. She really didn't want to sit near Stan Bookman and have him start talking business. The man never seemed to take a break from it.

Scott stood at the front with Lily, looking so handsome in his tux with his beard neatly trimmed and sandy brown hair mussed just the way Kelly liked it. When the music transitioned into the wedding march and Kelly stepped forward onto the impromptu aisle the chairs had formed, his eyes glowed with love for her. Sam felt her throat tighten with emotion. Beau gently took her hand.

With a minimum of formality but heartfelt words about love and partnerships, Lily read some beautiful poems from Rumi. Behind her, Sam could hear Zoë sniffing discreetly, while across the way tears were flowing down Riki's cheeks, although she had a smile on her face. Kelly and Scott read beautiful vows they'd each written—Sam had no idea her daughter had such a way with prose—exchanged rings, and were pronounced married. Cameras snapped and Sam hastily dabbed her eyes with a tissue.

The newlyweds walked among their friends, beaming hugely. Sam saw Zoë and her kitchen helper rush to the food tables to check the Sterno heat under the serving pans. Somewhere in the background several champagne corks popped.

"Introduce me to your daughter," Stan Bookman said, appearing at Sam's elbow. "I have a little gift for them."

"Um, okay." She was surprised he'd come to the ceremony, despite the fact that she had invited him when he showed up unannounced at her bakery yesterday. But a gift? She started to tell him it wasn't necessary, but his attention had wandered to the group standing around Kelly and Scott.

They held back a couple of minutes until the bridal couple was nearly alone, then Bookman approached and Sam introduced him. "I understand, from our little walk up the hill here, that your new husband is a history buff," he said.

"It's way more than a passing interest," Kelly said with a laugh. "He teaches by day and haunts the library and internet by night."

"I hope you don't think it presumptuous of me," Bookman said, "and feel free to say no if this interferes with your existing plans …"

What was he getting at? Sam wondered.

"Your mother may have told you that we fly private charters all over the world, and well … I'm taking off tomorrow morning for England. If you'd be interested, and if it's possible to change your existing plans, I can offer you a visit to a town with a fascinating history."

Kelly looked puzzled. Scott's attention seemed riveted. Sam wondered what Bookman was up to.

"I'd planned some time in this little Suffolk town called Bury St. Edmunds, and now it turns out I won't be able to stay. My wife and daughter were to join me but their plans have also changed, and the house will go unused. I need to be there two days, at most, to transact a little business with a local travel agency, but after that …"

Scott piped up. "Bury St. Edmunds? The town where

Mary Tudor was buried? My lord! I've heard of the abbey and the old ruins …" He turned to Kelly. "Honey, this is a place I've always been fascinated with. Would you—?"

"Give up a drive through Colorado to go there? Absolutely!" Her eyes were alight now too.

"Can we get tickets on such short notice?" Scott asked, wondering aloud.

"Oh, sorry, I didn't make myself clear enough," said Stan with a twinkle in his eye. "I'm offering to have you ride along with me on one of our private corporate jets. We'll fly into London and my driver will take us up. It's a couple of hours northeast of London. Near Cambridge— you might enjoy that as a side trip during your stay. I can leave the car and driver at your disposal."

"Are you sure? This sounds like a very expensive—" Kelly's fingers were mangling the stems of her bouquet.

"The only part that costs me a thing out of pocket will be the nights I'll book for you at the Angel Hotel, and that's a very minimal—"

"The Angel Hotel! Charles Dickens stayed there," Scott inserted.

"The very same. I'll put you up there for the couple of nights I need to stay in town, then the house is all yours. Stay as long as you like, and one of our planes will certainly be able to bring you back."

"I—wow—I'm not sure what to say," Kelly stammered.

"Say yes," Bookman said. "One or two phone calls from my end will get it arranged."

"And I can easily cancel our first night's reservation in Durango," Scott said. His face reminded Sam of the little kid who'd just thought of a way to scrounge a penny for the gumball machine.

Kelly smiled at her husband's enthusiasm. "You're right, we only reserved one night. The rest of the trip was going to be purely impromptu." She turned to face Bookman. "So, yes. The answer's yes!"

Scott reached out and shook their benefactor's hand enthusiastically. "Sir—thank you! This is the best gift ever."

Sam watched with mixed feelings. She was happy for the fantastic windfall trip Kelly and Scott had received, but Bookman's rich-man way of pushing his agenda through reminded her a little too vividly of her own experiences with him. It might be wise for her to get a private word with her daughter before it was too late.

Chapter 2

Sam never did figure out a way to handle the 'private word' with Kelly. The rest of the afternoon mountain reception had gone by in a blur of friends and food, while music played from someone's portable speakers. Stan Bookman was the picture of generosity as he saw how happy his gift had made the couple, and Sam couldn't bring herself to rain on Kelly's bubbly cheer as their friends danced in the grassy clearing.

When a late-afternoon thunderstorm began to build, everyone grabbed decorations, leftovers, and utensils and headed for their cars. The newlyweds had been deliberately secretive about where they would spend their wedding night, hoping to avoid pranks by their friends and students. Sam could only give Kelly a quick hug as the first raindrops began to fall and assure her daughter that she and Beau would drive them to the Taos airport to see them off on their adventure in the morning. Kelly had suggested breakfast together, the four of them—a little time together before the big trip.

Now, the young couple were grinning as they watched their private jet taxi to a stop. Stan Bookman arrived at the same moment in a black Suburban with darkened windows. He and his driver each opened one of the back doors and out stepped a couple wearing expensive ripped jeans and pricey leather jackets which had been buffed to shabby perfection.

"Oh my god, do you know who that is?" Kelly whispered to her mother.

Sam shook her head. She still didn't know, even after Kelly gave their names. A pop singer and her tennis pro husband. They walked across the tarmac and up the steps to the plane.

Stan walked over, beaming at Sam. "Now don't forget to get that contract back to my office. I'll be back there on Thursday, and we'll set up some meetings with the cruise line food management."

She nodded.

"Kelly and Scott, I hope you don't mind the extra passengers. They made a last-minute itinerary change—something we deal with all the time in the travel industry. Koko said they're exhausted and will probably do nothing but sleep during the flight. Shouldn't affect your plans at all."

Kelly did her best to act as if rubbing elbows with stars happened all the time. She had, after all, once bathed two of Julia Roberts's dogs.

A fuel truck had pulled alongside the jet and now appeared to be finished. Two crew members had wheeled the luggage away.

"Well," said Stan, "I guess we're ready to be off." He headed for the steps, giving the others a moment to say goodbye.

Beau and Scott shook hands, but Kelly and Sam unabashedly held each other and choked back tears.

"You guys have a wonderful time, take lots of pictures, and be ready to tell us all about the place," Sam said, with a faint tinge of jealousy. She had loved her trip to Ireland and only wished she could visit England as well.

"Heck, we'll share it right away," Kelly told her. "Facetime works over there too."

Beau put his arm around Sam's shoulders as they watched the young couple board the plane. The steps retracted and immediately the pilot turned the aircraft to face the long runway.

"Well, there they go," he said. They had stepped into the shelter of the airport's tiny terminal building to avoid the blast of air from the jet engines.

"Hard to believe she's a married woman now," Sam said. "I suppose every mother says that. It wasn't too many years ago she showed up on my doorstep with no job and nowhere to live, and I didn't believe she would ever turn into a responsible adult."

"So there—it happened. They make a good pair. Like you and me." He bent to kiss her before they headed out to his SUV.

The summer day was rapidly becoming warmer, with clouds building over nearby Taos Mountain. The blue sage which covered so much of the high desert landscape on the outskirts of town gave off its distinctive herbal scent, and Sam noticed yellow sunflowers had already begun to bloom along the roadside. Autumn would be here in another six weeks.

"So, home or bakery or chocolate factory?" Beau asked as they made the turn.

"Home. I left Bookman's contract on the dining table and I need some peace and quiet to read and digest it. The thing looks formidable." Even as she said so, she realized she should also have her attorney read the document.

So far, all of her business dealings with Stan Bookman and Book It Travel had worked out well. In the couple of years she'd been supplying handmade chocolates for the passengers on his private charter service, she'd received high accolades. The volume of business had required a separate facility and more employees than she'd begun with at her downtown bakery, Sweet's Sweets, but the offset had been financially very lucrative.

A mile later, Beau turned onto the smaller county road that led to their ranch property, and within a minute they were entering the long driveway to the large log house where Beau had lived before they married. He swung the cruiser in a loop, delivering Sam right to the door. The dogs, Ranger and Nellie, raised their heads and their tails began to wag.

"I'll be at the office unless I get some fantastic break in this robbery case," he said. "Come by for lunch if you're finished by then."

"Let's play it by ear. It could take a couple hours to read this thing and make notes, then I'll probably want to run it over to Nancy Olgado's office."

"You seem a little stressed, darlin'," he said with a concerned look on his face. "Is it just the wedding, or does this new contract have you worried?"

She opened her door and shrugged. "Some of each, I guess. The wedding is over now, and once I get this new contract done, I'll relax." She leaned over and kissed him. "I miss helping you with your cases. Life has gotten too busy."

He caressed the side of her face. "Yes, it has. Let's plan a little trip or something just for the two of us."

She nodded, knowing it wouldn't happen right away. Summer, with the huge influx of tourists in Taos, was a busy time for the sheriff's office second only to winter when the weather played a big factor in traffic problems. This time of year it was a whole other set of crimes, such as this recent outbreak of robberies at several of the merchants on the Taos Plaza.

Their fingertips lingered together, another kiss, and he was on his way.

Sam tickled the border collie's ears as the dog rose to go inside with her. Ranger, the black Lab, stayed on the porch, watching Beau's cruiser leave. She deposited her bag on the sofa and headed for the kitchen to heat the kettle for tea. She needed comforting. Maybe Beau was right— her only daughter's marriage was a big step, even though Kelly had been on her own for more than ten years. No, it wasn't that.

The weariness that had settled over her recently was most likely due to Sam's overextending herself. She loved to stay busy, but this was something more, and the secret source of her energy didn't seem to be having the same effect these days.

While the kettle heated, she went upstairs and picked up the carved wooden box she'd left on her dresser. The antique piece had been given to her a few years ago when an old woman told her she was meant to have it. All Sam knew was that she'd experienced a reaction between herself and the box every time she'd handled it—until recently.

She cradled it in her arms and waited. The wood warmed slightly, and the dark color lightened a little. But five minutes later, when the tea kettle began to screech, the box still hadn't changed much. Was the artifact losing its power? Was she losing hers?

Just when she could have used some spare energy to deal with the new cruise line contract, it appeared her old standby wasn't going to provide it. She set the box aside and went downstairs where she brewed a cup of very strong tea and grabbed a cereal bar Beau had left months ago.

A caffeine and sugar boost was most certainly *not* what she needed, but it was handy at the moment. She carried them to the dining table in the great room and stared out the wide French doors at the open fields beyond. The thick contract waited. Finishing the cereal bar and taking a few sips of her tea, she began reading the first page. By page three, she felt herself nodding and realized she would need to have legal advice to interpret it.

This was a far more complex document than her previous agreements with Book It Travel. Although he had described the cruise line as a small company that ran boutique cruises to exotic places, the parent company behind it was mega-big and they wanted all sorts of assurances from their vendors. She'd picked up the phone, hoping to get an appointment with her lawyer on short notice, when the dogs began barking.

A glance toward the driveway showed that a white sedan had pulled up near the front door. A woman in her forties and a man who was probably a bit younger were getting out. When the woman turned to face the house, Sam recognized her.

Isobel St. Clair from The Vongraf Foundation. What on earth would the antiquities expert want here? Sam had a sinking feeling.

Chapter 3

S amantha. It's good to see you again." Isobel St. Clair
wore a deep plum dress that flattered her slender
frame, her green eyes, and shoulder-length dark hair. She
indicated the man with her, a twenty-something who wore
black jeans and T-shirt, his hair sticking out in the random
angles favored by his age group. "This is my assistant, Tony
Robards. May we come inside?"

It took Sam a long moment to shift mental gears, to get
her mind away from chocolates, cruise lines, and contracts
and remind herself of Isobel's position as head of the
world's leading institution that studied ancient artifacts,
especially those with unexplained powers. On the woman's
last visit to Taos she had delivered a warning, to save Sam
from some evil people who wanted to take the wooden
box. Sam would have believed the visit to be a prank,

except that Isobel provided the credentials, even spoke the correct words to let Sam know she was legitimate.

"What's this about?" Sam asked.

"I'd rather not discuss it out in the open. If we could just ..."

Sam stepped aside, mainly because neither of the dogs seemed overly concerned. Nellie had nudged Tony and the young man smiled easily as he offered his hand for a sniff of approval.

"Can I offer you some tea, a soda or something?" Sam asked, her inner hostess speaking up before she had the chance to think it through.

"Nothing, thanks. I'm afraid I have some rather frightening news."

Sam felt her muscles tense, her expression freeze in place. She ushered them to the sofa and chairs near the fireplace.

Isobel perched on the edge of a chair. Tony studied Beau's collection of arrowheads, framed in a shadowbox, on the mantel.

Sam tried to behave as if she was patiently waiting, but she couldn't maintain it. "What's going on?" she asked.

"Marcus Fitch is back." Isobel pulled a photo from her small shoulder bag and placed it on the coffee table. It showed a candid shot of a dark-haired man with blue eyes, sitting at an outdoor bistro table.

"Back—here in Taos?"

"Not yet, as far as we know, but he is definitely back in the US."

"I wasn't aware he'd left."

"Sam, please don't take this lightly." Isobel's expression was more pleading than scolding. We—The Vongraf

Foundation—enlisted the help of the CIA after the incident here."

"More than a year ago, isn't it?"

Isobel nodded. "He was tracked to Italy last winter, then to Vatican City. Apparently, OSM maintains its connections there and Fitch has enlisted some powerful help."

"I thought you told me this *Offici* ... the ... whatever OSM stands for ... I thought you told me they were a very powerful group. Why do they need help from the Vatican?"

"Let me backtrack a moment. We at The Vongraf have documented two carved boxes—one is yours, the other belonged to your uncle. Mr. O'Shaughnessy brought his to us for testing when he bought it in the late 1960s. Despite the fact that yours has small colored stones on it and his didn't, apparently the two boxes tested positive for the same types of powers."

Sam leaned back into the depths of her chair. "Uncle Terry was planning to tell me more about the box, there in his study in Ireland. He died before we had the conversation. I took the box with me, hoping to learn more, but it disappeared from our rental car. I had hardly turned my back on it ..."

"Some of our staff members have attempted to trace it, but with no luck. So, you've no idea where it is now?" Tony asked. Obviously, he was privy to at least some of the information about the carved boxes.

Sam looked back at Isobel, who shook her head. "However, the point of our visit now is not about the box missing from Ireland. We know there is a third box."

If Sam thought she'd heard all the surprises, this one took her breath away. "Three?"

"We believe it was hidden away deep in the Vatican archives for a very long time, possibly hundreds of years."

"You told me you had carbon dated mine to somewhere around the 12th century."

"Yes, and your uncle's, as well. If all three boxes were created by the same woodcarver, the third must be the same age. The carver had scratched names inside the lids. The one at the Vatican is called Facinor, which means 'evil'."

Sam digested this bit of information before she spoke. "That's a long time to keep something like this in hiding."

"The Church is a very old establishment," Isobel said with a wry grin. "It's entirely possible the box was there all this time."

"You said it *was* hidden. What has changed?"

Tony took a seat on the sofa, leaning forward with his elbows on his knees. He looked at Sam and spoke frankly. "Marcus Fitch. He has declared himself on a mission to get his hands on all three boxes."

"And you know this … how?" Sam asked.

"I've been in touch with the leader of OSM in Washington, a man called Elias Swift."

"I thought this was a super top-secret organization?"

"It is, but things have changed. Fitch appears to be acting on his own to some extent. Elias Swift is being very cagey about it."

Sam blew out the breath she realized she'd been holding. "What does any of this have to do with me?" *And why now? I've got my hands full with way too much already.*

"We only wanted to caution you. Watch for Fitch, but also keep an eye out for anyone prowling around—we don't know who else he might have enlisted as help."

Sam stood. "Would you like to take my box with you?

Maybe I'm not the person who should be responsible for such an artifact."

"Oh no, Sam. You are absolutely the right person to have it. The boxes have always come into the right hands at the right time in history. When Bertha Martinez gave it to you, it was meant to be."

Tony had followed Sam's lead, standing and moving toward the front door. The discussion was nearly finished, she sensed. Isobel rose from her chair and hitched her thin purse strap to her shoulder. Together, they walked out to the log home's covered porch and Isobel fished a car key from the purse.

"Please take great care, Sam," she said. "We've uncovered clues that the boxes are most powerful when together. If Fitch has managed to locate the one from Ireland, and we're fairly certain he has the one from the Vatican—well, he only needs yours to complete the trio. I hope you have been careful with it, making certain to keep it under lock and key—you might want to consider a safer place, a bank or somewhere."

Tony had taken the car key and unlocked the sedan. Isobel stepped toward the passenger side, pausing a moment to reach into her purse. At that moment a shot rang out.

Tony fell to the ground, a neat round hole in the center of his forehead.

Chapter 4

Quick! In the house!" Sam shouted, grabbing for Isobel's sleeve. Her heart was pounding louder than a boom-box as she shakily dialed Beau's cell phone. "Keep away from the windows," she told the other woman.

Isobel moved like a robot, stiff and compliant to Sam's directions. Her eyes never left the locked front door and the window beside it, where she could see Tony's body lying still and pale next to the rental car.

Sam quickly told Beau, in a few terse words, what had happened. He asked no questions. "I'm on my way. Stay indoors."

Five and a half minutes later, his cruiser roared up the drive with full lights and sirens. A short distance away, the sounds of more sirens surrounded the property. He'd made the fifteen-minute trip in record time. She took a deep breath, finally, and opened the front door a few inches.

Beau took one glance at the body on the ground and positioned himself behind his cruiser, gun drawn, while he surveyed the open fields, the barn, and the trees beyond. Sam had already scanned the property before he arrived, standing at the edge of one window then another, but seeing no movement.

"Did you see anyone moving out there?" he asked Sam after he'd holstered his service pistol and checked the body for a pulse.

She shook her head and Isobel did the same.

"Nothing. We were standing by the car. It happened instantaneously—one shot."

Isobel spoke up. "I wonder if I was the target. I'd dipped my head, looking at something in my purse, a split second before the bullet passed over the roof of the car and got Tony instead."

"It could have just as easily been me," Sam said. "Considering the things you just told me."

Beau stared at her.

"No—it's just too weird to think about. I mean, here in Taos?" Sam couldn't wrap her mind around the idea that some international killer would come here, would try to murder her.

"You can give me all the details later," Beau said. He was already pulling out his phone, giving orders to his dispatcher to bring a forensics team from Santa Fe and the medical investigator from Albuquerque.

Another cruiser came up the drive and Deputy Rico got out. "I drove the county road down to the point where it intersects 64. No sign of any vehicle but Hector Martinez in his old pickup. Waters was out near the Gorge Bridge so he set up a checkpoint. So far, he hasn't stopped anyone of interest."

"Damn. Well, we can't even make a guess as to what direction he took until we figure out where he fired the shot from." Beau stared toward the woods at the edge of his property. "There are a million places out there."

"But not that many where he could have quickly gotten to his vehicle to get away," Rico said.

Beau looked down at the body. "That was a precision shot, the kind a sniper makes," he murmured.

"He could've been lucky," Rico said. "Or maybe he was closer than we think. How about over by the barn?"

"We'll have to check the whole property. He would've had to park on the county road and walk in. There'll be evidence." He ordered Sam and Isobel to remain in the house to avoid adding footprints and messing up the ground.

Within an hour, more vehicles began to show up. Lisa, the department's local forensic technician, came first followed by Deputy Evan Richards. Someone from the Office of the Medical Investigator arrived soon after. Sam felt a pang of sorrow over the body of Tony Robards lying on the ground in the summer heat, although Evan had erected a hasty awning above.

There didn't seem to be any quick way to properly conduct a crime scene investigation, what with all the technology, chain of evidence, and special handling to pass muster in court. Long gone were the Old West days of throwing a blanket over the dead man and digging him a quick grave.

Sam watched the proceedings for a while but became restless. She couldn't see Beau or Rico and assumed they were circling the perimeter of their land in search of evidence. It was going to be a long day.

Isobel had settled on the sofa in the great room and was making calls, first to her office in Alexandria, Virginia, where she informed the office manager of Tony's death and asked him to withhold an announcement until she'd had time to call the next of kin, his parents. Isobel dropped her phone on the coffee table and rested her head in her hands.

"I don't know how to do this," she said when Sam passed through the room to stare out the French doors again. "He's their only son."

"Would you like Beau to make the call? It's the hardest part of his job, but at least he has some experience."

Isobel shook her head. "I should do it. I just need to decide if calling on the phone is all right, or if I should wait until I return to Virginia and pay them a visit. Either way, I dread it."

Sam patted her shoulder and made soothing noises. "I'm going to make a platter of sandwiches. The team will be here a long time and it's almost noon already. Want to help?"

"Sure." She gathered her hair into a low ponytail and reached into her purse for an elastic band.

Her fingers pulled out a business card. "I was going to give you this, Sam. It's Tony's—his contact information in case you couldn't reach me." Her face crumpled. "I was looking down when the bullet got him. This card probably saved my life." Tears flowed in streams down her face. "I can't … I …"

Her words were lost between sobs and she leaned into Sam's shoulder, accepting the embrace. Sam held her and patted her back, feeling completely at a loss for words of comfort.

The front door opened. "Ms. St. Clair? Could I ask—?" Beau paused until Isobel raised her head and wiped her eyes with her sleeve.

"Certainly. Sorry about this …" She waved a hand in front of her face.

Beau gave her a moment to compose herself. "Lisa and I have some questions, about the moment it happened. I'm sorry to put you through it, but the quicker we put together the events, the quicker we can start after the killer."

Isobel pulled a tissue from the box Sam kept on a nearby dresser, blew her nose delicately, took another tissue, then followed him out to the porch. Sam listened from the front door as he asked Isobel to recreate for him the exact positions where everyone had been at the time of the shot. Isobel approached the passenger side of the car. She mimicked ducking her head and showed exactly where Tony had been standing. Using a long dowel rod, Lisa indicated where the bullet had most likely come from—a stand of trees somewhat separated from the rest. The nearest spot to where the county road passed the north side of the property. It would have been less than fifty yards for the shooter to dash from the tree line back to his waiting vehicle.

Beau thanked Isobel and asked Rico to accompany him. He took a compass reading where Lisa indicated, and the two men set off across the pasture of green alfalfa, following a straight line toward the likely spot where the shooter had waited. Sam stared out in that direction, searching her memory for a clue but she couldn't remember seeing a vehicle or movement of a person. She'd been far too absorbed in the information Isobel and Tony had just shared with her.

Why? Why hadn't she been more observant? She might have saved his life.

A bleak feeling overtook her. This whole thing about the boxes and the two rival organizations had returned to haunt her.

She shook off the vision of the field and trees. Regret, she decided, would not serve any purpose. All she could do was move forward from right now, so she headed into the kitchen to finish her mission of feeding the crowd. Isobel wandered in and unwrapped packages of sliced ham and turkey. Little conversation passed between them. Sam knew Isobel was still wrapped up in thoughts of facing Tony's parents with the horrible news.

By the time she carried the platter outside, the OMI's vehicle had already left but Lisa and the deputies were more than ready for some lunch. They dug into the cooler of sodas Sam had brought home from the wedding—was it only yesterday?—and helped themselves to chips and sandwiches. They sat on the sturdy wooden chairs on the shady porch, talking about plans for bowling tonight, the small traveling carnival some were taking their kids to, anything but the crime that had happened way too close to home.

In the distance, Sam saw Beau and Rico studying the ground at the base of one particular tree. They didn't seem ready to come back to the house right away, so she covered the remaining sandwiches with plastic wrap.

Isobel looked up from her seat on the top porch step. "I was—well, Tony and I were—booked on a flight out of Albuquerque late this afternoon, Sam. If I leave here soon, I could still make it. Guess I'm feeling the pressure to get back and make the visit to his parents. I suppose I'd better clear it with Beau, though, before I take off?"

Sam set aside her plate and joined her. "Yeah, he'll need to know your plans. Are you sure you're okay to drive? Should someone go with you?" She was thinking of the fact that the killer was still out there. If it was Fitch himself, he was especially dangerous.

"I've thought about it. I'm going to turn in this rental car here in Taos and get another one—something of a different make, model and color. I'll be okay, and once I get to the airport in Albuquerque, I'll be surrounded by security."

"Do you think it was Marcus Fitch himself?"

"I don't have any idea. I don't know much about him, apart from OSM. And things have changed. I wouldn't put it past the organization to be behind this."

Sam would discuss it with Beau. To her way of thinking, it seemed this killer had the skills of a trained sniper.

"Isobel, I want you to take the box with you. Store it away someplace at The Vongraf Foundation where it won't put anyone else in danger."

The woman shook her head and strands of dark hair loosed themselves from her ponytail. "I can't do that, Sam. The foundation doesn't keep artifacts you know that. Our mission is only to—"

"Study them. I know. But this has gotten bigger than all of us. I don't know what to do."

"The law will take care of Marcus Fitch, especially now that he's become violent. You should remember back to your original purpose when the box came into your hands. Bertha Martinez wanted you to take it and use it for good, to help people."

And she *had* been doing that, Sam realized. Helping

Beau to solve crimes, helping people with illnesses and injuries. She felt her resolve weaken, to be rid of the box. But she didn't remind Isobel that Fitch had already been violent in the past, when he ran her car off the road during her last visit to Taos, and the law hadn't been able to catch him then. Would they get him this time?

She walked with Isobel back into the house. While the visitor gathered her belongings, Sam called Beau's cell and made certain it was all right for Isobel to leave. He told Sam to be sure he had contact information but okayed the trip. Sam wrote down several numbers for Isobel and saw her out to the rental car.

Tony's suitcase lay on the back seat, another reminder of the sad nature of the trip and a heartbreaking thing to take back to his parents at home. Sam didn't envy Isobel the task.

Chapter 5

Marcus Fitch strode past the signs pointing to the baggage claim area in Reagan National. He prided himself on traveling light, leaving nonessentials behind. Even on international flights he rarely took more than a carry-on bag. As with his trip to Italy back in January, he'd managed to be productive in a very few days. Staying on track with a mission went way back to his CIA days, training that served him well even now.

He thumbed the app on his phone to order a car, and by the time he reached the pickup area at the curb his ride was waiting. True, he could have requested an OSM Towncar, which would have delivered him to his condo in finer style than this pale blue Prius, but then his movements would be known to someone. And right now he didn't want the board members knowing exactly when he'd arrived back in the capital.

His eyelid twitched as he contemplated arriving at the office in the morning. He hadn't quite worked out how he would explain the fact he hadn't come back with the one item he'd promised he could deliver. But the risk at the other end had suddenly amplified, and if there was one thing Marcus put first and foremost it was his own skin.

Doesn't matter, he told himself. I'll have plenty of chances.

He tamped down the impatience that hovered just beneath his every conscious thought. Isobel St. Clair and her staff at The Vongraf Foundation continued to frustrate him. He'd tried confronting her directly outside her office once, only to be grabbed by the security guards. That had involved long explanations to the local cops to assure them he'd only wanted to talk with Ms. St. Clair—he'd meant her no harm. Really. And that Samantha Sweet woman out in New Mexico—he would have to deal with her at some point. He caught himself grinding his teeth.

"Here we are, sir," said the driver over his shoulder.

They'd arrived at his Georgetown condo and Marcus got out without a word.

"Have a nice evening," the driver called out.

Yeah, sure.

Marcus walked inside, switching on lights and requesting soft jazz on the music system. Shedding his jacket, he wheeled his small suitcase to the laundry room where he tossed all the clothing, including what he wore, into the machine and started it. Nude, he walked to the bathroom and started the shower, a huge rainfall fixture he'd installed to replace the inadequate one that came with the place.

Twenty minutes later he toweled off and stepped into soft black sweats and a black T-shirt. He smiled at the memory of a woman he'd dated five years ago. Clarice. She'd told him how great he looked in black, how it complimented his raven hair and brought out the vivid pale blue of his eyes. Black was the only color he bought now.

Twilight Time was playing through the speakers when he went into the kitchen, a marvel of stainless steel and granite designed and installed by a decorator, although Marcus didn't cook and rarely brought anyone here who did. A sandwich and a drink would fill the bill for tonight. He would transfer his clean clothes to the dryer, and once done, would fold and repack them into his same carry-on bag.

He piled sliced ham on bread and sighed with his first warming sip of the Glenlivet 18. Basically, all he had to face in the morning was giving his report to the board at OSM, then he would be out on another plane tomorrow night.

He pictured the discreet doorway on the stone building just off Dupont Circle, the brass plaque with only three letters: OSM. No explanation, no address numbers. Anyone passing the place would assume it was some government office—everything in this city had something to do with the government, after all. The door was always locked and the thumbprint and retinal scanners, which gained one entrance, were so subtly mounted most would never notice them.

Marcus would pass the eye scan and fingerprint without a hitch and make his way from the tiny marble vestibule, up the elevator behind the brass doors, through the warren of offices until he came to his own. The narrow profile of the building at street level was deceiving. Inside were more than twenty private offices, a conference room where the fifteen-member board met, a dining room and kitchen.

Not to mention the cubicles where staff operated and the little-known "secure room," a magnetically shielded space where computers operated in completely untraceable ways and the most private of conversations took place.

He debated calling the Director, Elias Swift, and setting up one of those private conversations for the morning. He'd prefer a one-on-one with the irascible old man than to be grilled by the entire board. But such a step would only call attention to his dilemma. Better to treat it as inconsequential, brush past the report as if it were nothing.

The washer buzzed its end-of-cycle alert. Yes, that's what he would do. Breeze through tomorrow's meeting, grab his things, and catch his flight.

Chapter 6

The London airport was huge and crazy and would have been entirely intimidating without the guiding hand of Stan Bookman, who saw them through customs and immigration with barely a blink. Kelly felt like a minnow fending for itself in the ocean as she tried to adjust her ear and respond to the various English accents from each official who addressed her. Scott seemed only slightly less in awe—he had been to the UK once during his post-grad studies. The famous singer and athlete had been met by a kid with turquoise and purple hair who whisked them away to a private section of the airport, apparently for those who would be recognized in a crowd.

"I travel internationally quite a lot," Bookman said, as they walked past the last of the customs officials. "And I have to say, arriving in your own jet makes a huge difference.

Now let's see … where's our ride?"

A dozen or more uniformed drivers waited in the greeting area, holding up signs with various names on them. Nowhere did Kelly spot anything with Bookman or Book It Travel, but she realized looking for one marked her as a newbie when Stan called out, "Graham! Good to see you again."

"How was the flight, sir?" asked a tall man, impeccably dressed in a dark suit, white shirt, and narrow tie. "Better than the last one?"

"We ran into a terrible storm two weeks ago when I came in," Stan explained to Kelly and Scott. "Graham waited hours while we were rerouted." He introduced them all around. "Graham lives in Bury and he'll be at your disposal while you're here, unless, of course, he has to dash back to London to pick me up."

That led to a discussion between the men about Bookman's upcoming schedule. Meanwhile, Graham had taken the handles of their wheeled bags in each hand and was striding purposefully through the exit toward a multi-level parking garage.

"Right, then," he said after unlocking the Mercedes, which must have set someone back a hundred grand, at least. "Mr. B likes to ride up front, so you've the back seats to yourselves. TV on the screens in front of you, bottled drinks in this little—" He stretched over to reveal a compartment between the two seats. "Snacks in the pockets just there—but if I recall, you've been well fed aboard your flight."

They had, indeed. Champagne and hors d'oeuvres immediately after take-off, a sumptuous dinner of lobster and filet mignon with fresh veggies, and waking up to eggs Benedict and fruit for breakfast right before landing. Kelly thanked him but indicated she couldn't hold another bite.

Bookman had told them the drive would take between two and three hours, and she couldn't imagine a better way to make the trip. This treatment was certainly going to spoil them for anything involving economy class planes or crowded trains in the future. She burrowed into the deep leather seat and reached over to take Scott's hand. Married at last. He smiled at her and planted a tender kiss on the back of her hand.

Although she'd slept well on the plane—with those heavenly reclining seats, who wouldn't?—she caught herself dozing in the car, lulled by the soft conversation from the front seat and the view of softly rolling green hills outside the windows as they traveled the motorway. A peculiar scent caught her attention and she looked up to see that they were passing a factory of some kind on the outskirts of a town.

Graham noticed the direction she was looking. "Sugar mill," he said. "Wherever you go, they have a distinctive odor, don't they?"

Stan Bookman spoke up. "Take me by my place first, would you, Graham? That way Mr. and Mrs. Porter can see where the house is that they'll be staying. Then you can take them to the Angel and see that they get settled."

Mrs. Porter. Kelly smiled.

"Very good, sir. Have you told them much about the Angel Hotel?"

"Not a lot. Figured they'd love to discover it for themselves."

Kelly and Scott exchanged a look. He'd been reading up on the history of the famous hotel that dated back to 1452 and during their flight had given Kelly the condensed version of the parts he knew. Of course, he'd told her, there's bound to be more.

The car wove through curving narrow streets lined with redbrick row houses whose doors opened immediately onto the sidewalks. They passed the Green King Brewery (as an aside, Scott told her it had been there since 1799) then made a right turn onto a lane of well maintained homes with leafy trees in front.

"I'd say we're in luck on the parking," Graham said, pulling to the curb where he expertly angled the Mercedes between two smaller vehicles. Technically, it didn't seem like a legal spot, as he was blocking the entrance to someone's garage door, but likely he would only be here a few minutes.

Stan understood the need to move quickly. Either that or, Kelly guessed, the man always moved at a fast pace. He was out his door and standing near the back of the car before she or Scott had realized this was the place.

"I'll just grab his bag," Graham said. "Mind the traffic—cars will come opposite to what you're used to. Watch to the right."

They followed through a high gate, which Stan unlocked, through a tiny garden that held two English dogwood trees and two flowering butterfly bushes which flanked the front door.

"Here we are," Stan said, "your home away from home. As I said, stay the full month if you'd like. Or simply call this number and my secretary can tell you when our next plane will be heading stateside." He handed Scott a business card.

They were standing in a living room, smallish but impeccably furnished with a comfortable sectional sofa, two side chairs, a bookcase filled with novels, and a small gas fireplace. The lounge, Bookman told them.

"And through here is the kitchen and dining area, fully equipped. Just pop out to the shops for some food and you're all set, if you like to cook. If you don't, there are at least a dozen very fine restaurants within ten minutes' walk."

The rest of the home consisted of two spacious bedrooms and a bath. French doors led outside beyond the dining area and master bedroom, to a cute garden where plants grew in profusion, and a brick patio with two lounge chairs looked like the perfect place to share a bottle of wine on a summer evening.

"It's not large," Stan said. "None of the homes here are large compared to American suburbs, but the wife and I feel it's the ideal little English getaway when we don't want the world intruding. A honeymoon place, in other words."

"It's perfect," Kelly assured him. Already she was in love with the town and the little house, an ideal setting to begin their life together.

Near the front door, Graham discreetly cleared his throat.

"Ah, yes," said Stan. "The car. Graham will take you now to your hotel. Explore and have fun. I'm out of here Tuesday morning, and Graham will be happy to bring you and your luggage here to settle in."

"Of course," Graham said with a smile. "You may call me at any time during your stay in Bury."

The newlyweds climbed back into the car and, with Graham at the wheel following a series of winding turns, they were pulling up in front of a very old building five minutes later. Three stories of windows faced the street, their flower boxes overflowing with bright purple petunias, and the rock façade was covered in ivy that encroached upon the white-painted window trim. Beyond the parking lot, cars whizzed by on the two-lane street. Kelly gaped, taking it all in.

"It seems a bit confusing at first," Graham said, holding the door for her, "but you'll get the feel of the town straightaway. We're right at the center of things. That's the Abbey across the road, and the Abbey Gate just there. Walk over and stroll the gardens if you fancy stretching your legs. The flowers are glorious this time of year."

He pointed to the right. "Walk that direction and you'll see the streets with all the shops just there, directly behind the hotel. And, well … you'll sort it out as you spend time. And for anyplace you'd want to go beyond walking distance, you have my card."

A dark-skinned porter in white jacket with gold trim met them and carried their bags up the three stone steps to the front entrance. They quickly said goodbye to Graham and followed the man, past a restaurant, to the reception desk. True to his word, Stan Bookman had arranged a room for them and the check-in process went quickly.

"Breakfast is included from six to ten in the morning," said the slight girl with long blond hair done up in a clip. She handed over a metal key attached by a ring to a rectangular slice of wood. No magnetic keycards here, Kelly noted. "Sanjay will show you to your room, and we hope you'll have a lovely stay with us."

With a quick nod toward them, the porter grabbed both bags and headed up a staircase to their right. They climbed creaking wooden stairs, made a sharp left turn and realized Sanjay had already covered the length of a short corridor and was out of sight. Going the only direction available, they figured out he'd gone down three small steps and was waiting at the bottom.

"Watch your heads there," he cautioned, tipping his chin upward.

A couple of warning placards said the same thing. Parts of the hallway clearly had been built before modern man began to grow quite so tall.

Sanjay was already well ahead again, passing in front of a trio of guest rooms where the wooden hallway floor groaned loudly. Traversing a hall with windows on both sides showed that they were crossing what must have been a carriageway in the old days. Below, the street was to their left, a courtyard on the right. Kelly could imagine horses and carriages halting there, ladies in finery being helped down to the cobblestoned surface.

Down two steps, a curve to the left, up one step, and Sanjay stopped in front of a cream-colored door. "Your key, sir?"

Scott handed it over and the man unlocked the door.

"The Pickwick Room," he announced. He preceded them, warned them to watch for the step down, and set their bags in front of a tall cherry armoire.

"It's huge!" Kelly marveled, remembering the tales she'd heard of hotel rooms in Britain and Europe being on the small side.

Indeed, the spacious room looked very comfortable, with its smooth green carpeting, tasteful wallpaper and drapes over the two large windows facing the Abbey. There was a small fireplace, which showed evidence of use in a previous era, a beautiful canopied bed, small TV set, desk, and a tea service complete with a variety of teas and cookies. The ensuite bath featured a large tub, a complex-looking shower head, along with thick towels on a warming rack and a variety of shampoos and bath gels.

Scott offered Sanjay a tip, which the porter politely refused as being unnecessary. When they were alone, he grabbed Kelly's hand, pulled her close, and danced her around the open space until they landed—by design—on the bed.

"Happy honeymoon, Mrs. Porter," he said with a leer as he began to slide his hands beneath her shirt.

"Mmm … yes." Her lips found his, and articles of clothing began to drop to the floor.

* * *

The light had changed subtly in the room when Kelly awoke, the bedcovers tangled around her legs. Scott murmured in his sleep and tightened his embrace around her waist. She rolled to face him and started planting little kisses around his ear.

"What time is it?" he murmured.

She reached past him to pick up her phone from the nightstand. "Twelve o'clock. That can't be right. This must not have changed over to UK time."

He shifted and glanced at his wristwatch. "Seven. We slept more than four hours!"

"Well, we weren't asleep *all* that time," she teased.

"True." He grinned again. "But now I think I'm hungry—for food."

"We didn't make any dinner plan. Maybe we should just get out and walk a bit and see what's what. If nothing else, we can surely come back to the hotel and eat here."

They showered (leisurely) and dressed (quickly), and were out the door thirty minutes later.

"I'm so sorry, sir, all our dinner bookings are taken tonight. Shall I set up something for tomorrow evening?" The hostess at the Angel certainly knew how to deliver a pleasant rejection.

They hit the street and began walking. It was evident that the road behind the hotel, where Graham had recommended shopping, was not the direction to go. Storefronts were in night mode and the few pedestrians were hurrying elsewhere. They set out along the busier street and within a couple of blocks came to a place called The Fox.

"I do happen to have one cancellation," said the host. "Right this way."

Kelly opted for the most English thing she spotted on the menu, steak and kidney pie, while Scott ordered a lamb dish. An hour later, they were satisfied and impressed, deciding they would definitely be back.

"I should call Mom," Kelly said on the walk back to the Angel. "I told her I'd let her know we arrived safely and find out how things are going at home."

Chapter 7

The phone rang a little after three o'clock. Sam turned from staring out the back windows and absently picked it up. Beau and Rico were only now hiking back across the pasture, a few evidence bags in hand.

"Mom, hi! We're in the UK and it's fantastic here!" Kelly's voice conveyed all the excitement and happiness that had been missing from Sam's day.

"How was the flight? Are you best friends now with your favorite pop singer?"

"Oh, them. They weren't friendly at all, didn't even talk to us. There was a little private bedroom section on the plane and they disappeared in there right after takeoff. I thought they felt too important to talk to us but Mr. Bookman said she had a concert in London tonight, so I suppose that explains it. Anyway, you should see this hotel.

It's got that whole shabby, historic thing going on. The floors creak like crazy, but our room is really nice and we have an incredible view toward the Abbey and gardens. And Mr. Bookman's house is really nice, where we'll stay after Tuesday ..."

Sam laughed. " I bet it's amazing. I'm glad you're having a wonderful time."

"We are. How are things going at home? Does everyone miss me?"

Sam paused. "Fine. Things are ... Well, Beau's working a murder case." No way she would spoil Kelly's honeymoon by going into all the gruesome details, nor the reasons behind the killing.

"Mom? You okay?"

"Absolutely. It's been a very busy couple of weeks, but I stayed home today." Her gaze traveled to the dining table where the Book It Travel contract lay, untouched since early morning. "I'm going over Bookman's contract right now, in fact."

"Great—he seems like such a nice man, doesn't he? And what he's done for your business—wow."

Sam's memory flashed back to a time, not that many years ago, when she was scrounging to make a living, breaking into houses and cleaning up messes just to pay the bills. Things had certainly changed, very profitably, since Bookman came along.

Kelly chatted a few more minutes before they hung up.

Beau walked in, but not before slipping his boots off outside. "Rico's heading back to the office. I'm getting a quick shower. I stumbled and landed in some horse—well, anyway. Soon as I'm cleaned up I'll go in too. It could be a late night." He said this last bit as he leaned over to kiss the top of her head. "You doing okay?"

Sam nodded and put on a smile. "That was Kelly on the phone. They arrived and are having a great time already."

He sent her a compassionate look. "It's been a tough week for you, darlin'—take a couple days off."

He squeezed her hand and headed upstairs. Sam's attention wandered back to the contract. There was no way she could concentrate well enough to read the entire document now. The day had been far too crazy. Aside from the terms with the cruise line, most of what she'd covered in the first few pages was standard Book It Travel lingo. They'd worked well together so far. She flipped through the pages, scanning the clauses, then to the end where Bookman had already signed. She dashed off her own signature, jammed the document into the large envelope he'd left with her, and sealed it. She ignored the flutter of nerves in her gut. It was a done deal.

Beau came down the stairs at a trot, smelling of Irish Spring soap and his favorite shampoo. His hair was damp, with comb marks running through, and he was still buttoning the clean uniform shirt he'd found in the closet.

"You gonna be home or at the bakery?" he asked, barely glancing up as he looked for his keys.

"I should probably run to the bakery and see how things are going. It's still wedding season and Becky may need me. Or the Victorian—the crew making the chocolates doesn't yet know about this big contract I just signed."

She looked at the brown envelope. It had postage already on it; all she needed to do was drop it at the post office, which was on her way.

"Beau … when you questioned her, did Isobel St. Clair mention the name Marcus Fitch?"

Now he looked up. "Yeah, actually, she did. She seemed pretty certain he's involved. I've got Evan already checking on him."

"Apparently he lives in the Washington, DC, area. Did she tell you why she thinks he might have come around here?"

He shook his head. By now, he'd loaded his pockets with wallet and personal things and had strapped on the weighty leather belt with his pistol, Taser, handcuffs, pepper spray, and extra loaded magazines. His movements were quick and impatient. Sam decided not to drag him into a theoretical conversation about Fitch and his motives. It could wait.

He gave her a quick kiss and picked up his straw Stetson. "Not sure when I'll be home, so don't plan on me for dinner."

She nodded with a small sigh and watched him walk out. His SUV sat slightly skewed in the driveway, where he had roared to a stop hours ago when she'd called about the shooting. He maneuvered neatly back toward the road and drove away.

Sam moved around the great room, picking up tea cups, a stray napkin, a couple of the paper plates she'd taken outside earlier for the deputies' lunch. Cups went into the dishwasher, paper in the trash, pillows and throws rearranged where people had moved them to sit down. Upstairs, she wiped steam from the mirror and hung up Beau's towel.

The carved box sat on the bedroom dresser, blatantly ignoring all of Isobel's concerns for its safety. Sam had to admit she'd become lax again. After the last time Fitch had made a move to get the box she'd been diligent about locking it in Beau's hidden gun safe and keeping it there. Except in cases of emergency need of its help. But in the past few months, it had sat here in plain sight.

She chided herself, picked it up, and carried it downstairs. The box might have been given to her on a whim—she really didn't know. She'd certainly treated it as a convenient gadget, something to make her day easier.

Now, things had gotten serious. A man had died.

She pushed aside the coats in the downstairs closet and entered the code on the safe's keypad. Isobel might be right—was the box secure *enough* here in the house? Should she take it to the bank and get a safe deposit box? The alternative would be to destroy it, get it out of her life forever, but something told her to reconsider. Don't make any changes yet, she told herself.

She swung the safe door open and placed the box inside, then locked it and arranged the closet contents to conceal the secret.

Ten minutes later she was on the road toward town. As the miles slipped away, she realized how tense she'd been at home. Getting out was the right thing to do. She dropped the large brown envelope in the mailbox at the post office, circled the block and headed toward the old Victorian house she'd purchased as the location for her chocolate factory.

She'd first seen the building as a fixer-upper, fairly easy to renovate for her purposes, and the project had been a lot of fun. The rental turned into a purchase, and the old building appeared on the company logo for Sweet's Traditional Handmade Chocolates. The chocolatiers, consisting of herself and two helpers, had quickly grown to a larger crew with the expansion of Book It Travel and

Stan Bookman's numerous ideas for his exclusive—and wealthy—clientele.

Now, another major change was coming, and Sam realized she needed to give it serious thought. She parked her pickup truck under the portico and walked through the kitchen door, greeting the chocolatiers at the marble-topped work table, stopping to admire the exquisitely delicate pieces Benjie Lucero was turning out these days. Then she checked in at the packing and shipping rooms to be sure there were no obvious crises. All seemed under control.

Upstairs, the floors squeaked as she walked to her office in the rounded tower section. She chuckled as she remembered Kelly's description of their hotel; old buildings had their similarities. On her desk, everything waited just as she'd left it. Not exactly pristine, but neat enough not to drive her crazy for a few more days. She turned on her computer and opened a spreadsheet.

Nothing she'd spotted in the new contract specified how many pieces of chocolate Sweet's would need to turn out per day, or even per cruise. Stan had told her this was a boutique cruise line, small ships that made longer journeys. The food was always chef quality, and the desserts and little amenities were expected to be the same. It was how he had sold the line on the idea of handmade chocolates—well, that and the fact that Sam herself had made the samples for their inspection and tasting. Samples that included a little extra of her 'magic touch.'

In her browser she went to the cruise line's website and began taking figures from the sales pitch. 'Small ship' meant only about ninety passengers. Compared to the mega ships with two and three thousand, these truly were exclusive. But—the cruise was thirty days long, sailing from New York, through the Panama Canal, and circling the entire length of South America before returning.

Assuming two pieces of chocolate per passenger each day of the cruise, an estimate she thought conservative, they would need to produce more than five thousand chocolates and send them before the cruise ever left port. Otherwise, she would be faced with shipping a delicate commodity into foreign ports where heat, delays, and bureaucratic red tape could cause any number of serious issues and create horrendous costs.

Making matters worse, as she continued through the various cruise itineraries, she realized the ninety-passenger ship was the smallest in the line. Others—still 'exclusive'—carried as many as five hundred. She plugged numbers into her spreadsheet, including her costs and markups. Her chocolates didn't come cheap, and Stan Bookman was well aware of her charges and so were the cruise people.

The problem wasn't so much that she wouldn't make money at this venture. It was down to logistics—could she and her small company produce true handmade chocolates in the quantities she'd just agreed to do?

A flutter of nerves went through her gut.

Chapter 8

The angle of the sun drew a sharper, longer swath across his desk as Beau stared at the stack of evidence bags piled there. Considering the murder had taken place in broad daylight in front of witnesses, there was precious little to go on.

He and Rico had combed the area around the copse of trees, based on Lisa's estimated trajectory of the bullet. The forensic tech was good—he had to admire her. They'd found tire tracks showing that a vehicle had come to a stop nearby and had turned around, the shooter most likely positioning the car for a quick getaway. He may have even left the engine running, since the prevailing wind would have carried the sound away from the house. Or, he may have hidden himself in the trees much earlier and waited for the ideal moment. Beau realized he would likely never know exactly how it went.

All he had to go on was the scanty evidence. They'd taken molds of the tire prints and Rico was running the pictures through some databases.

The dry, dusty road hadn't preserved footprints well, but they'd found some at the point where it appeared someone had stepped between strands of the barbed wire fencing. Most prints were smeared from movement, but one was clear enough to take a mold. That, too, was going to the law enforcement knowledge banks to find out the brand. If they got lucky and it was an unusual one, they might have something to go on.

Moving into the stand of trees, the footprints became lost in the ground cover of leaves. It had been impossible to tell which of the dozen or more trees their guy stood behind. No sign of where he'd braced his shoulder to be certain his shot was straight and steady. Based on the distance and accuracy—the fact that it had taken only one shot to hit his target—the shooter most likely had training or lots of experience. And that meant he probably wasn't the man Sam and her friend named.

Generic tire tracks, generic shoe print, no snags or scraps of fabric on anything, and no spent brass casing from the bullet. Could possibly be a hired assassin.

He pushed the evidence bags aside. Until he had more information, there was no point in speculating. A good law enforcement man never made guesses until he had all the facts. He sighed and walked into the squad room. Rico sat at a computer where the photo he'd taken of the tire print filled half the screen; the other half had a dozen other pictures.

"Any luck on the footprint or those tire tracks yet?"

"Not yet ... still going through these ..." Rico didn't

take his eyes off the screen.

For the hundredth time Beau wished his department had the budget for a separate forensics section with the most up-to-date software and resources. It was crazy to have a deputy sit here for hours staring at tire prints. But unless he wanted to send these things to the state crime lab in Santa Fe and wait weeks for results, this was his immediate choice. He was lucky to have Lisa. At least she was close by and was great at gathering evidence at the crime scene.

"Any chance of ordering in some dinner?" Rico asked. "Assuming we're going to be here late?"

Evan Richards was on the phone at his desk, and Deputy Waters had just walked in the back door. If he planned to keep them into a second shift, he'd better feed everyone.

"Waters, why don't you run out and get a bag of tacos from Rosarita's? Couple dozen should do it, even if the patrol guys come back in." Beau handed the senior deputy some cash.

Evan hung up the phone and turned to the boss. "That was the OMI's office. They've retrieved the bullet from the body and will be sending it to ballistics at the crime lab for testing. I'm going to call them next, try to nudge them to give us quick results."

"Good luck with that," Beau said with a wry grin.

"I've got one buddy there in Santa Fe, so I'll try him. We were in the same criminal justice class at Colorado State."

Beau paced for a minute, wishing this part of an investigation went quicker. The thought flashed through his head: Why did this have to fall into his lap? An out-of-state victim who, for a moment in time, had stood in the path of what was most likely an out-of-state killer. He'd rather spend department time and resources on protecting the citizens of his county.

But that was unfair. If one of his loved ones were killed in unfamiliar territory, he'd like to think the law enforcement teams there would work hard to see justice done. He couldn't pick and choose his cases. This was the one fate had dealt him today.

His stomach rumbled. He was grouchy because he was hungry, a simple fact.

"Hey, boss," Rico called out. "Take a look."

He was pointing to a tire print on his computer screen when Beau stepped over for a closer look.

"Enlarge it."

Rico clicked the picture in question and made it the same size as the print they'd found.

"Looks like it," Beau said.

Rico dragged the picture on the right over the one on the left, superimposing it. The tread pattern aligned perfectly. "We got it!"

"Nice job," Beau said, giving him a pat on the shoulder. "Now, what can we find out about it?"

"I'm on that next." The deputy entered an identifier number from the photo and got a page of statistics. "It's a Bridgestone P22570R16, and it says here they're a stock tire commonly used on many light-duty trucks and SUVs. Toyota, Chevy, Ford …"

"Doesn't narrow it down a whole lot, does it?"

"The tire is also used on a lot of rentals, such as SUVs and minivans."

"Kind of fits with what we're thinking about this being

some guy hired for a job. He'd rent a car, probably not under his own name, in case anyone spotted the vehicle and got the plate number." Beau chewed at his lower lip for a moment. "Let's try this—get hold of the car rental companies in nearby cities: Albuquerque, Santa Fe, maybe even as far as Denver. See what they may have rented recently."

"Boss—"

"I know. It's probably a huge list and maybe not worth the time. Then again, maybe it is, and it could be our first solid lead." Even as he said it, Beau realized what a dead end it would probably turn out to be.

Deputy Waters returned just then, and the scent of corn tortillas and spiced pork filled the room. The four men pulled chairs around an empty desk and reached into the bags for the best tacos in Taos. It took a mere fifteen minutes to fill their bellies and improve their spirits, and they were soon back at the phones.

An hour later Beau decided to call it quits for the night. It was after nine p.m. and he was either reaching voicemail services or endlessly ringing phones with no answers. He locked the day's take in the evidence locker, then gathered his things and put on his Stetson.

"We'll get back on it tomorrow," he told the deputies. "I'd like the ballistics report and anything we can learn from the car rental places as early as possible."

Rico and Evan had been on duty since seven a.m., and their eyes showed fatigue. Beau told them to go home. Waters and the three men on patrol would work until eleven, and the regular night shift would take over. "Get some sleep. It's going to be an interesting week," Beau said as he pulled out his keys.

At home, Sam's damp hair told him she'd recently showered. She wore her favorite light flannels and was sitting up in a corner of the sofa, staring into space, when he walked in.

"Hey, darlin'. I thought you might be in bed by now."

"Can't sleep. There are at least a hundred thoughts in my head."

He draped his heavy belt on a rung of the bentwood coat rack and set his hat on top. "I know. We're struggling with the few clues we got. There's not much to go on."

She folded her legs in, making a space for him. He settled there and draped an arm around her shoulders.

"You okay?" he asked.

She nodded.

"I spent all afternoon thinking about it," he said. "Can't come up with a reason for Robards to be the target, and I can't get it out of my head that the shooter was really aiming at Isobel St. Clair. She had a close call the last time she visited Taos—I looked it up. Do you think either incident has to do with her job, with that special organization back East?"

"I don't know, Beau. What she does in her job doesn't sound at all dangerous, but she's had contact with some other group, some men who do sound pretty unscrupulous. They're known by the initials OSM and are somehow tied to the Vatican."

"Hmm." But he didn't say what he was thinking, that it was pretty farfetched for someone from the Vatican to give a hoot about anything going on in Taos, New Mexico. And to use violent means? That made no sense whatsoever.

Chapter 9

Marcus loved the airport in Shannon. Small, for an international airport, easy to get around and he'd already pre-cleared customs back at JFK after the short hop from Washington to New York. And the Irish were very friendly, assuming his dark hair and blue eyes belonged to one of them. His stay here wouldn't be long. He had basically one mission. He sent a quick text to the man he was supposed to meet. No response. Perhaps his plane from Italy had been delayed. So, wait around the airport or go ahead to the hotel?

He glanced around and spotted a coffee place. While the barista mixed his half-caff latte he took a deep breath. The meeting yesterday morning at OSM had gone all right, although Marcus had found himself skimming over facts as he deftly steered the conversation away from his last journey and directed the board's attention to his mission today. *This* was the important one, he'd assured them. Their expressions varied; he hoped most of them bought it.

His phone pinged with a text only a moment after he took a seat at a tiny table.

Just landed. Are you still at airport?

Yes. Find me at Coffee Point.

Marcus had just drained the last of his beverage when he spotted the floor-length robes of a Roman Catholic cardinal. He gave a small nod with his chin and the man walked toward him.

"Seriously, cousin? Full uniform when you travel?"

Maurilio Fitch smiled. "Hey, it's a Catholic country and I get first class treatment this way."

"Hm, I suppose. Did you—?" Marcus gave a nod toward Maury's shoulder bag.

A faint nod. "Everything's fine but let's get to our hotel. I got our rooms upgraded to a suite."

Apparently the 'first class treatment' comment was for real. Marcus couldn't believe the accommodations—a two-bedroom, two-bath suite, complete with living and dining areas and a well-stocked bar with no prices on the goodies inside. He wheeled his bag into one of the bedrooms and was back, pouring an Irish whiskey, when his cousin appeared wearing dark slacks and shirt, with the simple collar of a clergyman.

"Really? The collar here in the room?"

"Really—whiskey before ten in the morning?" Maury stared at the size of the generous shot in the glass. "Let me take you out for some breakfast."

"Let's order room service. I want to see the box."

Maury shook his head. "Still all business." But he picked up the phone and ordered two full breakfasts.

Marcus paced to the large living room windows, carrying his glass.

"I might as well get this over with," Maury said.

He vanished into his bedroom and returned a few moments later with a shoebox-sized parcel wrapped in soft black cloth.

Marcus hardly waited to have it handed over. He set down his glass and reached for the box, swiping the material aside and tossing it on the floor.

The box was magnificent. Glossy black. It gleamed as if covered in a hundred coats of varnish, and the colored stones mounted in the intersections of the carved X shapes had a deep luster. He couldn't take his eyes from it.

"Marc—wake up!" Maury touched his arm and Marcus shook off his hand.

"I wasn't asleep," he protested.

"No, but you looked like you were in some kind of trance." Maury glanced at the box. "What's with this thing? It looks different. Shinier or something."

"It's even more magnificent than I imagined."

"Yeah, well, you should have seen it yesterday. Coated with a thousand years' worth of dust. But I swear, all I did was give it a decent dusting. It was *not* this shiny. And those stones—I couldn't even tell what colors they were. Now they look like emeralds and rubies and sapphires."

A tap came at the door and the muffled call, "Room service."

"Quick, hide that thing," Maury whispered. "I'd be in big trouble if—"

"Yeah, I know." But Marcus grabbed the cloth, draped it over the box, and carried it to his own bedroom.

By the time he returned, the waiter had set their

breakfast on the dining table and gone away. Marcus found he had an appetite, despite the breakfast served on the plane a couple of hours ago. He wanted to ask his cousin more about how he'd found the box in the Vatican archives and whether he'd encountered any problems getting it out, but somehow he knew the subject was better left alone. He had the box now. That was the most important thing.

Chapter 10

Kelly awoke gradually, savoring the warmth of Scott's body next to hers in the luxurious king-size bed, under the elegant canopy. It wasn't as if she hadn't awakened beside him most mornings for months now. Ever since they became engaged he slept over at her house most weekends, and she'd stayed at his place two or three nights during the week. After the end of the semester, back in May, he had vacated his apartment and moved in with her. Some day, especially once children began to come along, they would look for a home larger than the little two-bedroom where Kelly had grown up. She wasn't sure whether Sam would want to rent or sell the little place, but that was a conversation for another time.

She stretched and brushed her fingertips across the web of hair on his chest, planting firm little kisses on his shoulder. A smile crossed his face and he rolled toward her.

Everything else came naturally, and they didn't leave the big bed for another hour.

"Did we miss breakfast?" she asked as they stepped into the large shower together. "Suddenly, I'm starving."

"I'm sure we can find something," he said, picking up the bath gel and drizzling a trail of it across her back. His motions, soaping and massaging her, brought back the desire, if not the energy to do anything about it.

It was nearly noon before they emerged from the hotel with the determination to see something of the quaint town that had been part of their windfall gift. As Kelly pointed out, they had the rest of their lives for sex.

They wandered around the corner from the hotel and found a lively restaurant that promised "Eggs all day!" The décor was sort of Euro-modern with blonde-wood tables and black metal chairs, dark wooden floors, and light fixtures of brightly colored glass. Vintage food and restaurant posters covered the walls, and the patrons at this time of day consisted of multi-generational groups—sort of mom-daughter-grandma gatherings who were talking animatedly to each other rather than checking their cell phones.

They studied the menu written on a chalkboard on the wall, placed their orders for omelets, and settled back to take it all in.

"You know what I love best about the UK?" Kelly asked, once the server had delivered their drinks and walked away.

Scott merely smiled.

"Aside from their accents … it's the tea. I mean, you don't have to explain that you don't want herbal, you don't want flavored … you just say 'tea please' and you get really good authentic tea."

"The coffee's not bad either," he said.

She shook her head slightly. "I may try it later. I'm so spoiled by Mom's special blend at the bakery I rarely order coffee anywhere else now."

She picked up her teacup and sipped luxuriously, her body satiated and now her tummy getting its due.

"So, what do you want to do today?" he asked. The omelets had arrived and looked scrumptious.

"Everything! I want to see it all. Britain's smallest pub is nearby, and I heard about some great antique stores, bookshops, and then there's a museum or two." She knew the historic sites would be high on Scott's list.

"We're only one train stop away from Cambridge. Talk about history."

She laughed. "I can see we'll need to pace ourselves."

They agreed the first day should be purely for exploration and getting their bearings, then they would settle on one historic site and one shopping destination per day. A slow stroll after breakfast was the perfect way to begin, but the one-per-day plan got sidetracked when they came to Moyse's Hall Museum, a 12th Century stone building, where the sign out front said it was the final day of the Implements of Torture Exhibit.

"Oh, Kel, we have to do this one today," he pleaded. "Look, they're switching it out for something else tomorrow."

"I can see it now—we get home and Riki asks what we saw on our honeymoon and I tell her our first stop was to check out implements of torture."

"It's actually our second stop," he reminded. "I did treat you to breakfast already."

She couldn't stop chuckling, even as he paid the small

admission fee and received a descriptive brochure from the polite docent. The brochure's wording promised they would "Enjoy the magical to the macabre." They meandered through a couple of rooms with low archways and ancient wooden beams supporting the thick walls and ceilings before Scott paused at a glass display case.

"This will interest you," he said, "a lock of hair from Mary Tudor. She was the favorite sister of Henry VIII and is buried at St. Mary's Church right here in town. We *have to* go there."

Kelly wasn't sure why a single lock of blonde hair would be the thing of interest—she supposed he thought all females were interested in hair—but she had already wandered to a display called Witchcraft and Superstition. "Honey, it says here that 'some people got rid of awkward neighbors by accusing them of witchcraft.' You might watch out—some women could try getting rid of awkward husbands that way, too."

"Ha-ha." He sent her a look. "Wouldn't matter. In this day and age it's kind of a cool thing to be a witch, right?"

His gaze was drawn upward and his mouth went open. "Oh, my gosh. Look at this thing. A gibbet cage."

Kelly didn't need much imagination to figure it out. Sturdy metal strapping formed the outline of a life-sized human, the straps designed to enclose the body, a heavy ring at the top to hang the body from a high wooden post and ninety-degree crossbar. Did they actually put someone in this alive? Or was it the body of a hanged criminal, left to rot in the sun and get pecked to bits by the birds?

She turned her back on the macabre device, only to face a display with a book in a glass case. 'Bound in the skin of notorious murderer William Corder, who committed the Red Barn murders,' read the placard beside it.

"Okay … sweetie, I think I'm ready for some fresh air," she said.

Scott had moved on to read statistics on the violence of law enforcement in the 18th century, so Kelly made a quick stop at the gift shop where she purchased a souvenir mug.

"When my husband surfaces, tell him I've gone to the bookshop down the street," she told the docent.

She was well into the biography section, browsing a memoir by a woman claiming to be an Irish Traveller, when he found her. Sam had told her of meeting the Travellers during her own honeymoon trip to Ireland, and Kelly thought the book would make a nice gift. She noticed Scott clutched a shopping bag from the museum.

"Have to stock up on interesting reading material while I'm here," he said. More than half the boxes he'd moved into the house were books, and she'd teased him about needing a bigger house just so it could have a library.

She bought the memoir plus a beautifully covered journal for herself, and they started down the street. Taking in the brilliant hanging flower baskets, the historic dates on the buildings, the displays of chic clothing in the shops and watching people with their well-behaved dogs on leashes was fun, but the weight of their packages soon became a bit much.

"Let's drop off all this stuff at the hotel," she suggested, "and then take a walk through the gardens, the ones we can see from our room."

Graham had been right. The gardens were a delight— from formally planted sections done in brightly colored geraniums, dianthus, and delphinium to sections left to go almost wild. Scott was ecstatic over the old abbey ruins that dated back to 600 A.D. (and astounded that children were allowed to climb and play on them). The 'modern' abbey in use today was only a thousand years old, he told her.

By the time they'd walked the equivalent of a couple of miles, Kelly was ready for a drink and going to the Nutshell Pub was a must. From what they'd heard about the tiny bar, it was a museum in itself, and that proved true when they stepped inside. Old photos and memorabilia hung from walls and ceiling. The only seating, benches lining the walls, was filled, so they picked up their beers from the barkeep and walked around to gaze.

"Kel, look—" Scott said. "A mummified cat."

One of the seated patrons piped up with a story about how cats were often placed inside the walls of buildings under construction to ward off witches. Kelly wondered, what was it about this obsession with witches in those times, and then something on the wall caught her attention. She walked over to look at the framed black-and-white photo.

A woman with wild, dark hair sat at a table, tarot cards spread out before her. Her long skirts draped to the ground, and it appeared the scene was outdoors. There was a stocky pony and small cart in the background. The placard said "Romanian Gypsy of the 19th Century" but what caught Kelly's eye was a carved wooden box at the edge of the table. The woman's hand rested on top of it, but the carved pattern was clear.

The box looked very much like Sam's jewelry box. Kelly had seen it in various places—the master bathroom, the living room, Sam's vehicle. Hmm … she wondered … could it be that the box had originally come from this part of the world?

Chapter 11

Sam woke with a jolt. In the nightmare she was standing on the front porch and could see someone in the woods on the other side of the meadow. A glint of sunlight on steel. She shouted to Tony and Isobel but her voice was silent and they couldn't hear her words. She dove for Isobel, but the bullet got Tony anyway.

Adrenaline pumped through her, her breath coming out in gasps. Beside her, Beau slept peacefully on his right side. His words came back: *"I can't come up with a reason for Tony to be the target ..."* Tony wasn't the target. Sam swung her legs over the edge of the bed.

Could *she* have been the target? She possessed the box they wanted. But her death wouldn't necessarily give up the box. Shooting Tony, right in front of her, had been a warning.

She walked softly to the bathroom, pulled her robe from the hook on the back of the door, and padded down the stairs. Moonlight came through the French doors at the back of the house, lighting the great room well enough for her to see her way to the kitchen. She turned on a burner under the kettle and stared out the window while it heated. The driveway was quiet. Beau's cruiser sat in his usual spot—she loved the fact that he liked to park it where anyone driving up to the house would see that a lawman lived here. It made her feel safer.

His protective actions made her feel all the more guilty because she was hiding her thoughts from him, her virtual certainty that the killer had been after her. She should tell him.

The kettle whistled. She quickly turned off the burner and reached into the nearby canister for a packet of hot chocolate mix, stirring it into the hot water she'd poured into her favorite mug.

She envisioned how the conversation would go. *"Beau, the man who killed Tony was actually after me."*

"I'm putting twenty-hour guards on the house and I don't want you going outside—the guy could get you as you're driving down the street, he could come into the bakery, he could catch you getting out of your delivery van at someone's birthday party."

"It wouldn't happen that way."

"It could."

Of course, anything *could* happen, she thought as she carried her hot beverage to the living room. The world *could* come to an end tomorrow, if you believed the doomsayers. She *could* die of exhaustion from trying to keep up with her business.

The unbidden thought stopped her in her tracks. Aside from worries over the wooden box and the people it had brought into her life, wasn't her greater worry that she would simply stop coping? The pace of her life had been crazy for several years now. Kelly chided her for thinking she could do it all. Beau tried to protect her. Even Zoë, her best friend, had made concerned comments about how tired she looked.

She slipped into her favorite corner of the sofa and raised the mug to her lips. The comforting warmth soothed her and she breathed deeply to clear her mind of the tumultuous thoughts. I don't need to do it *all*, she reminded herself. I have employees and suppliers and contractors. It's a matter of managing the team and scaling up the process to cover the additional workload. And if there's one thing I do know how to manage, it's getting an amazing amount of work done. My company has grown before, I can do it again.

With the help of magic.

There was no way to know if the special power from the box would be available to her anymore. It hadn't been of much help the past few weeks, and now there was a concerted effort to take it completely away … She tamped down that train of thought as she drained the last of her cocoa.

Breathe, Sam, just breathe. She made her way back to bed and snuggled against Beau.

* * *

Sweet's Sweets was bustling when she arrived at seven in the morning. Becky was putting final touches on a tiered cake for a bridal shower, a three-tiered creation designed by Jen, the front-counter girl who'd developed quite an eye for pastry design. Julio, her baker extraordinaire, pulled a tray of banana muffins from the large bake oven as Sam walked in and greeted them.

"How's the mother of the bride?" Becky asked, without taking her eyes off the delicate piping on the cake. "I'll bet the extra day off helped restore your sanity. The wedding ceremony was so beautiful."

"The newlyweds are loving their hotel in England, according to Kelly's call."

"England? When did the plans change?" Becky paused in mid-scroll with the icing.

It was a reminder that the rest of the world, even their closest friends, knew nothing of the changes in plans or the traumatic events yesterday. Sam pulled herself into the current moment in the bakery world she loved and told them how the surprise trip had come about.

She kept a watchful eye toward Julio as she talked—at one point she'd wondered if he had romantic feelings toward Kelly, but she'd met Scott at nearly the same time. Julio nodded and smiled and kept on with his work. He had attended the wedding, and he'd seemed genuinely happy for the couple. Odds were, Sam had over-reacted to what was simple friendship.

She walked through the kitchen, automatically checking supplies and glancing through the order sheets to see what was coming up for the week. Out in the customer area the beverage bar was neat and tidy; Jen was helping a couple of elderly ladies decide among muffins, strudel, or cheesecake. The window displays were in good shape, although Sam thought it would be a good idea to switch out a couple of the cake designs. Sales always perked up when something new inspired her customers' imaginations.

Back in the kitchen, she mentioned the display idea to Becky but made sure to give it 'when there's a chance' priority. Until Sam could spend time here and do more of the decorating herself, she knew Becky was swamped. She'd be back soon, she hoped. When it came right down to finding the pure joy of the business, Sam most loved designing and decorating cakes.

Meanwhile, there were other details she discovered when she checked her email and saw an e-ticket to New York. Stan Bookman had set up their meeting with the cruise line execs a week from today, which opened a whole new set of to-do items for Sam, not the least of which was to figure out what a small-town baker from New Mexico ought to wear to a corporate meeting in the city. Preparations must be made.

She sat at her desk and downloaded the spreadsheet she'd started yesterday. It was time to work the numbers and figure out how much chocolate she could reasonably produce for this contract. By converting all the Victorian's downstairs rooms to production and hiring twenty more people, they might come up with something close. But that left the packing and shipping departments homeless. Moving them upstairs wasn't practical—too many heavy cartons to be toted up and down. She felt a headache coming on.

"Sam—Sam, take a break," Becky said, somewhere at the edges of Sam's consciousness. "You just moaned."

Sam veered her attention away from the computer screen. "I did?"

"Can I do something to help?" But Becky's worktable was covered in cake layers for the three birthday cakes she had going simultaneously, and she held a full pastry bag in each hand.

Sam smiled. "I think it's the other way around. I should be helping you. What can I do to get away from this computer for an hour or two?"

Becky made a face. "I actually have the birthday cakes fairly well under control, even though it doesn't look like it now. But that tiered cake I finished this morning … it's due at the party venue by noon. Could you, maybe …"

"Absolutely. Getting outside is exactly the prescription for my headache." She went to the walk-in fridge and transferred the cake to a box on a wheeled cart. "The van is out back, right?"

Julio took a minute to help her get the confection into the van and settled in a secure spot. With the delivery address in hand, Sam concentrated on what the next twenty minutes would bring. The bridal shower was being held at someone's home, and she found the address just off Cruz Alta Road. A long, paved driveway led to the low adobe, a sprawling place which, with the surrounding perfectly tended grounds and mown fields, must have set the owner back a couple million at least.

The mother of the bride met her at the door, and Sam recognized her as one of the town's leading philanthropists, wife of a lawyer whose main clientele consisted of the movie star crowd in Santa Fe. That explained the luxurious digs.

"I can manage the cake," Sam said, "if you'll show me where it goes and make sure there's a cleared spot for it."

Mom led her to a great room with all-glass walls revealing a view of Taos Mountain. She pointed out a serving table where plates and silver forks lay in haphazard confusion with garlands of flowers and a pair of Nambe candlesticks.

"Mind if I move some of this aside? I'm guessing you'll want the cake in the center?"

Two young women bustled in, both wearing short

kimonos and rollers in their hair. "Jess needs you, Mrs. B," said one of them.

The mother bustled away and Sam quickly stacked the plates and napkins, set the silver forks nearby, and shoved all the flowers aside for someone else to deal with. Ten minutes later the cake was in place and she was on the road again, shaking her head. With this much fuss and elaborateness to the bridal shower, she wondered what the wedding itself would be like.

She ought to check with Jen and see if the customer had discussed the cake yet. She envisioned one of those fairy-castle confections that would need to be baked and decorated in a dozen sections, then assembled on-site at the reception. Which was fine—she always loved the elaborate cakes—as long as the family didn't turn into a bridezilla and her vampire-mom. She'd dealt with a few of those. She shoved aside those thoughts, filing that scenario for later.

The ride back to the bakery gave her time to get some distance and perspective on Book It Travel and the cruise line deal.

"Don't freak out, Sam," she said to the empty space in the van. *Yet. I'll just set limits on what's possible. Yeah, right. Until I meet with them next week, I have no idea what their attitude will be.*

Still, a group of businessmen and women surely couldn't be any tougher than a richer-than-God family who wanted the perfect wedding for their daughter, no matter what the cost. "Limits. That's my watchword." The only problem was, how to know what her limits were.

She'd just pulled into the alley behind the bakery when her phone chimed the little tune for a video call. Kelly.

"Hey, Mom!" Her radiant daughter was clearly relaxed and happy.

Sam settled into her seat and watched as Kelly used the connection to show a quick tour of their hotel room, complete with huge windows and canopy bed. Scott was sitting on one of the pair of armchairs near the fireplace, reading a book, waving when the camera went by.

"This town is just the cutest!" Kelly raved. "Everything is *so* old, and Scott already had to buy another carry-on bag to bring all the books and materials he's picked up about the history. People have lived here since forever. He's gone completely over the edge in research mode. I'm in love with the shops. The clothes are cute and really different from what I can get at home, so yeah, I've bought a few things too."

Her bubbly descriptions went on, covering the wonderful food they'd had everywhere they ate and how friendly the British people were. "They think our accents are cute! I laughed 'cause I think theirs are the best. Too funny, right?"

Sam laughed along with her.

"So, how are things back home? Beau and you doing okay? Are Ranger and Nellie happy? Does Riki miss me at the shop yet?"

"How many glasses of wine did you say you had with dinner tonight?" Sam asked, rather than going into any of yesterday's gruesome details.

She could hear Scott chuckling in the background.

"So, tonight's our last one here at the Angel, and I'm going to be so sad to go. Scott even got the concierge to take him into the Charles Dickens room. Now he wants to come right back and stay in that room while he writes a book. Tomorrow our driver will pick us up and all our stuff, and we'll move into Stan Bookman's house. We saw it already—very classy, although small. It's the perfect cozy size for us. Isn't he just the nicest man, Mr. Bookman, to give us this opportunity? I have to think of an appropriate thank-you gift for him."

Sam had to admit she had no ideas about that. Her recent annoyance with Bookman over the complicated contract would have to be put aside. He really had given the kids a great gift. But Sam sensed the true price was yet to be revealed.

Chapter 12

Beau had slept well, awakened early, and used those gray-dawn hours to clear his mind for the new day. He performed a few ranch chores—tended the horses, mucked out stalls, and noted a couple of small barn repairs he would ask his part-time hired hand to take care of next week. The routine tasks helped him look at the bigger picture on his new case.

The thing about this one that ate away at him was the fact that it had happened here on his own land and Sam could have so easily been hurt or killed. He'd never forgive himself if anything happened to her. It gave him a personal stake in catching this killer and making sure the danger never returned to his personal world.

Back in the house, he showered and dressed quietly. He knew Sam had been up at least once in the night, and he'd left her to her own thoughts. She had her plate full now; with Kelly's wedding, this new contract that had something to do with her chocolate-making business, and the normal busy state of her bakery it had been a demanding couple of months. Add the horrific event yesterday, and it was no wonder she couldn't sleep.

She was just waking up as he got ready to walk out the door, so they said a very quick goodbye and promised to touch base later in the day. He needed to be at work before the night shift guys left; he'd left word that he wanted a debriefing with all deputies present. He knew Sam would offer to help with the case in an instant, if she had the time, but that was more than he could ask of her.

Rico and Evan both pulled into the small staff parking area right behind Beau, and the three walked into the squad room together. One of the night guys had made fresh coffee, so after everyone had helped himself to a cup, Beau gathered them for the briefing.

"Anything new during the night?" he asked.

"Streets were quiet, boss," said the newest man, Todd Weathersby.

"Sandoval—what about faxes, messages, texts? Anything new come in?"

The other deputy shook his head. Not that Beau had anticipated the forensics division in Santa Fe, nor the OMI's office in Albuquerque, would incur overtime by staying late for him, but one could hope.

"We've got one name to go on now," Beau told them. "My source doubts this would be the shooter, but we need to check him out. Right now, he's just a person of interest, someone we know to have a marginal connection to the victim. Name's Marcus Fitch. He works in Washington,

DC, but we're not sure if that's also where he lives."

He turned to his right. "Evan, I'd like you to get on that, see what you can learn about him. Rico, on the off chance that Fitch actually did come here, see if you can find any evidence of his being on a flight to New Mexico. Albuquerque, most likely, but check the other airports, even out to Denver, Phoenix ... He would have had to rent a car to get to Taos, and maybe he thought it would be less noticeable if he couldn't be traced to the nearest airport."

The night deputies were fidgeting and he dismissed them. It was nearly eight o'clock when the intercom on his desk buzzed.

"Yeah, Dixie?"

"Bill Smithfield, from Ballistics in Santa Fe, Beau. Line one."

"Hey Bill, give me some good news."

A chuckle at the other end. "I knew you'd appreciate an early morning call," said the expert he'd met at a law enforcement conference a couple years ago. "I hope it's good news. We like to see you guys wrap up your cases quick and easy."

Papers rustled for a second, then Beau heard computer keys clicking.

"The bullet from your victim was relatively clean, with clear lands and grooves. It's a 6.5 Creedmoor with polymer tip, and the only weapons I know of that make that pattern are either a Tikka T3 or a Bergara B-14, both high-power rifles with an impressive range."

"The shot came from more than two hundred yards away," Beau said.

"Easy. The Tikka, in particular has been known to be accurate at a thousand yards. Well, of course, that's in the hands of the right shooter. Anybody can mess up a shot like that. There's probably only a few dozen marksmen who could make it."

"The two-hundred-yard shot or the thousand?"

"Oh, the two hundred isn't all that challenging. But to hit a person—that's a moving target with a small kill zone. I, uh, saw the pictures. The victim was shot in the very center of his forehead."

"Right."

"In that case, I'd bet your shooter has military training and a place he can go for regular practice. I'd be checking on military snipers."

Or retired ones. Beau couldn't imagine there was a government or military force behind this particular death but then again, he reminded himself, anything was possible. He needed to keep an open mind.

"One other question, Bill. Is it feasible for either of those weapons you mentioned to be carried aboard a commercial flight?"

"In a locked case, checked with the airline, with proper documentation for both the gun and the passenger— sure. Hunters travel with their weapons all the time. So do government employees, but that's usually on a need-to-carry basis."

"For a guy who doesn't want his identity known …"

"If you're thinking along the lines of a professional sniper, someone whose business with the weapon is illegal. He could easily get hold of one of the new 'invisible' rifles. Made of plastic parts, disassembles into almost nothing. He'd hide parts in one or more pieces of luggage and walk right through."

So it was a good-news, bad-news situation, Beau

reflected after Bill hung up. They could narrow down the weapon and, if they found it, could match it to the bullet in evidence. Finding the rifle and the shooter … that sounded as if it had just gotten a lot more complicated.

A tap at his door—Beau raised his head to see Rico. "Boss, I've got calls in with TSA and some of the airlines. Nobody's getting back to me yet on that, but meanwhile I've been scrolling through some of the databases of shoe prints."

"Any luck?"

"Do you know how many different manufacturers make how many styles of shoes in a given year?"

"Can't exactly imagine."

"Exactly. But I'll keep working on it, boss. The size is probably an 8-1/2 or 9."

Beau nodded. It was a slim lead, at best, but at least they had an idea of the size of their shooter. One of those compact, wiry military guys who was trained as a sniper precisely because he could squeeze into nooks and crannies and still operate a weapon efficiently. Determined not to let his optimism leak away, he called Evan in and told him to see if he could find out how tall Marcus Fitch was. If he turned out to be six feet tall, well, at least they could eliminate a suspect.

Chapter 13

Kelly loved the food department at Marks & Spencer. She had made a quick scouting trip their second day in Bury, but now they were in a home with a kitchen and she was back to shop in earnest. Scott had cautioned her not to load up the fridge—there were still lots of excellent restaurants to be tried. With that in mind, she picked up one of the small wire baskets and looped the handle over her arm.

Teatime at home was a must—she'd already experienced that luxury in the hotel room anytime she wanted. The tea aisle was beautifully simple—three levels of strength in the black teas (she chose the middle one) and a couple of milder ones (she picked up a small box of the chamomile). The selection of cakes was slightly mind-boggling but she had to show restraint. She'd be the size of a house if she indulged her desire to try one of everything. She settled on a small Battenberg cake and a sticky toffee pudding, promising herself she would make them last a minimum of a week. And she would come back and take some home for her mom. It would be amazing if Sam could figure out how to duplicate the English treats for her customers at Sweet's Sweets.

"I saw that," came a voice behind her. Kelly snapped her hand away from the box of Bakewell tarts she'd nearly picked up. Scott had been at the Visitors Center, picking up more historical pamphlets and books, and she'd only casually mentioned where she was coming.

She laughed at his gawking gaze into the shopping basket. "Okay, that's all the desserts. I promise. Let's decide what we want for lunch."

She led the way to the fresh produce and ready-made meals section. The selection was large and varied—they would have no chance to become bored over the next couple of weeks. She chose a salad with a variety of greens, a packet of crunchy toppings, and its own special dressing. Scott chose a spinach salad and said he liked the looks of a small tray of turkey, ham and cheeses, a snack in place of a big dinner this evening. Some fresh fruit and a bottle of wine, and the basket was becoming heavy.

"Once I get more familiar with the stove and the pots and pans at the house, I'll come for things I can cook—one of these shrimp dishes, or maybe that stir-fry. They all look fantastic."

The clerk divided their purchases between two carrier bags, and they set off for home.

"Tomorrow, I'd like to ride the train to Cambridge," he told her as they put the groceries away.

"Graham could take us, you know. He offered, anyplace we want to go."

"Maybe a different trip. I think the train experience will be fun."

"You know what else will be fun …" she teased, popping a grape into his mouth.

He eyed the bedroom and wiggled his eyebrows. "What's a honeymoon for, anyway?"

Articles of clothing got strewn across the lounge and into the hall on the way to the bed. "I'm glad Mr. Bookman had a maid service come before we arrived," Kelly murmured. "It would be creepy to climb into the bed right after he'd left it."

"Shh, shh … mood killer," he said into her ear.

"Okay, then, let's start in the shower."

He didn't need to be convinced. The steamy water and luxurious bath gel put them both in the mood. Later, lying under a cool Egyptian cotton sheet, Kelly sighed.

"I really don't miss being at home, bathing dogs all day," she said.

"I really don't miss my students. Thank goodness we have the summer break away from each other."

"I wonder how Mom's handling the bakery and the chocolate factory. You did hear her say this new contract with Book It Travel was huge? Sometimes I worry that she's overloading herself with work."

"Your mom will do fine. I've never met a woman who could get so much done. She's a dynamo."

She laughed. "That she is."

"Hey, let's do that ride to Cambridge this afternoon. What are we waiting for, anyway? It's only thirty miles away, and we'll figure out what to do once we get there."

The local railway station fit exactly with the style of the other buildings in town—red brick, tan rock trim, slate roof, and what appeared to be a bell tower. They bought tickets in the small lobby and waited at Platform 2 to board the Greater Anglia train with the bright red doors. Forty-four minutes after stepping aboard, they emerged at the far busier Cambridge station.

Meandering the streets was fun, noting how many of the buildings and scenes were very similar to Bury; other areas with wide open parks and the River Cam running through felt different.

"Let's ride one of the boats," Kelly said with a light in her eyes.

The flat punts filled with tourists crowded the river, but they quickly got tickets and stepped down into one. Their guide gave a narrated tour as he poled the boat, pointing out the various colleges and important buildings. Scott's interest perked up at the sight of the four-hundred-year-old buildings and what felt like hallowed halls. They left the boat at the end of their tour and decided to walk through the gardens, admiring the low-hanging weeping willows and beds of brilliant flowers.

A small admission price got them into King's College, where Kelly stared in awe at the ceiling of the beautiful chapel, while Scott browsed every placard that explained the history of the renowned school. When they connected with each other again, he told her he had already met a fellow history professor.

"Kel, he gave me his card and said he could get me into the library as a visiting educator. How amazing would that be?"

She smiled at his enthusiasm, but insisted it was too

late in the day to turn him loose in a library. They decided to look for someplace to have an early dinner. Wandering through the market area, they spotted a chop house where the aroma of steak filled the air. They left, full and happy, in time to catch an evening train and be back in Bury by dark.

The next morning, plans came together easily. Scott had already declared that another visit to King's College was in order, so he was off on the early train to meet up with his new professor acquaintance.

Kelly played housewife in their borrowed home, unpacking their clothes, throwing a load of shirts and undies in the small washing machine, exploring the kitchen appliances, and setting the tea things on a tray where they would be convenient. She spent the morning in the garden, reading a book she'd picked up at Waterstone's and watching two robins fly back and forth to a nest they'd built under the eaves.

By two o'clock, laundry done and her lunch salad consumed, she felt the need to get out and stretch her legs. She set out, carrying an umbrella in case the clouds continued to build as rapidly as they had in the past hour. Strolling through the residential section, she admired the brick houses, so similar but each with special touches to differentiate it from its neighbors. The lane curved in a graceful arc and she found herself at an unfamiliar intersection. She knew the town center was to her right, and she turned in that direction.

She passed a tire center and a pharmacy, a pub and a B&B, and eventually spotted the familiar obelisk that marked the war memorial. From here, she knew her way back through the shopping areas on Angel Lane and

Abbeygate Street. She meandered, taking her time in a way that never happened when there was a husband at one's side.

Kelly had noticed the many charity shops—cancer, heart, Alzheimer's research—they all ran thrift shops for fund raising, and she'd noticed the window displays seemed always timely with seasonal merchandise that appeared of good quality. Maybe she would take a look, come up with little things to take home as gifts. Rupert, for one, was always up for vintage clothing—but it was tricky to find things in his size. He was, however, a big fan of scarves and shawls, and those might be attainable. She walked over to the window of Cancer Research UK and gazed at the display.

A mannequin in a '20s-style beaded dress, with a feather boa and lovely cloche hat sat at a cute little dressing table covered with sparkling vintage jewelry. On the floor at its feet were stacks of books, mysteries of the same era, Kelly noted. A bentwood rack held a half-dozen hats, and a couple of scarves were draped through its curving limbs. She decided to take a look inside.

A couple of shop employees were busily sorting and setting items out for display, leaving her to browse at her leisure. When the older woman noticed that Kelly seemed to have targeted one of the scarves in the window, she came over and spoke.

"May I assist you with something, miss?"

"The purple scarf with the paisley design, there on the rack—how much is it, please?"

The woman pulled it down and looked for the tag. "Two pounds even." She handed it to Kelly.

It appeared to be cashmere, and Kelly couldn't see any

damage other than a small section of the hem which needed to be tacked back in place. She could do that herself. And Rupert would love it. Surely her favorite adopted uncle was worth it.

"I'll take it, and I'd like to browse a little more," she told the clerk.

"Certainly. I shall hold this for you, there at the till."

I have to keep these gifts small, Kelly reminded herself. Even with a private jet to ride home in, she couldn't be toting home any of the wonderful lighting fixtures or unique furniture pieces—although that cute dressing table would make an adorable desk. She found a book on dog breeds published by the British Kennel Club, for Riki, and a set of Russian wooden spoons, hand painted, for Ivan. Her bridesmaids were both into Victorian vintage jewelry—a hard commodity to find in Taos—so she picked out two pairs of earrings.

By this time she had wandered into a small room near the back where two volunteers were unpacking cartons and bags of donations.

"Choose anything you like," said the young man. "It'll take ages for us to get it all marked and put on display, but Gwen is a gem at pricing. She'll set you right with whatever you want." He nodded toward the older woman who had already assisted her.

"Thanks. I'll look around."

"American?" he asked. "Tourists usually prefer the posher shops."

"I love old things, and most of my friends do too. My husband and I are staying a couple of weeks, so I'm just picking out a few gifts to take home."

At the mention of a husband he went back to a carton

of books. Kelly gazed over the table tops and shelves against the walls, where several sets of china and crystal glittered. Pretty, but not her style. Definitely not something to wrestle nearly five thousand miles back home. Then her glance fell on a pile of dusty items on the floor, things that apparently didn't merit enough attention to immediately be put up for sale. One box caught her attention and she bent to pick it up.

"What's this?" she asked, holding it up to get better light.

Gwen had just walked into the room. She craned her neck forward and coughed slightly as the dust hit her nostrils. A pair of glasses hung from a cord around her neck and she slipped them on to have a better look.

"I actually don't know. Some old thing that's probably been here just ages. I don't remember it coming in, do you, Robin?"

The young man shook his head. "Never noticed it."

Kelly pictured a good dusting and a coat of furniture polish for it. "How much would you charge for it?"

"Oh, no more than fifty pee, I should think."

Fifty pence. Less than a dollar, Kelly calculated. Even if it didn't polish up nicely, she wasn't really out any money. "I'll take it."

Gwen picked a plastic shopping bag from among the packing materials near the two volunteers. "Just slip it in there," she suggested, clearly not wanting to get her hands dusty.

At the register Kelly pulled out the coin purse she was using to keep her British money separate from the dollars she'd brought from home, paid for her purchases and let Gwen place everything into one bag.

She just had time to get home and enjoy a cup of tea and a slice of her new Battenberg cake before Scott would be back.

Chapter 14

Sam needed time alone, to think. She woke with that realization at three a.m. Quietly slipping from bed, she dressed in black slacks, a plain white T-shirt, and her baker's jacket. She wrote a quick note for Beau and patted each of the dogs on the head before getting into her truck and heading for the chocolate factory. Many of life's problems were solved while deeply engrossed in kneading, rolling, stirring, or otherwise working with chocolate.

The old Victorian house stood dark and quiet at this hour. She pulled under the portico and walked into the kitchen. She turned on only one light, admiring the gleam of the copper pots hanging from their hooks and the smooth marble worktop. Deep breath.

Don't stress over what may come in the future, she told herself. *Spend a little time being creative and enjoying the process.*

She went to the pantry and gathered a few simple ingredients—cacao, butter, sugar, cream—then picked up the box containing the tiny bottles of pure flavors, and finally the canister where she kept a supply of the secret ingredient that made her chocolates the best in the world. The process of melting the chocolate slowly, stirring it to the perfect consistency, and adding the other elements was like an elixir to her soul. She stared into the double-boiler pan at the pattern her wooden spoon made in the thick mixture.

When it had reached the perfect temperature, she poured it on the marble slab and began to work with it, smoothing and folding, watching it cool. Soon, the glossy chocolate was ready for molding. She took a tiny pinch of the ethereal green powder she'd obtained from her mentor, the odd Romanian chocolatier who had appeared at her doorstep one Christmas. Bobul still could create chocolates that astounded Sam—his touch with the chocolate itself and his imagination and dexterity in executing beautiful and intricate designs were beyond anything she had yet mastered. And still, her own creations had delighted people all over the world.

She paused as the iridescent powder dissolved into the chocolate, reminding herself of the joy she'd brought to others. No matter how arduous the business felt at times, *this* was what it was about—creating things that made people happy.

Quickly, before the chocolate could cool too much, she scraped the mound of it into a pastry bag and began filling her favorite mold. The shapes came from nature—a pine tree, a holly leaf, a bird, an egg, a pinecone. When the two dozen spaces were filled, she set the mold aside, took a seat at the end of the table and proceeded, with childlike abandon, to lick the traces of chocolate from the pan and spoon. The act, so reminiscent of simple times, filled her with a pure joy and lightness.

"Thank you," she said to the smear of chocolate on her finger. "I needed this."

She spooned coffee into the basket on the coffee maker and started it to brew.

Dawn light had begun to show at the windows. Sam walked to the kitchen sink and stared out at the wooded land beyond. Although the old house had its share of peculiar squeaks and quirks, she had to remind herself how fortunate she was that her 'factory' sat here on an open spot of land surrounded by trees, rather than being in the midst of some industrial city with an uninspiring view of concrete and asphalt. She walked to the packing room, previously a dining room with a small fireplace, and stared at the view from there, then on to the bay windows in the old parlor, overlooking the shipping cartons now stacked against the walls. At times, the hustle and bustle of everyday production and the petty problems of her crew caused her to forget how good her life truly was.

The wide staircase with its ornate balusters and graceful banister led up to the area where Sam's office gave her a private work spot above the rest of the fray. With the new expansion she would be giving up some of that space, as various functions of the business would need to shift to accommodate more. She spotted the discreetly framed small door in the wall—yes, perhaps the house's original dumbwaiter would be put to use in moving product and materials. Her peaceful mood dimmed slightly as she again became caught up in logistics.

"Not right now," she said to the house. "I'm here to enjoy the morning, not to get myself in a twist over how much work I'm creating for myself."

Back in the kitchen, she checked the chocolate mold and saw the pieces had cooled enough to come out. In an upper cupboard was a beautiful English china plate she'd used a few times when serving samples to visitors. She pulled it out and unmolded the new chocolates onto it.

"My private supply," she said with a smile.

The coffee was ready. She poured a cup for herself and picked up the plate, taking her treasure upstairs to her office, where she watched the sunrise from the tower windows. Her first bite from the batch sent a feeling of peace and equanimity through her body. Yes, the few extra hours alone, the time to drop her concerns for the future and simply cherish the joyful moments—it had been exactly what she needed.

She turned on her computer, determined to hold onto the joy.

She took another chocolate and let it melt on her tongue. Below, her crew had begun to arrive. Benjie Lucero's little car was the first to pull onto the gravel parking area, followed by Lisa Gurule and Dottie. They were good people, good at their jobs, Sam reminded herself. The most experienced could be put in charge of the newer, larger divisions as the big orders came in.

She brought up her spreadsheet and rechecked her numbers, adding factors for the amount of output the kitchen currently achieved and multiplying by what would be needed. As long as she stuck with pure numbers, her mood remained level. Anxiety only crept in when she began to envision where the extra people and supplies would fit into the space which had once seemed large enough to swallow the entire operation with room to spare.

She popped a third chocolate into her mouth.

Chapter 15

Beau sat at his desk, forehead on palm, running his fingers through his hair. What possible leads could they check next? Everything in the murder case seemed to be at a dead end or a standstill. The shoe that made the one footprint couldn't be traced, the weapon was not a common one, but gun ownership was registered state-by-state and it could be a long process to track them all. So far, Marcus Fitch had not shown up as a gun owner, and certainly not of a high-power model such as the one they were seeking.

Rico was currently contacting airlines, asking for information on their manifests, hoping Fitch had checked in for a flight under his own name. Finding anyone who'd checked a locked gun case would be a bonus. Evan was wading through the crowded records of the DC authorities to learn more about Fitch—did he have a record, could he provide an alibi for three days ago? It was slow going; cops in other jurisdictions had their own cases, and helping with a crime in faraway New Mexico was low on their list. Beau and Evan shared a rueful chuckle when Evan had to explain that New Mexico was actually one of the fifty states, not in a foreign country. It wasn't an uncommon misconception, he'd learned over the years.

Meanwhile, all he could do was wait for responses and hope they provided usable answers. He picked up his mug—empty—and decided to see if the coffee maker had been refreshed in recent hours. The dark sludge at the bottom of the pot told him it hadn't. He needed to get out of here.

He phoned Sam. "You free for lunch?" he asked.

Her tone sounded more relaxed than in recent days. "I'd love that. I'm just leaving the chocolate factory and heading toward the bakery. Shall I pick you up or do you want to meet somewhere?"

"We'd better meet. I never know when a call might come in."

"I'll treat you to Lambert's, if you'd like," she said.

"Feeling in a good mood, huh?"

The menu was somewhat upscale, more their special-occasion date night place than for a quickie lunch. It was also only a couple of blocks from his office, so he readily agreed. By the time Sam walked in, he'd chosen a table outdoors under an old apple tree and was studying the lunch menu. A young waitress with the quick movements of a fox, and red hair to complete the impression, brought glasses of water. Beau chose a sandwich and Sam opted for something she'd never had before—tuna tacos.

He caught himself studying Sam's face. "You really are in a good mood today, way more relaxed than I've seen you in a while, even before …"

Sam reached into her pack and brought out a little plastic sandwich bag. "Here—have a chocolate."

"Save it for me for dessert," he said with a smile. In his wife's world, chocolate solved everything.

"How's the case going?" she asked as she dropped the baggie back into a side pocket.

"Slow. I don't want to say 'dead end' but nothing's coming together yet." He told her about the frustrating lack of clues.

Their food arrived and conversation lagged for a few minutes.

"This Marcus Fitch you told me about—have you ever met him?" he asked, dabbing his mouth with a napkin.

Sam shook her head. "I got a glimpse once from a distance, but never face to face."

"Based on the shooter's footprint, we think it's someone about five-nine or shorter. Could that be Fitch?"

She shook her head. "I'm sorry, Beau. I really couldn't say for sure."

"It's okay. Just clutching at straws." He picked up the second half of his sandwich. "So far, we aren't getting anything useful from car rental agencies or airlines, but Rico is still working all the angles we can think of."

"What about this OSM organization in Washington, DC?"

"I feel like I'd need to go there, talk to someone face to face. If the group is actually behind this attack, I doubt anyone's going to tell me anything on the phone. Even in person, it's iffy as to whether someone would open up and speak against their own members."

"True. From what Isobel has told me, they're very secretive."

"It would help if I had some idea about the motive. For all we know, it was some personal vendetta against Tony Robards himself."

"Someone followed him all the way to New Mexico to shoot him?" Sam's skepticism showed. "The man lived in Virginia. It would have been so much easier to get him close to home."

"So you still think Isobel was the target, but wouldn't the same hold true for her? She lives in Alexandria, doesn't she? Someone coming after her … close to home would be easier in that case too."

Sam pushed her half-finished lunch aside and looked around. He followed her gaze. Only three other tables were occupied, but one couple was watching the sheriff and baker with a little too much interest.

"All right," Beau said. "there's something more and you can't say anything here. Let's finish up and walk outside."

"Beau—"

"You never really told me why this Isobel came to visit, Sam."

"I know and it's—it's complicated."

"I'm ready when you are." He set aside the rest of his sandwich and swallowed the remains of his water, signaling to the waitress.

Out in front of the restaurant, they strolled down Bent Street. "It's a murder case, Sam. You need to tell me what you know."

"Isobel came to warn me about OSM."

"Right, so you said. Why? What's their motive?"

"It's got to do with that wooden box, the one I used to keep my jewelry in."

His forehead wrinkled. "It's an old chunk of wood. Why would it be important?"

"Well, I've told you parts of it, about the box's influence when I hold it … It's just that Isobel … well, she's convinced OSM is after the box."

"And would shoot a man because … why? What is Tony Robards' connection?"

"That's harder to figure out," Sam said.

They had come to a clump of tourists gathered near the entrance to the Governor Bent Museum. Rather than push through, they turned around, crossed the street, and headed back to the lot where they'd both parked. Beau's phone rang as they approached Sam's truck. She got in and mouthed "See you later" as he pulled the phone from his belt.

Still puzzling over her comments about this Isobel person and the connection with Sam's jewelry box, he looked at the phone readout.

"Yeah, Rico, what's up?"

"Got a hit from one of the airlines, boss. Air Italy."

Beau made him repeat it. A garbage truck pulled into the lot just then and began the noisy process of pulling beside a dumpster to pick it up.

"I'm gonna head your way," Beau said. "Can't hear a thing out here." He walked into the squad room six minutes later.

"Air Italy," Rico said. "Their manifest shows Marcus Fitch on a flight from Reagan National to Rome the night before our shooting happened here. Fitch definitely checked in for the flight and boarded the plane. They emailed me a copy of his passport. His immigration documents show him staying at the Piazza della Sol Hotel, and according to their information he just checked out this morning."

"So there's no way Fitch could have been our shooter."

Rico shook his head.

"But it doesn't mean he couldn't have hired one." Beau felt an odd mix of elation and defeat. Finding someone Fitch hired would be a lot more complicated than finding Fitch himself.

He walked into his office and put in a call to the TSA.

Chapter 16

Kelly set the dining table with some interesting dishes and linens she found in the cottage. A small roast beef was in the oven for their dinner. Scott would be back from his day in Cambridge soon, although she'd been surprised he and the professor acquaintance had found an entire day's worth to chat about.

The oven timer went off at nearly the same moment she heard his key in the lock. He came in, smelling of fresh air with a faint undertone of railway station fumes, and dropped his messenger bag and umbrella on a chair near the door. Kelly set the roasting pan on a trivet and met him in the living room.

"You'll never guess—" They both said it at once, stopped, and laughed.

"You first," she said. "Come in the kitchen and make

yourself a drink while I mash the potatoes, and you can tell me about your day."

"So, guess what I found deep in the library at King's," he said while he washed his hands at the kitchen sink.

She shrugged, busily rummaging through the drawers for a knife to slice the roast.

"A connection to Taos. And—more than just that—a connection with the house your mother bought for her chocolates."

"The Victorian?"

"Exactly. Remember how we discovered that an eccentric writer used to live there?" He opened a bottle of wine. "Eliza Nalespar was her name."

"Oh yeah, there was a strange family history, something tragic …"

"Yes! Her father died when he fell over the banister from the second story—some speculation as to whether it was an accident or not. Her mother went over the edge mentally. As Professor Midge says, 'quite mad' although I'm sure there are more politically correct terms for it now. All this happened before Eliza was nineteen."

Kelly was nodding while trying to concentrate on what she needed to do next to finish the meal preparation.

"What I didn't know about Eliza was that she actually left New Mexico for a time and came to Cambridge for her studies. According to the yearbooks, she was described variously as 'the moody one' and the 'one with great hidden creative genius.' And we know at least the creativity part was true because she did go on to write several books."

He carried the gravy boat to the table, dipping a finger and taking a taste.

"Eliza's most popular book, of course, was called *The Box*, which sold a few thousand copies in the US but which was enormously popular over here in the UK. Who knew, right? Professor Midge told me the college here adapted a course using Eliza's book as part of the material. It was sort of a fact-or-fiction-style class about the occult. I've got to tell your mom about it when we get home."

She handed him bowls of potatoes, carrots, and peas to set on the table, checking the kitchen to be sure she hadn't forgotten anything.

"Speaking of Mom and interesting things, after dinner I'll show you what I found for her in one of the shops."

Forty minutes later, meal consumed and dishes done, Kelly showed him the odd box she'd bought. "She'll be so surprised at this!"

Scott, although normally a fan of old and dusty things, gave the box a sideways look. "No offense, my lovely bride, but why would your mom want that?"

"She has a similar one—maybe they'd be a pair."

His skepticism didn't dim.

"Well, I'll show it to her on our next Facetime chat. If she absolutely doesn't like it, I'll leave it behind, maybe as a house gift for Mr. and Mrs. Bookman." She gave it a critical look. "I'd better clean it up first."

"Yeah, no kidding," he said with a laugh.

She set the box aside and they turned on the TV in the living room, where they laughed over the nearly identical format to the US version of a house-hunting show, followed by one in which two guys traveled the country looking for antiques in people's barns. Before long, they were bored with television. Scott spread his books and papers over the dining table, and Kelly took a novel to bed.

Over scrambled eggs and toast the next morning, Scott announced that he wanted a day at the museum today—a guest speaker was presenting 'Hidden Bury, Beneath the

Surface,' a lecture followed by a tour into the town's ancient underground passageways.

"Should be fascinating," he told Kelly. "You're sure you don't want to come along? There's lunch afterwards in an old crypt."

She swore he was beginning to adopt a slight British accent. She shook her head and passed the marmalade. "Narrow, dark spaces have never held much appeal for me," she said with a tight smile. "Reminds me too much of the time Cassie Woodhouse and Mary Ann Sanchez talked me into creating a 'clubhouse' in a cave near the ski valley. We were on a Girl Scout outing, and nearly got stuck in there. The troop leaders were on the verge of calling search and rescue to find us."

He patted her hand. "I can pretty well promise you search and rescue won't have to come get a guided tour out of the Bury St. Edmunds catacombs."

"That's reassuring. I'm glad you'll be perfectly safe. I had in mind spending the morning in the ladies clothing department at Debenhams, followed by Facetime with my mom this afternoon. You take your time and enjoy all the old, dusty things you can find."

Her glance went to the shelf where she'd set the box she'd bought yesterday, speaking of old dusty things. She would look through the cleaning supplies she'd spotted under the bathroom sink and see if the bucket included some furniture polish.

By nine, Scott was happily on his way out the door, his messenger bag slung across his chest. Low clouds hung above the chimney tops, with a hint of drizzle in the air.

Kelly washed the breakfast dishes and tidied the kitchen. She found a can of spray polish and a cloth. The layers of dust came off the old box readily enough, but the dark finish still was not very attractive. With a clean cloth she buffed it some more. Finally, deciding it was probably as clean as it would get, she set the box on the table. She ran her hands over the surface, feeling the smooth patina of wood that was, undoubtedly, decades old.

"Oh well," she said to the box as she set it back on the shelf. "I guess that's as good as you're going to get."

She washed her hands then hurried through a quick shower and shampoo, letting her curls air-dry. The sale at Debenhams began today and the store opened at ten.

There was something fun and liberating about being on her own on a cloudy morning in a small town in a foreign country. She watched as a clerk unlocked the front door at Waterstone's, a proprietor set up a window display in the candle shop, and the butcher cranked up his awning and set out a chalkboard easel announcing today's special on pork tenderloin. The six-block walk to the department store invigorated her, being part of the local crowd as some people bustled toward their jobs and others were, as she was, beginning their day's shopping and errands.

She made her way to the ladies clothing department and browsed the racks. A chic little dress called out to her—she even tried it on—but had to remind herself that there wasn't much call for chic little dresses in Taos. Dress-up occasions usually called for a clean version of her usual jeans and some kind of cute top. If she went all-out, it meant sparkles on the blouse and maybe a piece of jewelry. She put the dress aside. A couple of sweaters were appealing and she bought those. And there was a casual jacket made in a beautiful wool she could picture Sam wearing as autumn weather came on.

Feeling happy with her purchases, she carried her

shopping bag out to the street, where the earlier drizzle had turned to a steady patter. With umbrella up she decided to stop at a little coffee place she had passed several times. Inside, the atmosphere was warm and cozy, with a fire in the grate and plush upholstered chairs to settle into. She ordered tea and a scone, which arrived on a small tray, set on the low table in front of her, complete with pitchers of sugar and milk and a tiny saucer with a pat of butter and a little pot of raspberry jam. All of it proved to be delicious, and she watched out the windows as people hurried past.

When she was feeling thoroughly warmed and noticed the pedestrians no longer carried their umbrellas raised, she gathered her things for the walk home. She left a few coins on the table, although she'd been told tipping was not the mandatory practice here as at home, and picked up her bags. Water dripped from awnings and formed small puddles near the curbs. Kelly found herself walking, along with many others, in the middle of Abbeygate Street, which became pedestrian-only during business hours.

She strolled along Buttermarket and passed the museum, wondering briefly whether Scott and the group might be immediately below her feet at this moment in their tour of the tunnels. As she made the short dogleg turn that would put her on the narrow Brackland Lane and home, a man stepped out in front of her.

He wore loose-fitted clothing and a rough brown beret, much more Eastern European than British in style. His imposing height and width caused her to dodge to the opposite side of the passageway.

"Wait," he said. "Miss Kelly?"

At the sound of her name she hesitated.

"Miss Kelly, daughter of Miss Sam. Is correct?"

"Do I know you?"

He removed the hat and gave a funny little half-bow. "Bobul. I work at Miss Sam bakery."

"Bobul?" No one could fake both his appearance and his accent. Kelly remembered he had worked at Sweet's Sweets one Christmas season. In fact, her mother had said he was the one who taught her the fantastic chocolate-making techniques which had led to expansion into the business of creating handmade chocolates for Book It Travel. Without that connection, Kelly and Scott would not be here in the UK, would not be staying in Mr. Bookman's home here in Bury. It truly was a small world.

"Bobul, what are you doing here?"

"Bobul come to say, Miss Sam be wary or will be alone. And Miss Kelly, take great care with wooden box."

"Box? What are—?"

"Box you buy from small shop. Bring to your mother. She take care of it. But use great care to show no one. Tell no one."

"Why? What is special about it?"

"Hide it. Tell no one." He turned toward a narrow alley. "Tomorrow I tell more."

With that, he disappeared around a bend in the alley and the shadows swallowed him. Kelly stared, debating whether to follow. High brick walls hemmed in the constricted space and the shadows were deep. The light rain had suddenly become a downpour, and a man bumped into her, not watching where he was going.

"Sorry," he said, hurrying on with his collar turned high.

A shiver ran along her arms. She brought out her umbrella again and stared into the alley where water was now rushing over the cobbles. Bobul had said tomorrow he would tell more. Could she believe that? And how would he find her? How had he found her just now?

Chapter 17

Sam piped huge, full-blown buttercream roses onto small waxed paper squares, a task she could perform in her sleep. She'd chosen an easy one because the conversation with Beau still hung in her mind—the one at lunch and the one they would have later. She had to decide how much to tell of the rivalry between OSM and Vongraf, and how to break the news of the box's origins.

She didn't know all of it herself, not by any means, and he certainly didn't need to hear all of it either. But he had a real need to know the extent to which someone—most likely Marcus Fitch—would go to get the box from her. A murder had happened, right at their own front doorstep, and she couldn't take the chance the killer would realize the mistake and come back.

From her desk on the other side of the bakery kitchen,

her cell phone chimed with the Facetime sound. It would have to be Kelly; they'd made a plan to chat today. She quickly set down her pastry bag and wiped her hands.

"Hey, Mom. How's things?" Kelly was in the living room of their cottage in England.

"Great. Busy." Sam had purposely held back details of the shooting. Knowing it would only upset her daughter, she'd merely said that Beau was working a murder case.

"Looks like you're at the bakery. I see a tall cake there behind you."

Sam took a moment to pan the camera around the room. Becky and Julio each gave Kelly a small wave and hello.

"Um, Mom, is there a quiet place you can talk?" Kelly asked.

Sam walked to the back door and slipped out to the small porch. No telling what it was, but Kelly obviously didn't want Sam's employees to overhear.

"I ran into someone you know this afternoon. A total surprise that he recognized me. Bobul—that chocolate maker."

Sam felt her heart begin to pound. Bobul's appearances never seemed to be coincidental. "What did he say?"

"It was weird, Mom, and I wasn't sure what to say to him."

"What did he say to you?"

"Um, well, yesterday I was browsing in one of the charity shops, and—"

Sam felt her mouth draw into a pinched shape.

"Sorry. I picked up a wooden box that looks a lot like that old jewelry box of yours. It was really inexpensive and I thought you might get a kick out of having a pair of them."

"Oh, god, Kel." Sam's heart was in race car territory now.

"What?"

"Go ahead, about Bobul."

"Well, he knew about it. Truthfully, I got a little freaked. It means he's been watching me around town and he somehow knew I bought that box. He told me to take great care with it and not to tell anyone about it. That I should bring it to you." Kelly paused for a breath. "Do you think he's following me? Maybe peeping in our windows here at the house or something?"

Sam's own encounters with the quirky Romanian chocolatier had followed similar patterns. The man seemed to know where she was and what she needed at certain points in her life. For instance, just as she was nearly out of the special powders for her chocolates last Halloween, he'd appeared at the Victorian and brought more. He'd taught her everything she knew about making special chocolates that seemed to change people's lives. But she'd never got the feeling that his interest was anything akin to stalking or peeping. His knowledge went more to the mystical, something beyond.

"I think he's fine, Kel. I mean, always watch your back—any woman should. But as long as you see him out in the open, I don't think he means any harm at all."

"And you think I should bring the box back with me? I could just return it to the charity shop or dump it in a bin somewhere."

"No! Don't do that." *Better to know the whereabouts of the boxes than to have them on the loose, out in the world.* "Bring it home. But Bobul's right—don't show it to anyone. Wrap it in something and stash it in a hidden place. When you come back, keep it in your luggage and make light of it if

Customs should ask."

Kelly's mouth had formed a crooked little smile. "Okayyy … sounds very clandestine."

"It's a long story. We'll talk more when you're back home. I'd rather you didn't even discuss it with Scott until you know the whole story."

"He has seen it. Thought I definitely should not take it as a gift to you. It's pretty rough."

"That's fine. Rough is okay." Sam had another thought. "Kel, does the box have any colored stones on it?"

"No. Just plain wood. Well, it's carved kind of … I don't know … quilted-looking or something. That's what caught my attention, that it looks a lot like your jewelry box."

Sam hoped her expression didn't give away the shocking nature of this news. She thanked Kelly and changed the subject. They talked another five minutes before Kelly cursed the fact that her phone battery was dying.

Sam walked back into the bakery in a daze. The other box had just come back into her family. It must be the one Terrance O'Shaughnessy had in Ireland. No stones but otherwise just like Sam's. She had a feeling she might be about to learn what her great-uncle was going to tell her right before he died.

Would she be able to figure out where the box had been in the meantime? She'd believed the Travellers who hung around Galway had been behind the theft from the back of her rental car. Now she wondered. If it had, indeed, been taken by the gypsy-like Irish nomads why had they let it out of their possession, and how had it ended up in a charity shop in a small English town?

Chapter 18

Sitting on hold while a string of TSA agents passed him around like a virus they wanted to be rid of was getting on Beau's nerves. So far, he'd spent nearly an hour being shuffled between various offices and mired in government bureaucracy.

When a Colleen McWhittle came on the line he explained, for the eleventh time, that a wanted man, Marcus Fitch, was booked on Air Italy flight 23 from Rome, and he wanted him held at the DC airport for questioning in a murder case.

"Are you here in the District yourself, Sheriff … I'm sorry, what was your name?"

"Cardwell. Sheriff Beau Cardwell. I'm in Taos, New Mexico."

"Oh! I visited New Mexico a couple of years ago," Ms.

McWhittle exclaimed. "It's such a beautiful place."

He wanted to get impatient with her, but this was the friendliest greeting he'd received yet. He went along with a minute of small talk—what towns did you visit? Did you like the food?—before bringing her attention back to his request.

"Yes, so this Marcus Fitch you're looking for—will you be questioning him yourself?"

Beau had already thought it out. His department didn't have the budget for him to go buzzing off to the capital, especially since he already felt doubtful Fitch himself was the killer. This was an information-gathering interview, at best. He needed to enlist the help of the FBI, but pictured another hour of phone tag. He dodged the question.

"At this point, I need to know when he arrives back on US soil, and I'd like him available to answer questions."

"Let me check the flight manifest for you," she offered.

He thanked her a little too profusely.

"Hm, it seems Mr. Fitch was booked on the flight, and he did pick up his boarding pass and actually passed through security. No checked luggage, only a carry-on bag. But when the flight attendants did the head-count he was not aboard."

"How does that happen?"

"I wouldn't know. Most likely he just changed his mind. Or maybe there was a family emergency and he left the airport."

"Or boarded another flight. Can you check that? Find out whether he's coming on a different airline?"

"Sheriff, there are nearly three thousand flights a day between Europe and America. It's a huge number of people."

"You have computers. Can't a computer tell us what I

need to know—please, Colleen?" He was suddenly glad for the budget shortage and that he wasn't sitting somewhere at Reagan National waiting for a plane load of Italians and no Fitch.

She'd been about to cut him off but the politely worded request caused her to pause just long enough.

"I don't expect some impossibly instant information, but if you could call me back I'd really appreciate it."

"All right. I can do that."

He gave his number and set down the phone with a thump. He held little hope she would follow through, but he had things to do in the meantime. A call to the Italian airline's main office in New York got him an English-speaking agent who first resisted giving information but relented when Beau gave his law enforcement credentials. Mr. Fitch checked in for his Rome to DC flight, used his boarding pass to clear security, but never showed for the flight. They did not show him on a later flight, nor was he booked on any other Air Italy flight.

"So he must have booked something on another airline?" Beau posited.

"*If* he left Rome, that would appear to be the case," said the agent.

Why would an innocent man make such a sudden and complicated change, Beau had to wonder once he'd hung up from the call. Unless the TSA agent called him back, he realized he was in way over his head. This wasn't the level of investigation for a small town sheriff's department.

It was time to call in the big guns. He dialed the FBI field office in Albuquerque.

Chapter 19

By the next day Kelly found herself peering out the windows, both toward the lane and into the back garden, multiple times. She hadn't told Scott about the mysterious man who'd approached her. Men tended to go all protective and she didn't want trouble. Bobul wasn't exactly a mystery. She'd met him before; he knew her mother. But she knew her carefree days of strolling the lanes and shops here in Bury would now be tempered by watching for his next surprise appearance.

She looked at the carved box she'd casually set on a shelf in the dining room. Mom had said to keep it concealed. She picked it up and carried it to the bedroom. Now that it was no longer coated in grimy dust, she figured the logical thing would be to wrap it in some item of clothing and carry it back to the States inside her luggage. She picked up the cashmere scarf she'd purchased for Rupert. It wound several times around the box, the perfect wrap.

Sticking the parcel into one of the dresser drawers she realized how many things she'd purchased already—clothing for herself, small gifts for friends at home, and she definitely planned to get more tea and cakes to take back. Not to mention all the books and documents Scott had already collected for his studies. She might need to make another stop at one of the thrift shops to pick up a spare tote bag to fit it all.

And that reminded her she ought to be touching base with Mr. Bookman to find out when they needed to leave. Week one of their two weeks had already flown by, and she felt a pang of sadness. She and Scott had lain in bed talking, and both agreed they couldn't very well visit England without a few days in London. Once they knew when their plane would be heading back stateside, they could make a hotel reservation and arrange for Graham to drive them to the city. She picked up her phone and sent a text.

"Hey there," Scott said, emerging from the shower. "What's the plan for today? Looks like we have clear and sunny weather again."

"I want to drop back by M&S for a few things. I'm taking one of those fabulous Battenberg cakes back to Mom. Wouldn't it be great if she could figure out the recipe and start making them at Sweet's Sweets?"

"And the sticky toffee one—that thing is addictive."

She laughed. "Absolutely. I'll get some of each for us, as well. So, anyway, what's your pleasure today?"

He ogled her. "Aside from the predawn pleasure we already had … one thing on my list has been to see the Abbey, and the sign out front said there's a guided tour at ten this morning. Want to come?"

"I peeked inside a couple of days ago when I was just killing time, so I think I've got the gist of what it looks like. You go ahead and hear what the tour guide has to say. I know you'll be taking notes like crazy." She playfully tweaked his beard. "Why don't we plan to meet afterward in the Abbey Gardens, and we could walk somewhere for lunch?"

"Great idea." He reached for his messenger bag, which lay on the chair in the corner. "I will see you then, Mrs. Porter."

Her phone pinged with a text: I'm in NY this week but have a flight arranged for you next Tues. London to Denver. Denver to Taos. He gave the phone number of his secretary in Houston and said she would be sending specifics.

With that information in hand, Kelly called Graham and set it up so they would drive back to London to spend the weekend. She booked a room at the hotel he recommended on The Strand, 'quite convenient' to Covent Garden, Trafalgar Square, Piccadilly Circus, the theaters and the Thames. Making the plans—getting train passes and tickets for events—sent a bittersweet pang through her. Although she missed her mother and friends, she didn't want their time here to be over so quickly.

By the time she'd handled all those details, it was nearing eleven o'clock. The food shopping could wait— she hurried out the door and made her way to the Abbey Gardens. Walking under the massive Abbey Gate across from the Angel Hotel once again brought a sense of awe. A sign said the gate had been burned by the villagers in 1327 and rebuilt twenty years later. The stone version with its heavy steel portcullis was certainly impervious to fire now.

She walked the familiar route into the garden, admiring

the way today's sunshine brought out the vibrancy of the neatly planted flowerbeds around the circular main pathway. Scott would surely be along soon, so she didn't take time for the luxury of walking on into the rose garden or herb gardens on the other side. She chose one of the benches facing the path and sat there, enjoying the sun on her arms.

Less than five minutes into her wait a shadow passed over her feet and the bench vibrated slightly as someone sat down at the other end. She glanced up. Bobul.

"Miss Kelly Sweet. Bobul have something." He reached into the pouch that hung from a strap over his shoulder.

Considering the rather warm day, he was still wearing his baggy clothing with the thick cloth jacket and the hat that made Kelly think of horsehair. From the pouch he pulled a book, about eight or nine inches square and perhaps three inches thick, bound in leather with worn places at the corners. The deckle-edged pages seemed warped and thick. He handed it to her.

She saw no title or other markings on either front or back cover as she turned it over. The leather felt soft, the way a favorite old jacket would become after a generation of wear.

"What's this?" She looked into his deep brown eyes as she asked.

"From Romania, my home." He touched the front cover of the book. "Very old woman used it, great-great-grandmother to … woman burned for sins."

Goosebumps broke out over her entire body. The placard in the museum came back to her, the one about getting rid of awkward neighbors by reporting them for witchcraft. Could this be some kind of spell book? She started to lift the cover to look inside.

"Wait. Take book to Miss Samantha. You read together."

She looked up and saw Scott coming through the Abbey Gate, walking toward the flower garden. Bobul noticed her reaction.

"Like the box, hide book. Tell no one until you show Miss Sam."

"But, what—?"

"Important knowledge. You will need to destroy Facinor." He stood and began to move away.

"Wait! What's Facin— What was that word?"

But he had moved on, cutting over on a narrow dirt trail past the bird cages.

Scott's footsteps left the paved main pathway and became muted on the grass. "Hey there," he said. "Who was the old guy?"

"I—I'm really not sure. Weird."

"You mean, like a pervert?"

"Oh, no, nothing like that." She had slipped the book into the canvas shopping bag she'd brought along for later. "Nice enough man, but he just said some weird stuff about an old Romanian woman. And the really strange thing is, he seemed to know Mom. I definitely have to tell her about that when we get home."

He held out a hand to help her up. "Hungry? I'm starving, and I spotted a pub about two blocks down on Crown Street, near St. Mary's. We could grab something and then take a walk through the cemetery."

"Ooh, fun," she teased.

The outing did turn out to be fun, from her steak-and-ale pie at The Wooden Duck to the stroll through the cemetery which boasted some revealing tombstones with inscriptions such as: *Here Lies Interred the Body of a*

Young Maiden of this Town, born of Roman Catholic parents and virtuously Brought up, Who being in the Act of Prayer ... was instantaneously killed by a flash of Lightning – Aged 9 Yrs."

Kelly shivered when she read that one, and quickly moved on to another, this one about an elderly man commonly agreed to be a curmudgeon.

As they strolled back to the cottage, she told Scott about their reservations for London. "I'm sad to be leaving Bury in a few more days, but it'll be fun to 'do' the city too."

The reminder of their short time here seemed to send Scott into action. He said he planned another stop at the nearby Visitor Center to pick up more historical information, and Kelly had thought of a stop she wanted to make, as well. They would meet back at the cottage and have a light supper, considering their substantial pub lunch.

She crossed Angel Hill road and took the familiar route past the hotel to Abbeygate Street, popping in at the Cancer Research shop. Gwen, the woman who'd helped her the last time, was there again, placing some designer purses on a shelf.

Kelly said hello and reminded Gwen that she had purchased an old wooden box a couple of days ago.

Gwen remembered. "Ah yes, from that dusty lot that were under the worktable in the back."

"Exactly. Do you, by any chance, have a record of who donated it?" She'd already formed a story to go with the request. "My husband is a historian and he seems to think it might be very old. We'd love to know more about where it came from."

Gwen smiled indulgently. "Dearie, everything in this town is very old, myself included."

"Do the volunteers keep records of what is brought in?"

"Only so far as writing up a receipt for the donor, for tax purposes. But we rarely itemize each piece. A receipt would likely say something like 'one bag ladies clothing' or 'assorted kitchen appliances, 4 pieces.'"

"So there's no way to know who owned the box before it came here?"

"I'm afraid not."

Kelly swallowed her disappointment. After Bobul's initial cautionary words about the box, and now his gift of the book and the same advice, she'd become curious. She thanked the woman and left the shop, walking slowly until she came to Buttermarket and turned right toward Marks & Spencer.

She filled her basket with boxes of teas and several of the small cakes to take home as gifts, adding two premade salads for tonight's dinner. The encounter with Bobul remained strong in her mind, his warnings, but also the underlying implication that both the box and the book were meant to come into her hands. And, for some reason, they were intended for her *now*, at this time in her life.

The clerk rang her purchases and Kelly removed the old book from her tote bag, tucking it under her arm while she arranged the groceries in the bag, then sticking the book in alongside them. With her attention diverted in several directions, she handed over a twenty-pound note and received some change and a polite thank you from the clerk.

Had she remembered to tell her mother that Bobul intended today's second meeting? She couldn't remember. Along the way to the cottage she pondered whether to mention the book or to simply show up with it when she and Sam might look through it together.

Her pace increased. She was eager to get inside, lock the doors, and bring out the book and see what it was all about. Bobul's hint that the old woman who owned it might have been a witch—it was enticing and scary at the same time.

Chapter 20

Sam parked in one of the park-and-shuttle lots at the Albuquerque Airport and caught her ride to the terminal, knowing this was probably the simplest portion of the next few days. Check-in and security went smoothly enough, although the queues of people and the relentless PA announcements reminded her to be grateful for her quiet and (mostly) peaceful existence at home.

She sat in the waiting area for her gate, constantly aware of each new person who jostled their way into the row, the noise of their whining children, the impersonal way people stared at screens and didn't speak to each other. It was just as well. She wasn't in the mood for conversation. Her mind buzzed with anticipation over the upcoming meetings tomorrow.

Stan Bookman was flying into New York from

Stockholm or some such place. He'd insisted on meeting her flight at JFK and providing a car to take them into Manhattan where he'd booked rooms at the Carlisle. He had enthusiastically told her he'd secured a reservation at the city's hottest new restaurant for tonight's dinner.

Her boarding group was called and she picked up her bag and looked at the crush of people who seemed to think their reserved seat would somehow go away unless they forced the gate agent into letting them onto the plane more quickly. She sighed and hung back. The flight wasn't going to leave without her. She might as well brace herself. She was heading into a city where fast and pushy were the norm.

Another woman held back, standing near Sam. Dressed in a broomstick skirt and T-shirt, with a strand of turquoise heishi around her neck, she radiated calm.

"Are you from Santa Fe or Taos?" Sam asked as they bided their time.

"Santa Fe." The woman, who Sam guessed was in her early forties despite the tendrils of gray showing at her hairline, gave a nod toward the crowd. "Crazy, huh?"

"I'm not used to it, that's for sure," Sam said. She caught sight of the other woman's boarding pass, then glanced at her own. "Looks like we're sitting together."

"I'm Amanda. Nice to meet you."

"Samantha—Sam. From Taos."

The tide moved forward and their conversation stopped until they were tucked into Row 21 and the crew had gone through the standard spiel that no one listened to because they could quite easily recite it verbatim themselves.

"So, what takes you to New York?" Amanda asked.

"Business. I thought I'd be excited about it—a huge

new opportunity for my company—but I'm kind of dreading it."

Amanda nodded slowly. "Want to talk about it? Not the business deal, but whatever it is you're feeling."

"It's just moving along much faster than I anticipated and growing alarmingly." Sam smiled as she said it, trying to make light of the stress.

"So, a little overwhelmed …"

"Exactly. Plus, there's some other stuff right now."

"Can you put all this 'stuff' into separate compartments? Spread it out a little so it's not all in your face at once?"

Sam considered. It was good advice. "Yeah, some of it. I think so."

"Does it feel a little less pressing, even just thinking of it that way?"

Sam nodded. "A bit. Thanks. I guess the thing that's kind of bowling me over today is the way my largest client is taking charge, ramrodding the whole thing. He's a nice man, but he's built his business by dealing with high-power, important people. Then he steps into my life and just starts making plans for me. Like tonight. I arrive at the airport— he'll meet me. That's nice. I don't know my way around New York very well."

Amanda listened without saying anything.

"We're staying at *his* choice of hotel, going to *his* choice of restaurant, and all day tomorrow will be filled with meetings with *his* high-profile corporate client—although because of his connections they are now my corporate client too. Stan has meetings and events booked for two solid days and then I go back home."

"It's bothering you."

"Half of me is looking forward to the growth and the

challenge. The other half is terrified and resentful. What if I wanted to add a side trip to this one? What if I'd planned to take in a couple of shows, walk through Greenwich Village, shop on 5th Avenue?" She looked down at her clothing and thought of what she'd packed, the few pieces of businesslike attire she owned. A chuckle escaped. "Okay, *not* shopping on 5th Avenue. But taking time to gaze in the windows would have been fun."

A flight attendant came along and asked what they wanted to drink. Both Sam and Amanda said "Just water" at the same moment. Their eyes met and they laughed. The lighter mood felt good.

"So," Amanda said. "Recognizing that you're feeling stressed over this itinerary and this client, what can you do to reduce the tension? Perhaps say 'no' to some of the activities or meetings?"

"I doubt it's possible to cut back on the meetings, and I don't dare let my attention wander too far. I could sign on for a lot more than I want to if I'm not careful."

"Then remind yourself to be careful. With every suggestion, it's okay to say that you need a little time to think about it."

More good advice.

"It's also perfectly fine to say 'no' in the most polite way. 'I'm not quite feeling up to a big dinner tonight' is an acceptable answer. Choose the essential things and pass on the rest. Trust me, you'll find that a big portion of the things people ask you to do are non-essential."

Sam pondered that while she tore into her little bag of freebie pretzels.

"Are you a therapist or counselor or something?" Sam asked.

Amanda smiled and shook her head. "I'm an ex-overdoer. I know I look like a laid-back hippie type right now, but believe it or not I was married to the king of push-for-success for fifteen years. Practically every moment of every day was scheduled. If it wasn't travel, it was business meetings. If it was a vacation, we had to hit every amusement park and sightseeing spot within a hundred-mile radius. We'd drive a day out of the way just to be sure we didn't miss some famous rock or forest. We'd no sooner get there than it became 'okay, that was great, let's try to make the next spot by nightfall.'"

"Yikes."

"Yeah. With youth and ambition on my side, I did it all, went everywhere. I'm a person who absorbs the energy around me, so I kept up with him. Until I landed in the hospital."

"Oh no."

"Oh yeah. My parents stepped in and they were shocked. I was down to a hundred five pounds, looked like a refugee and had aches and pains in every part of my body. The doctors gave it a name that I don't even remember now. My dad called it nervous exhaustion. That pretty well described it."

"How did you get over it? I have to say, you look great now."

"I learned to say 'no.' Hubby didn't like it a bit. He was used to being fully in charge. A therapist taught me how to prioritize and how to make time for the things *I* needed—time to read a book for a whole day, to walk in the garden, to meditate and mainly just to *think*. I never realized how little control I had over my life because there was never the time to think about it. I ran full-throttle from before daylight until I fell into bed exhausted every single night. My family and my therapist stepped in and said that had to stop. When I came out of the convalescent center where they sent me, I'd learned a whole new way to live."

"And how did your husband react to that?"

"We split—within two months. It actually happened on many levels. Mainly, he couldn't handle not being in control of me. It's something I should have seen much earlier, even back when we met. I didn't, and I paid the price. But I came back from the experience as a stronger person."

"Good for you. I'm impressed."

Amanda reached for her bag beneath the seat. "I've learned to watch for signs. The things you really need will come into your life at exactly the right time. Everything else is the non-essential fluff. It takes some practice to limit intrusions into your time, but you can get the hang of it."

She pulled out a book—a real print-on-paper book— and leaned her seat back. "Now, if you'll excuse me. I'm needing some 'me' time."

Sam thanked her and leaned against the window with her eyes closed. She knew the truth and wisdom in Amanda's words. She could learn to say 'no'—couldn't she? She pictured Stan Bookman waiting at the airport gate in just a couple of hours. This wasn't going to be easy.

Chapter 21

Beau had worked with FBI agents from Albuquerque in the past, but it turned out his favorite contact there had been transferred. He felt as if he was starting from scratch and hoped he would get hold of somebody who didn't have an ego the size of the planet. Sometimes these Feds were the sort who wanted to insert themselves into a case without paying the slightest bit of attention to the evidence that had already been collected.

When a Rick Gonzales came on the line, Beau went through the basics about the shooting—how remote the location was, the skill of the shooter and use of a high-power rifle. He told about Isobel St. Clair's conviction that Marcus Fitch was behind it, although he'd already discovered that Fitch had an alibi, traveling to Rome on the day of the shooting.

"The biggest anomaly I've hit in the past twelve hours is this sudden change Fitch made in his return travel plans. He actually checked in and got a boarding pass from Rome to DC, then suddenly went off in some other direction," he told Gonzales. "Question is, why? It's devious behavior, almost as if he knows we're closing in."

"You think Fitch hired the killer."

"It's the best theory we've come up with yet. We'd just like to talk to him. There may be an innocent explanation, but if so I need to eliminate him as a suspect." Beau stared at the evidence bag containing the fatal bullet. "I was seriously trying to think of a way to drag money from my budget for a trip to DC to question Fitch, but we're a very small department. I can't go chasing all over the country."

"No, don't do that. It'll eat you up." Rick chuckled. "Not that we've got unlimited money either, but I can come up there and take a look at what you've got. We should be able to pull some of our resources together and see if we can help."

It took twenty-four hours, but Beau was glad to see Special Agent Rick Gonzales and Special Agent Patricia Draper arrive from Albuquerque the next morning. Gonzales was a seasoned agent, a fit and trim fifty, with generous gray in his black hair, a firm handshake and a ready smile. Patricia Draper looked as though she was straight out of college, petite, with dark hair in a sleek bun at the back of her head. She took in the layout of the squad room with interest; it might have been her first time in a small-town sheriff's department.

Beau invited them into his office and offered coffee, which both accepted. Once Rico had brought the mugs, they settled in and went through the evidence.

"It's not much, is it?" Gonzales said, looking at the bullet.

Draper took a long look at the mold of the shoe print.

"Probably the skimpiest crime scene I've ever worked. And I know the place well." He'd already informed them the shooting had taken place on his own land.

"If I may ..." Patricia Draper spoke up. "I think we need to look at the motive behind the killing, not strictly at who pulled the trigger. It definitely sounds like a hired assassin, from everything you're telling us. But what was the reason for that shooter to be out there in the first place?"

Beau shook his head. "My wife had two visitors at the house that morning. One, Isobel St. Clair, is someone known to her."

"A friend? Business associate?" Draper asked.

"Neither, exactly. The woman works at some kind of foundation that studies antiquities, according to what I know. My wife has some old object that was of interest. I'm afraid I don't know anything very specific about it. Just that Ms. St. Clair and her assistant came out to Taos and spent a day or two." Beau realized how inadequate his explanation sounded. He'd been concentrating on the actual killing and not asking enough questions about the reasons behind it.

"I believe you said it was this Ms. St. Clair who named Marcus Fitch as being behind the crime?" Gonzales asked. "Does your wife know anything about him?"

"Very little. She's never met him, but she agreed that he may have been watching her, waiting for an opportunity to steal this wooden box that seems to be the thing they're all interested in."

"Can we talk to your wife?" Draper asked. "She may be able to tell us more."

"Well, not at the moment. She's in New York for a couple days, some business meeting."

"I'd like to see that box."

Beau considered. Sam had always been very protective of the box and any information about it. And frankly, he'd never been curious enough to ask more. But he couldn't very well bring up the matter of the box and then refuse to let them see it. He knew Sam was keeping it in his gun safe now. "Sure. It's at home. We'll want to go out there anyway, so you can see the crime scene for yourselves."

What could be the harm?

Chapter 22

Sam had been to New York once in her life and never felt compelled to return because to her it felt noisy, dirty, and crowded. This time was a somewhat different experience, beginning when Stan Bookman met her just outside the security gates.

"Sam! Good to see you again so soon," he exclaimed.

Her reservations began to dim somewhat. He really did exude a vibrant energy that became contagious.

Don't let people push you into situations you aren't comfortable with. Amanda's words came back to her. She looked around, seeing several people from her flight, but there was no sign of the woman who had befriended her. Funny. Broomstick skirts and turquoise jewelry weren't exactly commonplace here. And Amanda's hair was fairly distinctive. But Sam didn't spot her.

"This is all you brought?" Stan asked.

"Just the one carry-on bag and my computer."

"Perfect." He sent a quick text on his phone. "Our car will be at the curb in two minutes."

He took the handle of her wheeled bag and pressed forward, Sam quickening her pace to keep up. She scanned the crowd but didn't catch any glimpse of Amanda. She'd wanted to thank the woman for her wise words. There was something almost beyond coincidence about her showing up in Sam's life just when the advice was most needed.

Bookman glanced at his watch as they walked out to the area where hired cars could pull in for pick-ups. "Great timing. We should be at the hotel by six, freshen up, and our dinner reservation's at seven. It's about a five-block walk from the hotel, or we can get a car."

Sam realized he had turned to her for a response. "Um, a walk would feel good. Too many hours of sitting already today."

"Great. That's the plan then."

She noticed that he liked to set up everything in advance. What would he say if, at the last minute, she changed her mind?

He nudged her elbow. The driver had already stowed her bag in the trunk, so she slid into the back seat of the long black car. The drive into Manhattan was in bumper-to-bumper traffic, and Bookman filled the time by asking about her flight, telling her about the four different European cities where he'd been since they last saw each other at Kelly's wedding. She contrasted his conversation to that of Amanda on the plane, realizing the man had a seriously hyperactive style. Whereas she had relaxed in Amanda's presence, now she felt herself tensing up again.

Everything comes along at the right time. Sam cleared her

mind while Bookman talked on, letting herself believe this was her destiny for the moment.

A beautiful little suite at the Carlisle also seemed to be part of her destiny, and Sam walked through the living room, bedroom, and bath while calling Beau to let him know she'd arrived safely. She took in the pastel bedding, shiny brass fixtures, the dainty writing desk in the bedroom, the classic styling of the living room furniture and sumptuous bowl of fruit on the coffee table.

Stan was in a suite one floor up, and since traffic delays caused them to arrive later than planned, he'd said he would meet her in the lobby in fifteen minutes in order to make it on time for the dinner reservation.

Sam sighed. She would love to get into her pajamas and order room service, but the first night in the city didn't seem to be the ideal time to assert her independence from her host.

As it turned out, the dinner was enjoyable and the wine a very good one. They were joined by the cruise line's director of marketing and their CEO's personal assistant—a good-news, bad-news situation. While Sam didn't especially like being careful of everything she said, fearing she would make a bad impression, it was nice to meet the high-power duo outside the conference room ahead of time.

Still, by the time she reached her hotel suite at ten o'clock, she was exhausted. The others had opted for drinks in the bar, but Sam used her long flight as an excuse to skip it. She had the fleeting thought that it would have been nice to bring the carved box on the trip with her. She could have used a shot of its energy. If that energy still worked.

* * *

Her phone rang the next morning as she was brushing her teeth, and she nearly ignored it. But when she saw Kelly's name on the readout, she quickly picked up.

"Hey, Mom. You're in New York?"

"Just got in last night. Meetings start in about an hour."

"Ooh. I'll let you go then. We're heading for London today. It should be fun but we'll miss Bury a lot. Tell Mr. Bookman we've really enjoyed it."

"I'll tell him." They compared schedules and Sam was pleased to know they would all be back in Taos soon. "I've missed you, Kel."

"You okay, Mom? You sound kind of down."

Sam assured her daughter she was fine, but privately she wondered. Things recently had felt *off* somehow. The minute she and Kelly ended their call, Sam felt tears rising.

What the hell? I am not a crier. And I'm definitely not meeting my clients with red eyes.

She let out a deep breath and paced the length of the suite twice. She'd better get her act together before going into what would be one of the more important meetings of her business life. She reached into the closet and chose the closest thing to a power suit she owned. The steel-gray pants and jacket brought out the darker tones in her hair, and the blue shirt complemented her eyes and added rosiness to her face. It was feminine but not fussy in any way. She smiled, remembering how Rupert had gone shopping with her and helped choose it.

She fluffed her hair and slipped the jacket on before picking up her purse. "Okay!" she said with a thumbs-up as she faced the mirror near the door. "I am ready!"

Kelly's voice started to play in her head and Sam shut it

out. *Later. We'll talk about the bigger things later.*

Then Amanda's voice came through. *Don't be afraid to say 'no.'*

Good advice, Sam thought, but she decided to remain open to the possibilities the day would bring.

Everything in this city was larger than life, Sam thought, as she sat in the back of the car next to Stan Bookman, watching the crowds on the sidewalks, the tall buildings, the expensive merchandise in the stores they passed. In less than twenty-four hours she already missed the open spaces of New Mexico, the ability to see fifty miles or more in the distance at a glance.

The car pulled to the curb in front of a gray stone building with lots of glass. Stan stepped out and the driver opened Sam's door for her.

"Ready?" Stan asked. "Just remember, our dual purpose today is to nail down the specifics for these boutique cruises. For you, that means finding out how much chocolate they'll want, to meet the needs for their various itineraries. Make it doable all the way, Sam."

"If I can," she said. "You know I'll do my utmost. I always have."

"Yes, you have." They walked in the wide front doors and headed to a bank of elevators.

"I also have to be realistic. We're a very small chocolate company. Boutique, if you will, which is, I suppose, the reason they want us for their smaller, intimate cruises. They need to understand our limits, as well."

He had pressed the button for the forty-third floor, and he turned to look more closely at Sam.

She sent him an enigmatic smile as the doors closed.

World headquarters for Cruceros Privados occupied the entire floor, as far as Sam could tell, and the décor reflected the South American origins of the company. They stepped off the elevator to face a huge reception desk. In the background were dozens of glass-walled offices. The receptionist greeted them with a smile and picked up her intercom phone to announce their arrival.

Within moments a young woman in a form-fitting dress arrived to escort them to a conference room, the scope of which caught Sam's breath. Her entire house could fit into a couple of these. The long table seated twenty-four, and every chair was occupied except the two reserved for herself and Stan. A blank screen filled the far wall, and she saw a projection setup facing it.

"Was I supposed to have a presentation ready for them?" she whispered to Stan beneath the rustle of two dozen chairs pushing back.

"No, not at all," he whispered through his smile.

The director of marketing, Arnold somebody, and the CEO's young assistant, Cindy, whom they'd met at last night's dinner, stepped forward to greet them warmly and proceeded to introduce them to every other person at the table. Sam made a point only to remember the faces that went with the names on the contract she'd signed. She took a seat between Stan and Cindy, becoming more nervous by the minute.

Arnold, seated across from Sam, reached for the projection machine. Automatic shades closed across the expanse of windows, and the room lights dimmed. "To give you the best feel for what our little cruise line is about, and since a picture is worth a thousand words, may we present … next summer's cruise itinerary." With a slight flourish he started the machine.

The video showed a ship, briefly, before switching to

scenes with laughing couples, champagne toasts, hot tubs, lounge chairs in the sun, and chefs in tall hats meticulously placing intricate food on plates. A pastry chef appeared to be working on a tiered wedding cake. Happy music flowed along with the mood of each vignette, along with scenery from exotic places interspersed with it all. "Let Cruceros Privados show you the experience of a lifetime!" came the closing pitch.

While potential travelers would be wowed with the whole presentation, Sam had her attention on one thing— the quality of the desserts. As the lights came back up, Arnold turned to her. "As you can see, we feel your very special chocolates would be a wonderful fit for our themes and our clientele."

Sam nodded. "It's very tastefully done. I assume there are none of those all-you-can-eat midnight chocolate soirees?"

Light laughter rose from around the table.

"No, nothing like that."

"Tell me, how do you envision incorporating my chocolates? As after-dinner treats, or as a menu item, or …" She left the question open.

Cindy spoke up. "Mr. Hidalgo asked me to talk about his vision, since he was unable to be here this morning. One of our feature events aboard ship is High Tea in the afternoons. If I may be quite frank? The dessert chef has come up with cakes and small tarts … but Mr. Hidalgo feels his efforts in chocolate making have been somewhat lacking."

A few chairs shifted slightly.

"Oh, *not* that the offerings for High Tea have been lacking. But he feels that adding exquisitely done chocolates will bring the quality of *our* tea service to a whole new level. When Mr. Bookman sent samples to us, the answer was clear. Sweet's Handmade Chocolates were the obvious choice. And we are thrilled to have finalized the contract with you, Samantha."

Arnold was on his feet again. "Of course, we hope renewed popularity in the High Tea event will lead to other features for your work. Your suggestion of placing the chocolates as after-dinner accompaniments was an excellent one, Samantha."

Had she suggested that? Sam didn't think so.

"And at a point we may wish to discuss wholesale pricing so as to offer boxes of your chocolates in our gift shops." As if the idea had just come to him, he brightened. "In fact … what would everyone think of offering boxed chocolates aboard all cruises, even on our larger fleet? Hm? We'd get more people interested, knowing if they took the boutique cruises they would be able to have these wonderful chocolates every day!"

The idea may have been a great marketing ploy, but Sam could see exponential increases in her workload with decreased income at a wholesale price.

"It's interesting," she said before the rest of the group could jump in and ratify the idea. "But I do feel we need to take it a step at a time, both from my standpoint as manufacturer and to test it with your passengers, as well. I'd suggest we not go further than your current plan right away. By next season, you'll have a much better feel for how the idea plays with your guests."

There were a few wrinkled foreheads and furrowed brows around the table, but Sam stood firm with the couple of men who tried to push for more. Other questions came up and she did her best not to make decisions on the spot. *Everything happens at the right time.*

By the end of the meeting that afternoon, she was exhausted by the number of people, especially the few whose critical comments served to sap her energy. When Stan suggested dinner that evening with the CFO and his department heads, Sam invented some friends in the city whom she'd promised to see. "Sorry, Stan, they're people I haven't seen in ages."

In truth, she sneaked back to the hotel in a taxi and burrowed into her room, where she pulled out the contract. Over a light dinner and a very strong cup of coffee she went through it, line by line.

Chapter 23

Their time in the UK was coming to an end all too quickly, Kelly thought as she rearranged everything in their luggage. They would be on the train from central London to the airport this morning. Mr. Bookman had promised an escort would meet them at the train and get them to the special area where the private planes flew out.

The wooden box was wrapped in Rupert's cashmere scarf, and both were stuffed alongside the book Bobul had given her, in the bottom of the leather tote bag she would be carrying herself. On top were the packets of teas packed to gently surround the delicate cakes. She wasn't certain she would have attempted so many fragile items on an airline, and once again she silently thanked Stan Bookman for the luxury of the flight as a gift.

Her mother's expression came back to her, the moment

when Bookman had offered the trip. Sam hadn't seemed especially happy about it. But, Kelly reminded herself, she was probably the only person who noticed. Sam was gracious with everyone and would never be rude to her biggest client.

Still—something was going on. Sam's usual vivacious energy had been lagging lately, enough so that her daughter easily spotted the change. There was something in her voice before the New York meeting. And Kelly's last contact with Bobul had not reassured her. It was a conversation she and her mom would need to have when they got home and re-acclimated after their travels.

An arm slipped around her waist from behind, and Scott nuzzled her neck.

"Sad to be leaving?" he asked.

"A little." It was the best explanation to cover her worries.

"What was your favorite part about London?" He stepped in front of her and took both of her hands.

"Wow, we did so much. I loved that city tour on the double-decker red bus, where we got a taste of everything. Walking through Covent Garden and seeing all the stuff people were selling—that was cool."

"The London Eye—getting to see everything up and down the river from such a height," he added. It was true. The huge wheel with cars the size of small rooms was amazing.

"The theater. I'd see *Phantom of the Opera* again tonight if we could. Ooh, and the Tower of London."

His eyes lit up. "Ah—and the wax museum. How cool was it to stand next to the prince and have our picture taken?"

"And your very favorite … Sherlock Holmes's house."

She held up the small tea canister she'd bought in the gift shop there. "Can't wait to get home and try this."

"I can't wait to get home and put my notes together. I'm definitely doing some writing this year, just have to narrow it down and decide on the topic." He couldn't stop smiling.

"Writing? That's wonderful, honey. What a great idea. Can you tell me about it yet?" She searched his face for clues, but he was shaking his head.

"I'd better figure it out myself first. Don't want to lose my momentum."

She checked the time. "Speaking of momentum, we'd better get ourselves to the train station."

Chapter 24

The FBI agents followed Beau in their government-issue sedan. He drove out Paseo del Pueblo Norte and turned on the county road leading to his ranch, bypassed the driveway to the house, and continued to the spot where the suspect's car had parked.

"This is where we believe the sniper's vantage point was," Beau said, after they ducked through the barbed wire fencing. He led them to the stand of trees and showed them where the single footprint had been before recent rain had washed the area clear.

Standing at the spot where he believed the shot had come from, the skill of the shooter became evident.

"The victim's car was parked there, near our front porch. The man was standing beside the car and the bullet caught him in the center of the forehead."

"Impressive shooting," Gonzales said.

Draper sent him a look.

"If it was a paper target, at that distance, I'd be hard-pressed to hit it," he said.

"I know what you mean," Beau said. "Had to be a high-power weapon with a damned impressive sight."

"I wish we had some kind of database of snipers for hire, someplace we could go and just pull up a name for you," Gonzales said. "Unfortunately, we don't. Most snipers remain low-key and unknown unless we happen to catch them."

Beau nodded. He'd been afraid of that.

"What about this wooden box?" Draper asked. "The item your wife thinks the killer might be after."

"Sure. It's in the house. Want to walk across the pasture or shall we drive back?"

The agents had already headed toward their car. He led the way back to the turnoff to his driveway and pulled up outside the house. The dogs rose to greet the visitors.

"These two always here?" Agent Gonzales asked.

"Yeah, and they're good at recognizing strange vehicles and alerting us. But Sam had been here that morning and since she didn't have a problem with the visitors, the dogs weren't skittish at all."

"What about out there?" Rick pointed toward the far stand of trees.

Beau shook his head. "The county road isn't exactly high traffic, but enough vehicles pass that way the dogs wouldn't have raised a fuss. By the time the shooter left his car and came onto my land, it's likely the dogs were inside with Sam. I can ask her, though. She might remember them barking if they were outdoors. Too bad they don't speak English and can't pick someone out of a lineup."

Both agents chuckled.

"The box is in my safe. Come on in," Beau said, leading the way.

The house was quiet, with only the ticking of the grandfather clock to fill the great room with sound. He closed the door, leaving the dogs outside, and ushered the two agents in.

"I keep my service pistol in this safe whenever I leave it home. Otherwise, it's just important papers—the stuff everyone puts in a home safe," he said as he pushed the coats aside in the closet.

He turned his back and tapped the code onto the keypad, and the door popped open. He extracted the wooden box and carried it to the agents.

"A while back, maybe a year or so, Sam asked if she could stash this in the safe too. Before that, she'd used it as a jewelry box and it usually sat on the counter in our bathroom or on the bedroom dresser upstairs."

Gonzales handled the box, turning it to look at the sides and bottom, his expression neutral. "Anything inside it now?"

"I have no idea," Beau said. "Take a look."

The agent raised the hinged lid, revealing a few pieces of costume jewelry, some thin gold chains, and hoop earrings.

Agent Draper poked a finger through the items. "None of it seems of great value," she said.

"I don't think it is. Sam's a pretty casual woman. She doesn't go for fancy dress-up occasions or anything."

"May I take these out?" Gonzales asked.

At Beau's nod, he walked to the coffee table in front of the sofa and dumped out the contents of the box.

"I'm no expert on antiques … I mean, I can tell this is

probably very old. It's a little beat up in places, you know. I get the feeling it's been through a lot of hands over the years, but I sure don't see anything about it that would make it worth a lot of money. Can't figure out why it might be worth killing for."

Agent Draper was also shaking her head. "I don't either." She took the box and held it, rubbing the pad of her thumb over the stones. "These don't look like rubies or sapphires, they're not especially well cut … I don't know. I can't figure it out. I suppose we could have an antiques expert take a look."

"Maybe later," Beau said, reaching for it. "I know Sam really looks out for this thing. There's some sentimental value because of the old woman who gave it to her. I really feel I'd have to ask her before letting it out of our hands."

"Understood." Gonzales moved toward the back of the room, where wide French doors faced open pasture. The barn stood to the far left and the two horses grazed contentedly in the field. "Where's that stand of trees where we were a while ago?"

"Look to your far right," he called out as he finished locking the box back inside the safe. "You may have to go out on the porch to really see the whole area, but it lines up visually with the spot where our cars are parked right now."

"Okay, I see that." Rick Gonzales joined them at the front door.

Both agents were quiet as they stood on the front porch, Gonzales looking toward the trees, calculating bullet trajectory. Draper turned toward Beau.

"That shoeprint you took," she said. "I can't help thinking it's the same as a pair of shoes I own. I'd like to get a photo of that mold and compare them."

"You think it might be a woman's shoe? That our sniper could be a woman?"

"Don't sound so surprised, Sheriff. Many champion shooters are women."

Beau smiled. "I didn't mean that at all. I've had female colleagues who out performed me big-time on the gun range. I'm just … hmm … looking at this in a whole new way now."

"Well, we can't jump to conclusions yet," she said. "First, I'll need to compare the treads on both. I could be mistaken. If they are the same, at least I'll know which manufacturer made them, and I can pursue finding out if they made a men's shoe with the same pattern."

Beau nodded. Maybe Draper had something there. What if the sniper really *was* a woman?

Chapter 25

The ride to the Cruceros Privados offices the next day was quieter. Aside from reminding her that their plane would be ready at one o'clock, Stan Bookman stayed busy with his phone. Apparently, he always operated a step or two ahead of real time. He seemed to be confirming meetings for tomorrow and the next day. The silence was fine with Sam.

Her evening in, reading the contract for the third time in the quiet and privacy of her room, had proved a godsend for her mood. She went into the second morning's meetings more fully prepared to make and yield to suggestions that were within her limits as a chocolatier.

Today's itinerary included a tour of the warehouse offices where the small cruise line stocked provisions for each departing ship. Everything from towels and robes to meats and veggies came through there before being loaded aboard. Every ten days a ship headed east, crossing the Atlantic, touring the British Isles and sailing north to Scandinavia. Another left port the morning after, southbound to the Panama Canal and South America. The line ran a total of five ships, and they were always on the move.

The offices were completely computerized and linked to each ship. Here in New York they knew when passengers purchased their robes to take home and therefore how many new robes would be needed for that ship on the next tour. Used ones were laundered aboard ship and returned to service. The same system told them how many pounds of potatoes, how many dozens of eggs, and—soon—how many pieces of chocolate from Sweet's would be needed for each day of each cruise. This is where Sam's shipments would come, once they were packed and on their way from New Mexico.

The warehouse itself was a massive space filled with pallets of goods, refrigerated rooms of food, and noisy forklifts to shuttle it all around. Every wrapped pallet was barcoded, and every driver and foreman carried a tablet computer that could scan and tell him where each particular pallet was to end up. There seemed little room for mistakes, and Sam had to admit she was impressed.

"This is the reason for our insistence that each of your cartons show our coded labels prominently," said the young woman who had been assigned to guide them, shouting to be heard over the din of warehouse noises. "If a label falls off, the pallet is shuffled outside where it may sit twenty-four hours or more until someone breaks the seal, unwraps it, and inventories the contents. Perishables are especially vulnerable."

She said it with a smile but the warning was clear. Sam remembered a contract clause about proper labeling and penalties to be incurred. She would have to keep a very sharp eye on her crew as they learned this new system. Scary, but she could manage it.

* * *

The flight into Albuquerque served to calm Sam's mind. Once more, Stan was engrossed in setting up his own future travel and Sam, with the stress of the New York meetings behind her, settled into a seat away from his and leaned back for a nap. Part of her was thrilled to be aboard a private jet rather than fighting the crowds within the terminal; the other part knew she had a hell of a lot of work ahead. The nap was her best defense.

She was happy she'd left her car in Albuquerque. The two-and-a-half-hour drive home would be hers alone, as Bookman was merely dropping her off before heading to San Francisco. She thought of Kelly and Scott, on another of Bookman's flights from the UK. They would clear customs in Denver and then make the short hop to Taos. As grumpy as Sam had felt with Stan at times, she could not fault his generosity when it came to travel.

Beau was home when she drove in. He took her suitcase and gave her a kiss that reinforced exactly why she was so happy to be home.

"I got some steaks out of the freezer," he said, "and I am cooking for you tonight."

She had probably never loved him more.

"So, how was the trip?" He was washing a couple of potatoes at the sink.

"Long. Exciting business-wise, but tiring. I'm just glad to be home. How about if I unpack and have a quick shower, and then I'll join you for a beer or something?"

The shower relaxed her weary muscles, but Sam didn't want to spend her first evening home with Beau as a puddle on the couch by eight o'clock. She thought of the box.

Downstairs, wearing her favorite pair of soft pants and a T-shirt, she went to the safe and unlocked it. The box sat there, dark and lonely, and she pulled it out. One of the things her seatmate, Amanda, had said during their flight was to embrace the things that give you comfort. "So little in the world gives us comfort these days," she'd said.

While Sam had initially resisted the idea—after all, her life was nearly perfect with a wonderful husband, loving daughter and son-in-law, and two businesses she loved— she had to admit that a bit of self-care might be in order after the week she'd had. She picked up the box and cradled it against her body. The familiar warmth began to come from it.

Beau walked in with the lighter for the grill. "I hope I didn't mess up your jewelry too much," he said.

Sam looked at him, questioning.

"I took everything out—for the FBI. But I put—"

"What? What was the FBI looking at it for?" She hugged the box closer.

"Turns out, nothing."

"Beau—nothing?"

He paused and started over. "You remember I told you I was calling the FBI in on the shooting investigation?"

She nodded.

"Two agents from Albuquerque came up, came out here to see the scene. We were just going over possible motives, and well, you had said the box might be—"

"—a reason for Marcus Fitch to come out here." It was true; she had told him about Fitch and the box.

"They just wanted to take a look. Didn't seem to think much of it." He continued toward the back deck where she watched him lift the lid on the gas grill, turn the valve, and touch the flame to it.

She felt a wave of possessiveness at the thought of strangers, government agents at that, having touched and looked at the box. She held it out and looked at it. The wood had taken on that familiar golden glow and the stones were beginning to light up reassuringly. Obviously, it had not reacted that way for Beau and the agents or else they would have taken a much closer interest. Looking inside, she didn't see any important differences.

Realizing she was likely overreacting, she returned the box to the safe, rubbing her hands over it one last time. She might need to talk to Beau about sharing information, but for now she was content that the box had lifted her tired spirits.

Beau returned and pulled her into an embrace. "Sorry if I worried you. It did seem like relevant information, but really, darlin' they were not interested in the box. It's Marcus Fitch they're going after." He rubbed her back and she felt herself relax into him.

If the law could find Marcus Fitch and get enough evidence to put him away, it would definitely be a huge worry off her mind.

"Let's get something to drink and put those steaks on the grill," she said.

Chapter 26

The announcement came over the plane's speakers, the standard stuff about stowing loose items, putting up tray tables, yada yada …

Marcus came out of a doze. Once again he'd been contemplating where the third of the carved wooden boxes could be. Wrapped in its purple sheath, inside a leather shoulder bag, the box he'd gotten from Maury rested against his foot beneath the seat in front of him. He knew with virtual certainty Samantha Sweet had one. But the third … having all three was key to possessing the ultimate in power.

Back in Shannon, he'd quizzed Maury at different times during the day, but it was evident his cousin knew nothing and wanted to know nothing. As a cardinal within the inner Vatican circle, he clearly felt uncomfortable at his role in taking this box from the archives. He'd mumbled some ancient Church doctrine about witches and dark magic—babble that seemed right out of the Middle Ages. Marcus gave up.

He'd already done a lot of research in advance, looking for the third box, the one they called Manichee. He'd come up with absolutely nothing beyond a rumor that the box had been examined by The Vongraf Foundation nearly fifty years ago. Supposedly, it had been in possession of a man called Terrance O'Shaughnessy in Galway, but no one could—or would—verify this. He'd made calls, followed online sources.

The box had apparently vanished when Mr. O'Shaughnessy died. Vanished from the possession of Samantha Sweet if the story was correct. That rankled. And made him all the more determined to get to Ms. Sweet and question her—to interrogate her within an inch of her life, if that's what it took.

The plane's wheels bumped the runway and the flight attendant welcomed them to New York's JFK airport, where the local time was eleven p.m. In typical fashion, it took forever for two hundred people to gather their belongings and get off the plane. Again, he had pre-cleared customs, declaring the wooden box as a cheap tourist trinket worth twenty dollars.

He walked into the immigration hall confidently, presented his passport, and looked for the exit signs.

"Welcome to America, Mr. Fitch," said the immigration officer. "I'll need you to step this way with me, please."

Marcus's thoughts went to the box. "Why? What's up?"

"Just step this way." The man had left his booth and two others in plain suits had come up behind Marcus. They ushered him toward a blank door that would have otherwise gone unnoticed.

"What's this about?" A hundred thoughts flew through his head.

"FBI, sir. We have a few questions," said one of the suited men.

A hand took a no-nonsense grip on his upper arm and the second man relieved him of his bags.

Chapter 27

Beau had no sooner walked into his office the next morning than the intercom rang. "Sheriff, it's that FBI agent," said Dixie. "The lady one."

A smile crossed his face and his eyes rolled upward. "Thanks, Dixie."

"Morning, Sheriff," Agent Draper said. "Well, I've got some good news and some bad news."

"Get the bad part over with."

"The shoe tread. It's an Asics running shoe, a model they made last year. Couldn't narrow it down to whether the shoe was a man's or a woman's—they used that tread pattern for both. And, I'm sorry to say, that brand is sold nearly everywhere. The tread pattern is from last year's most popular cross-trainer, so there are literally hundreds of thousands of them out there."

"Okay, thanks. I can't see wasting time by trying to track down where it was purchased."

"Wouldn't even be possible. If we had the actual shoe … there might be a way to find a batch number or something—I'm not sure, really. But with only one print to go on … Sorry, that didn't turn out to be much help."

It wasn't as if a definitive answer would have led them to a suspect anyway, Beau thought.

"The good news is that we got a call from New York. Your Marcus Fitch landed at JFK late last night. Immigration had him on a watch list and he's being interrogated right now. If you want to talk to the agents in charge, here's a number."

He thanked her profusely and dialed the 212 area code.

"Special Agent Rossetti? It's Sheriff Beau Cardwell in Taos, New Mexico. Patricia Draper gave me your number."

"Yeah, she said you'd probably call."

"You have Marcus Fitch in custody?"

"We got the call from Immigration 'cause he's on the watch list. So far, we've questioned him about his movements, done a search of his belongings. My partner's in there with him now. I can see them through the window."

"Did Draper tell you he's wanted here for questioning about a murder?"

"She did. I wasn't clear on whether you think he's a suspect or just a POI?"

"He's definitely a person of interest. It seems he had an alibi for the actual time of the shooting. He went to Rome and checked into his hotel there on the fifteenth."

"I've got his passport here. Hang on a second," Rossetti said.

Beau heard the swishy sound of pages turning.

"Okay, yeah. He flew into Rome on the fifteenth, left

there and passed through immigration in Shannon, Ireland, on the eighteenth. Must have liked the Emerald Isle—he stayed until yesterday."

"And he flew directly from Shannon to New York? Does he say what was the purpose of his trip?"

"Kind of vague on that. Said he has family in Italy. Claims his business has something to do with antiques, so that's what he was in Ireland for. He does have a couple of old-looking little gadgets with him—a box, like maybe for cigarettes, and another wooden trinket, a shillelagh or something. Nothing that looks valuable at all, and his customs declaration didn't exceed the eight-hundred dollar duty-free limit."

Beau took another tack. "I didn't find any criminal record for him. You guys discover anything like that?"

"Clean as a whistle," Rossetti said. "He claims he works for some organization called OSM that scientifically studies artifacts. Says that's the reason for the items he had with him. I've got somebody looking up the outfit, but they're pretty low-key."

"Let me know if you do find anything on the group."

"Fitch says this OSM has an office here in the city and that's where he'll be all week."

"Ask him if he's been to New Mexico and watch for his reaction. I'm guessing he'll deny it, and I need to know if your experts get the impression he's lying. We know he was here a couple years ago, but we suspect he's been back much more recently. Try to get specifics about what towns he visited and what his purpose was here, too. I'd like to know how that turns out."

"Will do. I'm going in the room now. You'll hear back from me soon," Rossetti said.

Beau thanked him and hung up, frustrated he couldn't be there to ask the questions himself. He wished Sam was available as a deputy right now, too. She always came up with insights to help with his cases. He missed the good old days.

Chapter 28

Sam set the bucket of chicken on Kelly's dining table, calling out to let her daughter know she'd arrived.

"Hey, Mom." Kelly walked in from the bedroom.

"Beau should be along any minute. Sorry your welcome home dinner isn't something fancier." Sam gathered Kelly into a big hug. "Missed you guys."

Scott appeared, setting a large shopping bag on the kitchen counter. "The trip was amazing but it's really good to be home," he said. "Jet lag is getting to us a bit, though. We fell asleep last night at seven and were both awake at two a.m. A meal at home is smarter than having us doze off in a restaurant somewhere. Thanks for bringing everything, Sam."

"You have to tell us all about it. Meanwhile, shall I grab some plates and silverware?" She turned to the familiar cupboards, catching sight of Beau's cruiser pulling into the driveway.

Sam had turned her house over to Kelly when she and Beau got married, and she'd noticed changes in the furnishings, which was fine. She'd expected her daughter to make the little house her own. Now that Scott's possessions had been added, it was decidedly more crowded here. She wondered whether they would declutter and keep the small home or find a larger place of their own.

"Hey, everyone," said Beau, walking in the back door. "Mmm, chicken smells good."

They filled their plates and took seats around the table. "So, what was the best thing about the trip?" Sam asked, pulling the crispy crust from a chicken leg and popping it into her mouth.

"Private jet!" they both said.

Sam laughed. "Well, obviously. That must have been a world away from the usual crowded airliner. Otherwise … tell us about the best parts."

"Cakes," said Kelly

"Cambridge," Scott added.

"Me first," Kelly said, "because this is quick. Mom, I brought back a couple of the English specialties. It would be so great if you could figure out how to make them for Sweet's Sweets." She nodded toward the shopping bag on the countertop.

"I'll give it a shot," Sam assured her with a pat on the hand. "So, Cambridge? What was the big attraction, Scott?"

"An interesting little connection to that Victorian house you bought for the chocolate factory." He launched into the story about Eliza Nalespar and her studies in England before returning to her childhood home to become a writer.

"Her books became enormously popular in Cambridge and that area of England. One was actually used as course material for a class on the occult."

Sam felt a ripple of uneasiness. "Really?"

"Yes, the class was sort of an exploration of whether Eliza's ideas were based on fact or whether she'd completely made it up as fiction."

"I'm going to vote for fiction," Sam said with a little chuckle to lighten the mood. "Remember, my office is in the same room where Eliza wrote her books."

"No ghosts so far?" Scott asked.

"None. And let's keep it that way." She turned her attention to her mashed potatoes. No way was she going to bring up the strange sounds she often heard in the old house at night. They would only lecture her on how she shouldn't be working so late anyway.

Kelly pushed her empty plate back. "Yeah, there were several interesting connections between that part of England and our lives here in Taos." She suppressed a yawn. "And when I'm more alert, I've got stuff to show you."

Sam knew about the box from the charity shop and couldn't wait to see it, but it seemed like something she and Kelly should talk about another time, alone.

* * *

Kelly texted at six the next morning. **You up? We've been awake so long it feels like lunch time.**

Sam was in the kitchen, pouring her first coffee of the morning. She pressed Kelly's number.

"Hey, good morning. Figured it would be just as easy

to talk than go back and forth with lots of texts. So, you're ready for lunch already?"

"Not really. But I've already finished unpacking and all the laundry is done. Scott's gone out for a run and then he's got some kind of meeting at the university. Thought maybe you and I could get together about the … you know."

"Definitely. I can't wait to see the box you found in that shop. I have a real feeling it's Uncle Terry's."

"So come on over. Any time."

"Give me thirty minutes."

Sam carried two mugs upstairs. Beau was just getting out of the shower and accepted his coffee gratefully. Sam pulled her standard bakery uniform of black pants and white shirt from the closet. It couldn't take more than an hour to get the full story on the box from Kelly, and she really did need to put in some time with her business. For one thing, now that she had more specifics about the upcoming orders for the cruise line, she needed to negotiate better quantity discounts with her suppliers.

She and Beau walked out the door at the same time, and she pulled into Kelly's driveway a few minutes later. Kelly ushered Sam into the living room where two new bookcases held some of Scott's huge collection of books. A dozen cardboard boxes were stacked beside them, presumably containing additional volumes.

"Well, here it is," Kelly said, holding out a rectangular object wrapped in a beautiful piece of cloth. "Oh, sorry, not the scarf. That's for Rupert once I do a little mending job on the hem."

Sam unwound the fabric. The sight of the box nearly took her breath away. She held it with both hands, closing her eyes and imagining. It was surely the one Terrance

O'Shaughnessy had given her in Ireland.

She looked at Kelly. "Did you handle it much?"

"Cleaned it up. When I spotted it in the shop, it must have had an inch of dust and grime on it. I dusted it and used a little furniture polish."

"Did the … did the appearance of the box change at all? I mean, other than being cleaner, did it …" She stared at the ceiling for a moment. "I'm not quite sure how to ask this. Did the wood turn a different color, did it … I don't know … *gleam*, or did it get warmer to the touch?"

Kelly shook her head. "Mom? What about it?"

Sam set the box on the coffee table and paced the length of the room. How much to tell? How much *should* she say? The powers of the other box had been such a closely guarded secret. But Sam had touched this one when she visited her uncle's home, and it had not exhibited the same effects. It was probably just a plain old box that just happened to look like hers. She turned back toward her daughter.

"Kel, I don't know whether—"

Kelly had picked up the box again and sat with it on her lap, the lid open.

"It looks like there was some lettering in here," she said. "Starts with an M, I think. Toward the end there's maybe an E, but I can't actually tell what it says."

She ran her fingers around the perimeter of the inside. "I don't feel any additional carving," she said.

All at once, when her fingers reached the fourth side, she let out a yelp. Her body stiffened and the box dropped to the carpet. She fell unconscious to the sofa.

"Kelly!" Sam shouted and ran to her side. "Kelly! Wake up!"

Chapter 29

Sam knelt beside her daughter and felt for a pulse. It was rapid, pounding. Kelly's eyes were moving beneath her closed lids, but she didn't respond to Sam's pleas.

This must be what happens, Sam thought. She remembered the night she had brought her box home from Bertha Martinez's house. The old woman on her deathbed had insisted Sam take the box, saying she was meant to have it, to do good things with it. She had taken it to her bedroom and handled it in a similar way to what Kelly had done just now. And she had apparently lost consciousness too, although no one had been present as witness.

Kelly's movements began to quiet down. Her eyes were no longer moving. Her pulse had slowed, but she remained unaware. Sam gently stretched her out on the sofa and draped a blanket over her. She sat on the floor at Kelly's side, holding her hand, for what seemed like a very long time.

Sam was wondering whether she should call for medical help, but what would she tell them? The truth certainly wouldn't work. Kelly began to stir in her sleep. By the clock it had been forty-five minutes when her eyes finally opened.

"Mom—*what?*"

"We need to talk. Can you sit up?"

With assistance, Kelly sat, leaning into the corner of the sofa that had always been Sam's favored spot. "This is about the two boxes, isn't it?"

Sam nodded. "Maybe I should make us a cup of tea."

Kelly perked up. "There's some of the really good English kind in that shopping bag on the counter."

Sam headed to the kitchen and put the kettle on. She found two mugs and the packet of tea bags from Marks & Spencer. Before the water boiled, Kelly had come into the kitchen, hugging the blanket from the sofa to her chest and holding the carved box. She sat at the kitchen table and set the box down.

"What happened to me just now?"

Sam switched off the stove burner and made the tea. With a sigh she said, "Same thing that happened to me once upon a time."

She set the mugs down and took a seat. "Back when I was breaking into houses, right before you came back from California ..." The whole story unfolded—Bertha Martinez, the town's reputed *bruja*, the old woman's deathbed, the bequest of the box. Sam's nearly identical experience the first time she touched the inner surfaces of it, the strange 'powers' she seemed to have acquired.

"Those times you worked late into the night, getting the bakery started, turning out so many fantastic cakes in record time ..." Kelly's eyes were wide.

Sam nodded. "Yep. It took me a while to make the connection between the box and all this amazing energy I suddenly had, but it was true. And now it looks like the second box is ... okay, this sounds really strange ... The second box seems to be *your* destiny."

"Does it seem weird to you that right now, after passing out for, what, forty-five minutes that I feel like jumping up and cleaning out my kitchen cabinets?"

Sam laughed out loud. "It doesn't seem at all weird to me, sweetie, but I doubt it's a good idea. Take your time. Get used to the box's powers gradually. I never told anyone, not even Beau, but those times I worked long hours ... afterward I would sleep for a very long time. We might feel like we have all the energy in the world, but the body can only take so much."

She finished her tea and took the mug to the sink.

"Kel, I'll also tell you this—I tried several times to get rid of the box and couldn't—it actually came back. It seems Bertha Martinez was right about it being meant for me. Others have said it, too, but you'll be on information overload if I try to tell you everything at one time."

Kelly was staring at the box, cupping her mug between her hands. "Mom, I have more to tell, too. I know you're busy at the bakery and with the chocolates now—we could do this another time."

Sam felt as if a shadow had passed over the room. "There are dangers involved with this stuff, Kel. At least give me the basics. Did anyone approach you, any strangers wanting to know about the box?"

"Not strangers, exactly. Just Bobul. I told you about that, how he showed up and talked to me in Bury St. Edmunds. Well, it wasn't only one time. He met me again, and he gave me something—a book. And he said some things, about you, crazy things about how you'll be alone."

Not the OSM people or the Vongraf Foundation people, Sam was relieved to know. "Look, I'm not alone. Beau and I are happy and doing fine, as you saw last night when we were here together. And I've got you and Scott. So don't fret over that."

"I haven't had time to really look at the book or read it," Kelly said. "I don't even know if it's anything important. He just said something about Fas ... no, what was it ... Facinor?"

Bobul and his tales. Sam felt her interest perk up, but her phone rang at that moment. She saw the caller was Jen from the bakery. She held up her index finger to pause Kelly and picked up the call.

"Sam, are you going to be here soon?" Jen asked. In the background it sounded like a crowd scene. "Becky's getting a bit behind and well, she was in tears a minute ago."

Poor Becky. She'd taken on the burden of so much of the summer business.

"I'm coming now. Tell her to hang in there." She hung up and looked apologetically at Kelly.

"They're swamped. I need to go. Will you be okay?"

Kelly smiled and sprang up from her chair to show off her newfound energy.

"Okay then. We'll talk about Bobul and his stories later. For now, please take this seriously." Sam put her hands on Kelly's shoulders and looked deeply into her eyes. "Find a safe hiding place for the box and don't leave it out in plain sight. Don't show it or tell anyone, and warn Scott not to talk about it either."

"He didn't seem interes—"

"That's fine. That's *good*. I'm not saying this to scare you, but there are bad people out there who want to get hold of these boxes. We both need to be careful and to keep the secret. Got it?"

"Got it."

Sam drew her close and gave her an intense hug. She went out to her truck and drove away, filled with a whirlwind of emotions. Happiness because the box from Uncle Terry was in the family again, fear for her daughter and the maelstrom she might have just stepped into.

Chapter 30

Kelly watched as Sam backed out and drove away. She cleared the tea mugs and thought about where she would hide the carved box. For now, a lower kitchen cupboard would work. She wrapped the box in a plastic bag and nestled it behind the toaster oven and a stack of saucepans. Between Sam's warnings and Bobul's, she knew she should consider having a safe installed. She would bring it up with Scott tonight.

She debated calling Riki. Her best friend and her boss at Puppy Chic had insisted she take a couple of extra days off to compensate for jet lag. But since the recharge she'd received from the box, she felt energetic and ready to work all day.

"No need," said Riki when she made the call. "Jen's

niece is helping and we can handle it. Take the time and I'll see you on Monday."

Well, there are certainly other things I can do, Kelly said to herself. She showered and used extra conditioner in her hair, then gave herself a pedicure. When she went into the bedroom to dress, she noticed only a half hour had passed. Was this what Mom had meant by having so much energy tasks just flew by?

Her gaze fell on the bags of gifts she'd brought back from the UK. This would be the perfect morning to deliver them. She made a few phone calls, gathered the presents, and carried them to her car.

Zoë and Darryl were her mother's best friends and had been secondary hippie parents to Kelly as a kid. She drove the few blocks to their B&B, where last night's guests had checked out and the hired helper was in the process of cleaning the rooms in readiness for the new people who would arrive this afternoon. The lawns were brilliant green from recent rains, and Zoë's touch as a flower gardener was evident both in the front beds near the road and surrounding the patio, Kelly noted as she parked near the back door.

Zoë had seen her coming from the large kitchen windows and she was standing in the doorway when Kelly got out of her little red car. She wore a calf-length crumpled linen skirt and loose sleeveless top, and her masses of wavy gray hair were pulled back in a thick single braid that trailed down her back.

"Kelly! You look radiant—such a beautiful bride. Well, come on in. I have some time between cycles on the washer and dryer. I tell you, the laundry is a never-ending thing when guests come and go all the time." Zoë led the way through a small room that served as mud porch and gardening catch-all, and they went into her large, sunny kitchen.

"When you called, I thought what a perfect time to take a break. Would you like coffee, tea, soda …? Well, you know all the stuff I usually keep on hand."

"Just a glass of cold water would be great for me." Kelly handed over the small gift bag she'd carried inside. "Keep these for your own special moments."

Zoë set the bag on the counter and pulled out the contents, a small version of the sticky toffee pudding Kelly had loved so much in England—that spiced, gingery, moist cake with the infusion of sticky caramel sauce which soaked right in. "And a box of real English tea!" Zoë exclaimed. "I know we will love it."

"I ate this cake in nearly every restaurant in town," Kelly said. "At least that's my excuse for the extra five pounds on my gut."

They sat on stools at the kitchen counter while Kelly told about the high points of her trip. She found herself focusing on Scott's finds in Cambridge and his research at the museum to avoid going into anything about the box or Bobul.

"Darryl and I have been wanting to have Sam and Beau over for dinner these past couple of weeks, but there hasn't been the chance, what with the shooting he's trying to solve and your mom's trip to New York."

Shooting? Kelly couldn't remember if Sam had told her about that.

Zoë caught her puzzled expression. "Honey, you know your mom wouldn't want to worry you with that. If she'd told you someone was killed right there at their house, well, you would've wanted to come right home."

At their house? She felt her expression freeze. "No, no, of course not. Mom never wants me to worry." *But it's about time she started to share some of this stuff with me.*

Kelly changed the subject, asking about Zoë's garden. While Zoë talked about her ongoing crop of tomatoes and offered zucchini to take home, Kelly thought again about Sam's warning to keep the carved box hidden and safe.

When Zoë fetched a grocery sack and filled it with her home-grown produce, Kelly took the opportunity to thank her and excuse herself.

"I've a couple other little things to deliver," she said as she hugged Zoë. "Plus, I've taken enough of your morning already."

"You come back any time. And we'll plan a dinner with you guys so we can get to know Scott better." Zoë watched from the back door, waving as Kelly backed out.

It was almost noon when she arrived at Rupert's house. Another of her mom's longtime friends, Rupert was a writer who kept his mornings as sacred, uninterrupted time to create the bestselling romances he wrote under the pen name Victoria DeVane. By now he should be ready to stretch his legs. He'd already told her he had a lunch date— no doubt the latest of his incredibly good-looking hunky lovers. Kelly wanted to time her arrival for a quick delivery of the cashmere scarf, a hug, and five or ten minutes of chitchat. And hopefully she wouldn't learn any other frightening news, as she had at Zoë's.

Rupert raved over the scarf and, as usual, was all hugs and love and blessings for Kelly and Scott. He'd spent some time in Cambridge himself, so the topic went that direction, and he asked whether they'd tried any of the favorite restaurants he named. When she admitted she had only been there for an afternoon and one meal, it brought the conversation to a natural close. She wished him a good lunch and said she was off to the bakery.

Heading back toward the center of town, she came within a block of Sweet's Sweets before she reconsidered. What she really wanted to talk to Sam about should be kept private. Meanwhile, she might learn more from another source.

Chapter 31

Beau was in the squad room, hovering over Rico's shoulder as the deputy searched for known offenders with the word 'sniper' anywhere in their profiles. He knew he was hovering—Rico had given off impatient vibes for the past half hour. He also knew the odds of their happening to stumble across the right one were minuscule. But the case was so damn exasperating.

The better chance for a break might come from the FBI where the main forensics lab in Quantico was running the bullet through their databases. If the lands and grooves on this particular hunk of lead matched a known weapon or even if it matched another bullet from another case, it could provide new directions for their questions. Rick Gonzales hadn't given much hope for a quick answer—it could take days, maybe weeks, for the computers to scan all the possibilities. But it was a thread of hope.

He became aware of movement in the hall that led to the front offices, and he looked up to see a fresh face.

"Kelly—hey. What brings you here?" He walked over and she offered a hug.

"Can we talk a minute?"

"Sure. My office? Or would you rather grab lunch? I was going to call Sam."

"Um, here is fine." She headed toward the door she knew to be his.

He'd no sooner closed the door than she hit him with the question. "Mom told me you were working a murder case, Beau. Why didn't she let me know it happened at your house?"

"Ah." He expelled a long breath. "My guess is that she didn't want to worry you. I take it she's not the one who told you about this?"

Kelly rolled her eyes and plopped into the guest chair in front of his desk. He crossed behind and took his own seat.

"Obviously, Mom wouldn't want to scare me and certainly wouldn't want me rushing back from my honeymoon trip, but geez, Beau. Didn't I have the right to know?"

"Hon, of course you do." He leaned forward. "What can I tell you?"

"I don't know anything—the basic who, what, when would be nice."

"Two people came out to the house to see Sam. She says they study old artifacts, at some lab in Virginia, and they had questions about that old wood box she keeps her jewelry in."

Kelly's expression shifted subtly, but he wasn't sure why. She stared, waiting for more.

"The man and woman were leaving, and someone took a shot from a great distance, killing the man. His name was Tony Robards."

"And?"

"We're investigating the fact that it was a sniper-like shooting. The victim had no personal ties to New Mexico, so we think it's someone who tracked him here, possibly from Virginia or the DC area." He spread his hands on the desk, metaphorically showing his cards. "The killing may have had to do with the young man's job. There's one connection, a man who actually had threatened the life of the woman, Isobel St. Clair. This man is our primary suspect but we've run into so many stumbling blocks and the fact that all three came from clear across the country … well, we've called on the FBI for help. Frankly, it's not at all the type of case that usually would fall to a county sheriff's department."

"Was Mom in danger from this killer? I suppose I should ask, is she *still* in danger?"

Wow. Right to the point. "We don't know, Kelly. We don't have reason to believe so. As far as we know, the killer left the area and hasn't been back."

She didn't look as if she believed him, but at least she didn't become argumentative. She sat there quietly, staring at a spot in the middle of his desk, for a full minute.

"Would you tell me, Beau, if you get any information that any of our family is in danger? Mom, you, any of us?"

He nodded. "I will certainly warn you and your mom if anything indicates the suspect has come back."

She gave him another hug and when she pulled away her eyes were moist. He walked her to the door and saw

her out to her car. She hadn't believed a word of it.
    And worse, he didn't blame her.

Chapter 32

Kelly's hands shook on the steering wheel when she left the Sheriff's Department parking lot. Asking Beau about the shooting might have been a mistake. For all his assurances that the killer would not come back, Kelly didn't believe it. And she couldn't put her finger on the reason why.

She didn't believe Beau had deceived her—there was no feeling about that. He'd honestly opened up, although there was more to the story. He had been married to her mother long enough, and Sam had been deputized for some of his cases. Kelly knew lawmen always held back a few facts of any case. There were good reasons to keep clues hidden from the media, and she supposed even family members needed to be unaware of certain things.

But this was more.

She couldn't define it, but somehow she knew, with a deep gut feeling, *knew* that Tony Robards was not the real target and the killer would be back. Traffic on Paseo del Pueblo Sur was bumper-to-bumper with summer tourists, and she nearly rear-ended a minivan.

"Gotta get home," she said out loud.

She seriously thought of turning off and going to the bakery, but talked herself out of it. Being around other people would be a mistake. She needed to pace the floor, or gnaw her nails or put her fist through a wall—she felt that edgy.

She did a few deep breaths and concentrated on the crawl of the traffic until she could make the left turn on Kit Carson Road and then the couple of short blocks to her house. It was a relief Scott's car wasn't home. She felt guilty at the sentiment, but knew she couldn't explain. It was simply a feeling. She had a ton of excess energy she needed to dissipate.

In the cool, dim kitchen only one word came to her. Mom.

She picked up her phone. "Is this normal?" she blurted out the moment Sam picked up. "My insides are churning and my head feels like it's buzzing with a thousand bees inside."

Her mother was quiet for a moment and said she was stepping out of the noisy kitchen.

"I'm thinking, trying to remember how it was for me at first," she said. "Yes, I think you're feeling the effects of handling the box. Did you get out and do something active? That seems to help."

"Riki already has help at the grooming shop, but I went for quick visits to take gifts to Zoë and to Rupert." She held back mentioning her talk with Beau. Sam was busy with the bakery and this was a subject that would take some time.

"It's a bit hot outside to go running," Sam said, "but if you can think of something like that, something to burn off the excess energy. It might help."

Kelly had paced through every room in the house during the time it took Sam to give the advice. Back in the kitchen she looked into the messy cupboards. Well, there was no time like the present.

Chapter 33

Sam finished the third tier of the wedding cake she'd been working on when Kelly called. Setting the topper in place, she stepped back to be certain it was perfect, then carried the cake to the walk-in fridge. Becky had gotten past her frazzled state from earlier in the day—she was contentedly piping big pink roses on a birthday cake for an eighty-year-old customer who had been coming to Sweet's Sweets since the first day Sam opened the shop.

"Mrs. Maldonado will love it," Sam said, receiving a smile in return.

She picked up the stack of order forms to see what was coming up next. Six wedding cakes for the weekend. She gave Julio a list of the sizes and flavors, and he immediately began pulling pans from the shelves to get started. No wonder Becky had felt overwhelmed. Sam made a note to call another decorator she'd used a few times. By Thursday they would need all the help they could get. Three more birthday cakes needed to be done by this afternoon, but only one of them was a bit complicated. She would start that one herself.

Becky carried the finished pink and white confection to the fridge and picked up the other two order forms. "Sam—thanks. Your being here saved my sanity."

Sam gave her a warm smile, while feeling a stab of guilt that she hadn't been more on top of the situation. She stepped into the walk-in to pick up the baked layers for the two-tier birthday cake, her mind fidgeting. Besides Becky's crisis, there had been the cruise line contract and meetings, the changes that would be needed at the chocolate factory, and now this new development with Kelly and the boxes. There didn't seem to be enough pieces of herself to give to everyone.

She remembered Amanda from the flight to New York and one of the things the wise woman had said: "It's essential to give to others. It's what makes us complete. But when you give from your own reserves, rather than your excess, you'll burn out." The only problem was, how to tell the difference?

She pushed the thoughts aside while she studied the sketch on the order form and began gathering the decorating tips and color pastes she would need to create a fairy castle from cake, icing, and sugar.

By six p.m. all the day's orders had been completed and delivered, and they'd done many of the basic steps to start on the weekend's wedding cakes. Becky gave Sam a hug and promised to come in early again the next morning. Sam walked through the shop, happy to see that Jen had kept the front room tidy and everything was set for the next day's early rush. She turned on the nighttime lights in the window display, and dialed Kelly's number as she was picking up her bag to go. Scott answered.

"She's conked out on the couch," he said. "I brought home a pizza and she'd barely eaten half a slice before she got really sleepy. Guess she had a busy day."

"I can imagine. Just tell her I called to check in. I'll see her tomorrow."

* * *

Sam woke at five in the morning. The niggling discontent from yesterday at the bakery was completely gone. She stretched and rolled over to see that Beau's side of the bed was already empty. His uniform hung over the back of a chair, so he must be outside tending to the early morning ranch chores. She tended to forget how much he did in addition to his more than full-time job as sheriff. Horses, barn, and alfalfa crops all required his attention too, even with the help of his part-time ranch hand.

She showered and dressed in her bakery clothes, remembering her promise to be there at least part of the day to work on the wedding cakes. She thought of the box locked away in the downstairs safe. Might be a good idea to gather some extra energy before she left the house.

Beau walked into the kitchen as the coffee finished dripping into the carafe. He smelled of hay and oats and fresh air. "Yes, I would," he said, holding out a mug before Sam had even asked the question.

"I don't suppose I should ask whether there's been any big break in the shooting case?" Sam asked as she served him a cinnamon roll from the box she'd brought home.

He shook his head. "Working lots of angles. The FBI is comparing ballistics on the bullet. We have surveillance on Marcus Fitch. It's just not much of a case without more physical evidence."

She patted his shoulder on her way back to the fridge for the cream.

"Kelly stopped to see me yesterday."

Sam stopped in her tracks.

"She seemed a little miffed that no one had told her the shooting happened here at our place."

Sam sighed. "I should have. I just didn't want to worry her while she was traveling, so I guess I kind of glossed over the facts. Did you tell her all about it?"

"The basics. I didn't want to worry her either. Plus, I really don't have many answers—for anyone." He stood up, bestowed a kiss on her forehead, and headed toward the stairs. "Gotta get ready for the office."

Sam sent Kelly a short text asking if she'd be up for a drop-in guest now or after bakery hours. The response came immediately back. **Now—yes!**

She arrived just as Scott was leaving. "I'm already back at the university, getting my material planned and my office organized. I'm teaching two courses this coming semester," he said through the open window of his Subaru.

Kelly waved from the back door, and Sam noticed the newlyweds gave each other a dreamy smile as he drove away. Young love—so cute.

The back porch had been freshly swept, the mudroom organized with storage bins for gloves and scarves, and the floor shone as it never had before.

"Looks like you did get busy after I talked to you," Sam commented.

"You wouldn't believe," Kelly said with an enigmatic smile.

Inside, the kitchen counters gleamed and the usual clutter of small appliances and kitchen tools were out of sight. Kelly opened one cupboard door to reveal neatly stacked canned goods and perfectly aligned cereal boxes on fresh shelf-liner paper.

"I did them all, and came up with two boxes of things to give to charity," Kelly said. "And ..." She led the way to the living room, where the previously boxed books were now neatly placed on shelves. "Alphabetical by author name." And the furniture and floors were immaculate.

In the bedrooms the closets had become an organizer's dream. "Someone could do a magazine spread on how great this place looks," Sam told her.

"You know, I had seriously thought about having a weekly cleaning service after we got back from our honeymoon. With both of us working, things were getting a little beyond me, but now I think I can handle it. I'm loving this."

Sam wanted to add a caution about overdoing the use of magical power, but she caught herself. Why rain on Kelly's happiness? She would soon learn the extent of the box's power as well as her own limits in using it.

"Coffee's made—you want some, Mom?"

They walked back to the kitchen where Kelly poured. It was the signature blend from Sweet's Sweets. As she handed one of the mugs to Sam her expression became serious.

"I stopped by and talked to Beau yesterday."

"He told me. I ... I'm sorry I didn't say more about the shooting earlier. I didn't want to worry you."

"He said the people who were there at the house came

from some organization in Virginia? That they came to see the box?"

Sam nodded. "It's called The Vongraf Foundation. In Alexandria they study various unexplained phenomena, according to what Isobel St. Clair, the director, tells me. She came here once before and showed me some documentation about the box I got from Bertha Martinez. The same box had been sent to Vongraf in the 1920s for verification."

Kelly's brow furrowed.

"There's more. Isobel believes there were a total of three boxes made by the same woodcarver. I told her about seeing another one at my uncle's home in Ireland. It was just like mine but without the colored stones. I'm pretty sure it's the one you have now."

"And it also apparently has similar powers."

"Yes." By now, Sam was pacing back and forth. "There's something else. Another group calling itself OSM—believed to stand for some Latin name that's roughly Office for the Study of Magical ... something. I'm not sure. Isobel believes this group may have the third box."

She came to a stop and held Kelly's gaze. "OSM desperately wants the other two boxes. They've tried twice now to get mine. If they ever learn about yours ... Kel, you could be in danger."

"Wow. So that's why you told me to keep it hidden and not tell anyone about it."

"Yes. I'm very serious about that."

Kelly's eyes went liquid. "Mom—you had all this going on in your life and you never said anything? How did you handle it?"

Sam gave a tight smile. "Some times better than at other times."

Kelly hugged her, but after a moment Sam stepped back. She had more to say.

"Isobel and The Vongraf Foundation have very limited information. Their role is to study these types of artifacts, but they don't collect or keep them. So their knowledge is only theoretical and mostly anecdotal. We—you and I—as far as we know, are the only ones to ever possess two of the boxes in the same place at the same time. Until we learn more about the power of the boxes, especially if two or all three happen to come together, we cannot be too careful."

Kelly had become jittery, shifting from one foot to the other. "There's more, Mom. I mean, I have more information."

"What kind—?"

"From Bobul." She took a deep breath. "Remember, I said he had told me things. And I mentioned a book."

She dashed from the kitchen and Sam watched her rummaging in the living room, pulling books from the shelves until she came up with one hidden toward the back, which looked different from the others.

"Have you ever seen this before?" she asked, handing the book to Sam.

The cover was leather unlike any Sam had ever seen on a modern-day book. Almost velvety to the touch, worn at the edges but still very much intact. The deckle-edged pages were of thick paper, most likely handmade. She started to open it, but Kelly's words stopped her.

"Bobul told me it belonged to a very old Romanian woman, and something about her being burned. I think it was for being a witch."

Chapter 34

Beau dispatched two deputies to a traffic accident scene, hoping it would turn out to be nothing major. When he turned toward Rico, he saw search statistics scrolling across the deputy's computer screen. He asked how it was going.

"There are several entities using the initials OSM somewhere in their titles, but none with a DC address, and none whose stated purpose seems anything like what you're looking for, boss."

"It was worth a shot," Beau said, "but if the FBI can't give us anything definitive, odds are we'll never find them either."

"Do you want me to stick with it?" Rico looked up.

"Nah. I'm going to call Rick Gonzales and see if Quantico has turned up anything. Meanwhile, I need somebody working that robbery at the trading post out on 285. Can you go out and take the woman's statement?"

"Sure, boss." Rico seemed disappointed at the lack of results on the shooting, but they all felt that way.

Beau went into his office, closed the door, and dialed the FBI Albuquerque office. Rick came on the line right away.

"I'll report what we know, but afraid it isn't much," Gonzales said. "Ballistics ran your bullet through our databases, first by region, then nationwide and then worldwide. *Nada*. The gun that fired it hasn't been used in any previous crimes—I should say no crimes with a matching bullet. So that seems like a dead end."

Beau wasn't exactly surprised. Everything about this case had been a dead end.

"We've got surveillance on Marcus Fitch in DC. Agents are watching his apartment and tailing his moves. Got taps on his phone and computer, but we're just not getting anything useful. He goes out for a run every morning, one-point-six miles through a nice Georgetown neighborhood and along a riverside pathway. Our agents have observed every step of the route, five days in a row now, and Fitch never pauses, never speaks to anyone, hasn't so much as thrown a gum wrapper in a trash barrel."

"And the rest of the day?"

"He goes back home after the exercise, cleans up and comes back out dressed casually. Khaki slacks or shorts, polo shirt, ball cap. Stops at the closest Starbucks. One of our female agents even observed inside and he orders the very same thing every morning. Sometimes pulls a laptop out of his messenger bag and goes online while he has coffee. Reads his email—nothing connected as far as we can tell—checks his Facebook page where his closest friend seems to be some guy from college. We checked him, and can't spot a connection there. Want more?"

"Summarize it for me."

"He has four regular stops: coffee, groceries at a small neighborhood market, a bookstore where twice he's come out with a new novel to read, and what appears to be his favorite take-out restaurant—Thai food."

"When he's home there's no additional email or social media activity?"

"Well, sure. But it's just more of the same. We haven't found anything that speaks of a compelling reason for his trip to Rome, much less to New Mexico."

"He doesn't go to work? To an office anywhere?"

"Nope."

"The witness, Isobel St. Clair, is really convinced Fitch was involved in this thing."

"My mother's convinced all priests are good men."

"We do have some evidence," Beau reminded him. "St. Clair's last visit to Taos a year or so ago, when Fitch followed her and ran her off the road, stealing some important—and related—documents from her car. Her offices in Alexandria also had an attempted breach, by someone in this OSM organization."

"And that's why we're giving the man this much attention and manpower. Just keep in mind, unless something breaks open here, we can't keep it up forever."

"I know, and we all appreciate the efforts." Beau hung up feeling frustrated.

He, too, was beginning to wonder about the point in following Marcus Fitch around his daily routine. But he believed Sam and he trusted the information from Isobel

St. Clair. This guy was involved, whether he was the shooter or he'd hired one.

Most likely, Fitch had spotted the agents tailing him and was leading them on a merry—very boring—chase until they gave up. Judging by the way Gonzales was talking, that day would come soon. The day when, Beau knew, he and his department would need to become extra vigilant.

Chapter 35

Bobul had told Sam bits about the Romanian witch, too. At the time she'd guessed him to be delusional or simply superstitious. Now she wondered. Too many of his predictions had come true. She turned the book over in her hands and opened it to the first page.

The printing was done by hand on what appeared to be the title page. The elaborate lettering was difficult to decipher and apparently in a foreign language.

"Hold on," Kelly said, picking up her phone and opening a translator app. "Do you think it's Romanian?"

Sam shrugged. Kelly tapped a few buttons and entered what she thought the letters represented.

"Well, either I'm not reading the lettering right or it isn't Romanian." She held the phone up to show Sam that the translation hadn't meant anything.

"Never mind. You can play around with that later," Sam said. "I think our more pressing worry is about the boxes. We have two of the three, and we know someone is after them. Urgently enough that they're willing to kill to get them."

Kelly chewed at her lower lip. "What shall we do?"

"We may find some answers in this book," Sam said, riffling through the pages. "But I'm afraid getting there may be a long, slow process. I can't read the words, and it's full of little hand-drawn sketches that probably mean something too."

"I'll work on figuring out what language it is," Kelly said. "And you know, we have a historian in the family. I could show it to Scott and see if he recognizes it."

"Umm … not sure that's a good idea. I don't want to put him in danger."

"I doubt he could read any of it, but he might recognize the characters and at least give me a lead."

"Be careful, Kel. Really careful."

Kelly laid a hand on Sam's shoulder. "I will. Meanwhile, I'll keep the book hidden away as long as I'm not working on it. Riki said for me to take another couple of days off—bless her, she thinks I have jetlag. I can spend this afternoon on the book. You're buried at work, and I don't want to add this as another worry to your list."

Another worry for the list—Sam almost laughed—there were already so many.

"You're right. The bakery is crazy this week, and if I don't get busy with some definite plans for revamping production at the chocolate factory we'll never be ready in time to start shipping to the cruise line."

"Exactly. Leave this to me," Kelly said. "I *will* report. And don't worry!"

It was like hearing 'don't worry' from your toddler who was about to step into traffic, Sam thought as she backed her truck out of Kelly's driveway. But it had been many years since her daughter was a toddler, and she knew she needed to have faith that Kelly was a grown, capable woman. She smiled to herself—*your kid is always your kid.*

She had no sooner pulled up to the back door at Sweet's Sweets than her phone rang. *Language translation already?* But it wasn't Kelly. The screen told her Isobel St. Clair was on the line.

"Sam, hi, just wanted to check in. Is there any news on the investigation? I realize I should probably have called your husband's office directly."

"It's okay. You caught me at a good time." Relatively good, Sam thought, considering there hasn't been a lull in weeks. "Unfortunately, I'm afraid Beau hasn't reported anything new about the shooter. The FBI is in on it now. That's about all I know. I'm sorry."

"Me too. I was hoping for some news, some closure, for Tony's parents."

"It's so sad. Heartbreaking for everyone he worked with, I'm sure."

"Yeah, definitely." Isobel's voice conveyed her disappointment. "Meanwhile, is everything all right with the, um, artifact? No mishaps, no inquiries?"

Obviously, she was asking whether anyone had been poking around, trying for information or to take the box away.

"All's well," Sam said. She debated for a moment then decided to trust. "I do know where the second one is."

"My god," Isobel said. "So it's true. It wasn't destroyed?"

"I believe it's the same one my uncle once had. More than that, I really shouldn't say."

"No, you're right. *Please* be vigilant, Sam. We are just beginning to learn the price—"

The call disconnected, leaving Isobel's sentence unfinished, but Sam knew the sentiment behind it. Yes, she and Kelly would definitely be watchful. Tonight she would tell Beau about Isobel's call and ask him to share any news with the Vongraf people. Sadly, there were no updates that could bring back their lost co-worker.

Chapter 36

His heart began to pound as Marcus Fitch dropped the connection to the line he had breached at The Vongraf Foundation. Tapping their phones had posed a real challenge—unlike the dink system at the Taos County Sheriff's Department, The Vongraf had invested in some serious security. But because of his persistence, he now knew Isobel St. Clair had just received a valuable piece of information. For Marcus, the news was priceless. His fingertips practically itched with the urge to act. Unfortunately, the time was not quite right.

He'd spotted the FBI tail the very first day, and he felt quite proud of the way he'd manipulated them. An agent—usually the attractive dark-haired female, sometimes the young hot-shot guy—was now at Starbucks every day. On the days he didn't see one of them inside the shop, pretending to leisurely sip a coffee while sneaking glances toward his laptop screen, one or the other would be sitting in a car a half block down the street.

There were two others, one a blonde who looked damn good in gray Lycra shorts and a blue singlet that hugged her every curve. She ran his entire route each morning, keeping about a quarter mile behind, although she was fit enough to have overtaken him anytime she wanted. The fourth character was actually the one who'd tipped him that the team was FBI—older guy, bald, tired blue suit that had gone baggy at the knees from too much sitting. He'd passed Marcus on the street when he paused to look in a window at some cool watches; in the millisecond when the suit jacket flapped open Marcus spotted the badge and holster at his waist.

None of this came as a surprise after that Special Agent Rossetti had questioned him in New York. He'd been a little freaked when they pulled him aside after the Shannon flight, but he'd kept his cool and walked away. Now, here in DC, all he had to do was keep up a boring routine and not make any sudden moves. They'd give up. With all the flap in the news about government cutbacks, they couldn't watch a guy jog and drink coffee forever.

"Morning, Fitch," said a voice at his shoulder. Marcus tried not to flinch.

"Perone. How's it going?" he asked without looking up from the computer screen in front of him.

"I could ask you the same. The director wants to know why you weren't at the last three meetings. Clearly, you're in town and you're here in the secure room nearly every day."

Marcus gritted his teeth behind the smile he sent to the junior OSM member. "I'm monitoring critical phone calls. The director knows about it. He gave the go-ahead."

"Well, yesterday afternoon he asked if any of us knew where you were." Perone's voice took on a whiny tinge as he tried to justify the interruption.

Fitch gave him a long stare and the younger man backed down. "Okay, then, guess it was nothing."

Behind the cool glare to his fellow OSM member, Marcus's thoughts were still reeling after listening to the call Isobel St. Clair had placed. Samantha Sweet had two of the magical boxes in Taos. If he could get his hands on them ... He practically salivated at the thought.

Another trip to Taos was in order. If only he could get rid of those damned FBI agents.

He erased his browsing history and shut down the ultra-secure OSM computer. Bypassing the director's office, he took a narrow hallway to an elevator that led to the underground parking level. What few people knew was that the unmarked door next to the elevator opened to the basement of the adjacent bookstore.

The agents had trailed him there, too. For the first three days he'd tested their patience by wandering up and down the aisles of the fiction sections, seemingly browsing every book. On day two he'd picked up one and taken it to the in-store bistro where he spent two hours eating a sandwich while reading. By day three the FBI had taken to watching from across the street, and by day four he could see the two agents having a lively conversation in their car while barely glancing toward the bookshop. That's when he began strolling toward the restrooms and veering away to the elevator. Many bookstore customers parked in the underground lot, so no one noticed Marcus.

For two weeks now he'd been able to accomplish miracles in tracking the moves of his quarries in Alexandria and in Taos without ever using his personal computer or phone. To keep his surveillance team thinking they were doing a great job, he always ended each session at OSM by walking back through the bookshop, grabbing a novel at random to buy, then tucking it under his arm as he strolled out the front door and went back in the direction of his apartment. He grinned. Oh *yeah*, these people would soon be *extremely* tired of Marcus Fitch and his boring routines.

Chapter 37

Kelly pored over the old book most of the afternoon. A few of the drawings were recognizable, but without the context of the words to go along with them, she couldn't take much meaning from them. The one sketch she definitely knew was that of a box shape, skillfully drawn in three dimensions, showing a quilted pattern carved into the surface. It had small circular shapes in each X part of the design, identical to the box her mother owned.

Beneath the picture was one word, but Kelly couldn't read it. Sam had said the boxes had names. Perhaps that was it.

Outside, a car pulled into their driveway. She shoved the book under the edge of the sofa and hurried to the kitchen. It was Scott.

"Hey, baby," he said with a warm smile. "Were you napping?"

She couldn't tell him how much energy she had, so she merely shook her head.

"I was dozing at my desk. Can't believe it's only three o'clock. Decided to come home early, grab a little rest, then I thought maybe we could go out for Mexican. Those burritos at the Taoseño keep coming to mind."

"Sounds good. Hey, before you fall asleep could you take a look at something real quick?"

He followed her into the living room and she pulled out the book. She opened it to a page without pictures. "Mom and I were looking at this earlier but we have no idea what language it is. Do you recognize it?"

He held it at arm's length, staring intently. "Not really. The characters are similar to Cyrillic, which is what Russian and several other languages are based on … but I don't think it's exactly that. Some of the letters could almost be Runes. But I'm no expert on languages. I could show it to one of the linguists at the university and see if they recognize it."

She took the book back, watching him yawn. "Go have your nap, and we'll think about this later."

She watched as he dropped his jacket over a chair and dragged himself toward the bedroom. Within five minutes he'd kicked off his shoes, flopped fully clothed onto the bed, and was snoring heartily.

The book should definitely not leave her possession, Kelly knew. And she had a feeling even making a copy of a page or two wouldn't be smart. What if the linguist who looked at it could do more than identify the language, could actually read it? If the book had indeed come from a line of Romanian witches, having someone know it was here might not be good at all.

She found a sheet of tracing paper among a bin of art supplies and set about tracing a sampling of random characters, with a full word only here and there. Surely, this couldn't be comprehensible. What she wanted at this point was just to identify the language so she could go online and look up the meaning.

By the time Scott woke up, she had a half page of what looked like scribbles.

"Can your language colleague help us with this little bit to go on?" she asked when he came into the kitchen and saw the page on the table.

"No idea, but we can ask."

She had expected him to fold the page and take it to the college the next day but he pulled out his phone and snapped a picture. In under a minute he'd found the email address of the linguist he'd been thinking of and had sent the photo and request.

"Now, how about that burrito?" he suggested.

Kelly had loved the Taoseño since she was a kid, from the family who owned the place to the consistently good food. And, come dinner time, you could have a drink with your meal. She and Scott ordered Tecate, which seemed the ideal match for the chicken burrito smothered in green chile sauce. The scent of the steaming hot meal that arrived in front of her caused her to salivate, even before the hot chile tingled her taste buds.

Scott's phone rang just as he was pushing his empty plate aside. "Hmm, that was quick."

"Hey, Ben. Are you a whiz with languages, or what?" He put the speaker on so Kelly could follow.

A chuckle came through. "Well, can't say I'm a whiz at this one. Can't read a thing it says."

Kelly felt a stab of remorse. Maybe she should have at least copied an entire sentence verbatim.

"Actually, I don't think it's a recognized language. Based on the characters, I believe this is a made-up communication using two or more different languages. Some of the symbols are Glagolitic, which is an ancient language—generally thought to be created in the 9th century by Saint Cyril, who was a Byzantine monk from Thessaloniki."

Scott sent Kelly a wide-eyed look. She was scribbling notes on her rumpled napkin.

Ben continued. "Certain of the characters are from one of the runic alphabets. Those were the earliest of Germanic writings, but they can also date back to Greek or Phoenician. It's fascinating stuff, but I don't think what you sent me can really be translated. It's such a mishmash of word patterns … Perhaps if I had a whole page of it … but I'm thinking someone wrote it almost as a code. If you had the answer key, you could figure out what character stands for what. Then we might be able to apply it to one specific language and get somewhere with it. Sorry I don't have more positive news. I'd love to give it a shot if I had a longer text and if there existed an answer key of some kind."

Scott looked at Kelly with the question in his eyes. She shook her head.

"Well, thanks anyway, Ben. What you've said is most appreciated." He tapped the button to end the call.

"So I guess my translator app isn't going to work on this one," Kelly said.

She put a smile on it so he wouldn't think he needed to follow up further. His colleague's information had probably been exactly right. Somewhere in that book there was most likely an answer key of some kind. She couldn't wait to get home and look further.

Chapter 38

Beau rubbed his itchy eyes and sighed. It was nearly seven p.m. and he'd intended to get out of the office by six. Not a smooth-running day, for sure. The traffic accident this morning had involved a fatality, which dramatically increased the time and paperwork to process everything, not to mention his having to visit a family out in Talpa and deliver the news that their teenage daughter wouldn't be coming home.

Rico had been in a mood after taking the theft report from an elderly Tewa woman who ran a little trading post-slash-curio shop out on the highway. He'd spent two hours taking details on what amounted to less than a hundred dollars' worth of stolen tourist junk. The foul mood came about because he couldn't call it like he saw it and could only advise the lady to report the loss to her insurance company, when no doubt she didn't carry insurance.

Sam had called to say he'd better grab something to eat for himself—she was tied up at the bakery and Jen would bring her a sandwich or something. She hadn't sounded exactly chipper either.

So, he was sitting at his desk now, staring once again at the sorry collection of evidence in the shooting of Tony Robards. What he wanted to tell the grieving parents was that the FBI had taken over tracking the lead suspect, so they could call them instead of him. But of course, whatever he said would have to be couched in the most polite of terms.

When his phone rang and he saw that it was Rick Gonzales, he had a feeling he knew what was coming—in the politest of terms, of course.

"Sorry, Beau, HQ has spoken. The higher-ups have decided it's a waste of manpower to keep 24-hour surveillance on Marcus Fitch. The man hasn't deviated from routine or made a suspicious move in more than two weeks. The case will remain open but they've called off the team."

"Damn."

"I know. But it's not like we have a database of snipers for hire or that they all belong to some social club or something. If we could have caught Fitch meeting with someone or paying them off ... but that was probably done well before the shooting ever happened."

"It's just been that kind of day all around," Beau said. "Okay, Rick, thanks for at least doing this much."

Gonzales offered to buy him a drink next time Beau was in Albuquerque, and they promised to let each other know if there were any new developments in the case. Beau hung up, feeling the weight of it all on his shoulders.

There was no doubt in his mind that Sam was still in danger from this guy. If he thought Fitch was only after the stupid wooden box, he'd set the damn thing out on the porch and just let him steal it. Hell, he'd pack it up and mail it to him. But somehow it went a lot further than that; other lives would be in danger if Fitch got away with this.

He was on his own to protect his family until he could figure out a way to take Marcus Fitch down.

Chapter 39

The blonde runner wasn't on the path this morning, Marcus noticed. He sharpened his lookout for someone else. Maybe she was on vacation. Or the Feds could have switched the whole team so he'd have to look for new faces everywhere, dammit. Or … he might have gotten lucky.

He skipped coffee at Starbucks and went straight to the bookstore. With a magazine and a coffee from the bistro there, he parked himself at a table where he had an overview of the entire store. For ninety minutes, people came and went, buying books, browsing and leaving, having a pastry and leaving. No one paid him any mind and no one hung around very long.

He followed his usual path to the elevator and parking garage, then slipped through the doorway that led to the

OSM building. He went to the section of the computer room and to the machine he'd been using to encrypt his logon and access the recordings he'd set up to happen anytime Isobel St. Clair's or Sheriff Cardwell's phones rang. The time stamp showed Cardwell had received a call after nine o'clock last night, 7:14 New Mexico time.

Marcus fast-forwarded to that one. *Sorry, Beau, HQ has spoken.*

That sounded promising. He listened to the entire phone call, backed up and listened again. It explained the absence of the tail this morning. Unless … could they have any idea he was listening to their calls? He went back and listened to all of Beau Cardwell's calls for the day. No, the sheriff wasn't on the verge of a breakthrough in the case. He'd sounded discouraged all day and by evening wasn't surprised when the FBI called.

Marcus drummed his fingers on the desk. He would break with routine, get out and about, be visible, for one more day. If he didn't spot a tail in that time, he knew what he would do.

Chapter 40

All the way home Kelly thought about what Scott's colleague had said about the made-up language used in the old leather-bound book. It made perfect sense that there would be an answer key somewhere, and she would find it. She was on a mission.

They made coffee and turned the TV on to a sitcom, but within a half hour of sitting down Scott was dozing again.

"Hey, why don't you go ahead and hit it early?" she asked.

"I never remember jetlag hitting me quite so hard," he said. "Aren't you tired?"

"A little, but I think I'll read for a while."

He gave her a kiss and went to brush his teeth. By the time he went into the bedroom, she was digging into her secret storage space in the kitchen cupboards and came out with the carved box and the old book.

"If I have a prayer of staying awake long enough to look through the book, I'd better help myself to some extra energy," she mumbled.

Remembering Sam's cautions about not overdoing the box's influence, she carried the box to the living room and sat in her favorite corner of the sofa. On her lap, the artifact began to change color, going from its normal dark, muddy brown to a light honey color. She laid her hands flat against the top and the warmth grew. She wanted to hold onto it, to soak up more energy, but reminded herself she was new at this. She set the box aside.

It was true—she felt more alert already. She picked up the book and felt the soft leather cover.

"Okay, if there's a key to the code, it would probably be on a loose page." She held the book up by the covers, letting the pages hang downward. Nothing fell out. She riffled them but no loose page showed up. "Maybe in the back …"

But if she expected some kind of chart, such as A=B, it wasn't apparent. She set the book on her lap, allowing it to fall open to a random page. When she looked down, she found that she could read the page perfectly. One page written in English when the rest was in code? Odd.

She turned to the first page, the one where she had traced characters for the linguist to look at.

There exist three boxes, created by an Irish woodcarver, made from the wood of an alder tree that was struck by lightning. These boxes have enormous power. Great care must be taken when accessing this power.

Kelly blinked. There was nothing code-like about the words she saw on the page. And yet …

"Whoa. Okay, weird."

She flipped to look at the inside of the front cover. *Property of Maria Obrenivici. Only the chosen shall receive this text.*

"Chosen." A chill ran up her arms. *Isn't that what Bertha said to Mom?* She turned back to the first full page of text.

The woodcarver named the boxes, in order to describe and also to warn. They are:

Virtu, who conveys good powers and is helpful to the possessor.

Facinor, the bad one. Beware should this box come to any person with evil intent.

Manichee, whose powers are neutral and changeable. Manichee takes on the intentions of the holder. A good person will achieve good things. An evil person will achieve his intents as well.

Now behold this~~

When the boxes come together in the same place, be warned!

Virtu and Manichee together will accomplish great things

Facinor will turn Manichee to his own purposes and the two will overcome Virtu. This evil influence will become very powerful.

To you who possess this book, bear in mind the power you have to bring powerful changes to the world. For good or for evil—the choice is yours.

Kelly slammed the book shut, her heart racing. Choosing between good and evil, of course she would choose for the good every time. But what if it was not in her power to choose? What if the boxes exerted so much influence that she might be helpless. The feeling of being struck unconscious, as if by lightning, only yesterday. She could relate to feeling helpless.

Her hands began to shake uncontrollably. She stood and her knees felt weak.

Not again!

But when she gripped the back of a chair for a minute the feeling passed. She made her way to the kitchen table where she'd left her phone.

"Mom, you aren't going to believe this."

Chapter 41

One of the best perks of being associated with OSM was the virtually unlimited funding at his disposal. The organization had members worldwide, but most had no idea that the money they sent 'for the furtherance of scientific research' actually went into a huge fund that the board of directors used at their own whim.

Marcus's private meeting with the director had not gone well, even though he played the recording which revealed the FBI had stopped looking for him. Elias Swift was every bit as hungry for the power of the three boxes as Marcus himself, but the old man wanted credit for obtaining it, and he wanted the three boxes under his own control. Marcus persisted in his argument that he alone should make the journey to New Mexico. Eventually his request for a chartered plane was approved. A car would be waiting when he arrived in Colorado Springs, but his name would be nowhere on the lease. No one would connect this trip with a flight to Albuquerque last month, that trip also under a different name.

He stood in the bedroom of his Georgetown condo, pondering what to take. Although accommodation for baggage wasn't as restricted on the private plane as on a commercial flight, he must be careful. His disappearance could not appear to have been planned in advance. He needed time to accomplish his mission, including his escape to the west coast and a last-minute flight, paid in cash, to a destination unknown. One suitcase for clothing, a carry-on bag containing the valuables—this must look like a casual trip of a few days.

He pulled a few shirts from the closet and tossed them on the bed. Shoes, sports gear, and luggage were pushed aside and Marcus reached for a certain board on the closet floor. He'd rigged it so a push in the right place would raise it gently, leaving no scratches or gaps to reveal the existence of the hidden compartment he'd created.

Shining a flashlight into the space, he brought out a Smith & Wesson .45 handgun in a lockable case, three rubber banded stacks of cash, and a rectangular parcel wrapped in a black cloth pouch.

"Thank you, Maurilio," he whispered. It paid to have a cousin who'd achieved a high position in the Vatican, even if the man didn't have a clue that influence from OSM had gotten him there—and quite by design, into a position at the Vatican archives.

He carried the items to the bed, where he placed the cash and pistol into his waiting carry-on bag. From the black cloth he withdrew a carved wooden box, sat down, and set the box on his lap. As he stroked the wood finish, the color became darker and darker, turning to a shining black within a few moments. Small colored stones of red, green, and blue glinted like the eyes of mysterious creatures hidden deep in the wood surface. He lifted the lid.

A name carved there—Facinor—intrigued him.

When they had met in Ireland last month, he had asked Maurilio what the name meant, but his cousin shrank away from the artifact. "This should have remained in the Vatican archives, deep in that niche. I should never have brought it out into the open."

Warning vibes told Marcus not to reveal anything more to his cousin. Just because they looked nearly identical, as children enough so to switch places in school sometimes, didn't mean the two of them had turned out anything alike. Maurilio was the 'good boy' and his place among men of piety, wearing the collar of the Church, was exactly where he should be.

In retrospect, it was amazing Marcus had been able to convince the wimp to switch places one more time, to take his flight to Rome and then swap their passports and tickets so Marcus could fly to Ireland and back to New York, foiling the authorities' attempts to prove he'd been in New Mexico.

Well, this time it wouldn't matter. By the time he finished his visit to Taos, he would be in possession of all three boxes, and if the legends were true he knew what that meant. Virtually unlimited power. Not even the vast OSM or the powerful Vongraf Foundation could stop him from having anything he wanted.

His eyes gleamed as he put the box back into its black pouch and stowed it beneath the gun case and cash in his travel bag. He hastily tossed the clothing and his shaving kit into the larger suitcase, rearranged the closet items neatly, and gave a final farewell to his condo before he was out the door. He had a plane to catch.

Chapter 42

Sam spent the morning at the chocolate factory, going through and revising her cost spreadsheets, putting new numbers into the equations based on what she'd learned at the meetings in New York. Seeing the cruise line's massive warehouse and methods for supplying each ship gave her a whole new perspective on the intricacies of packing and shipping her delicate product.

By eleven o'clock, she'd been at it for hours and was developing a throbbing headache. When her phone rang and she saw it was Kelly, she gladly picked up the call and closed her eyes.

"Hey, sweetie, what's up?"

"I hate to interrupt, Mom, but I've discovered the most amazing thing about the book Bobul gave me. I can read it!"

Sam sat up straighter.

"If there's some point in the day when you can take a break and come by … well, I'd love to see if you can do it too."

Why would I be able to …? Had Kelly figured out some kind of invisible ink trick or something? "Tell you what. Let me finish a few calculations on these spreadsheets, and I'll come by in a half hour or so. We can take a break and have some lunch."

Sam hung up, her mind suddenly whirling. This was more than a parlor trick. If they could read the book, they might learn all kinds of things Bobul had hinted at. She looked at her computer screen. What the hell. Spreadsheets could wait.

She picked up her phone and bag and told Benjie she would be gone a couple of hours. Out in her truck, she remembered she'd intended to ask Beau if he had purposely left the barn door open—she'd noticed when she left home this morning. If not, she could offer to drive out there now and close it. She thumbed his number as she backed out of her parking spot.

No answer. It went straight to voicemail. She left a message. At the corner where she would either turn left to go home or right for Kelly's place, she paused. For all she knew, Beau might have remembered the door and gone home himself. Eager to see what Kelly had to show her, she turned right.

An unfamiliar car sat in the driveway. Hm. Someone must have arrived in the last few minutes or Kelly would have said something. Sam stuffed her phone into the pocket of her slacks and locked her bag in the truck. Kelly's back door was unlocked, so she walked into the service porch and then tapped lightly on the kitchen door as she opened it.

"Kel, it's me," she called out.

"Mom—no!" The shout was interrupted by a smacking sound and a thud.

Sam ran through the kitchen to find Kelly sprawled on the living room floor. She hurried forward when she caught movement to her left.

Marcus Fitch stepped behind her, blocking her exit, pointing a gun directly at her face. Sam knew him from the photos Beau had shown her. She spun toward him, ready to lash out.

"Don't do it, Ms. Sweet. Even with magical power, you can't move faster than a bullet." He seemed to find humor in this, in a you're-no-Superman kind of way.

He looked at Kelly, keeping the gun aimed at Sam. From his back pocket his left hand pulled a fistful of plastic ties, the kind used to strap things together, the same type Beau's men used in criminal apprehensions when handcuffs weren't practical.

"Tie her wrists and ankles," he ordered. He tossed the plastic strips on the floor beside Kelly, motioning with the gun that he wanted Sam to do the work.

Frantic thoughts raced through her head, but she couldn't see a way to defy him without one or both of them being hurt. She knelt and looped a tie around one of Kelly's wrists.

"Huh-uh. Not in the front," he said "Hands behind the back."

There went her first idea. But she complied, leaving the tie cinched loosely. Same with the ankles after Kelly sat with her back against a wingback chair. Marcus was no fool—he waved Sam aside and stepped in to give a firm tug to each of the ties, adding another one to strap her ankles to the chair leg as well.

"Ow! That's tight," Kelly said.

"Too bad." He edged his way to the coffee table and picked up Kelly's carved box, tucking it under his arm.

"Don't let him, Mom. If he gets both—"

He quieted her with a sharp kick to her hip. "I can send a stronger message. If you're not crazy about your ribs or that cute face of yours." His icy blue eyes narrowed to evil slits, his words coming in a rasp.

Kelly's face paled and she curled up protectively.

"Leave her alone. Just go," Sam said, trying for a firm tone but thinking she sounded shaky.

"Oh, no, that's not how this works," he hissed. "You and I have an important errand."

He jabbed Sam's ribs with the barrel of the gun. With a final backward glance at her daughter and a meaningful look, Sam walked to the kitchen door. Marcus paused and turned to Kelly again. "If I don't get what I need from your mom, I'll be back."

Sam knew what he wanted. The man would not stop until he had both boxes. Would he kill the two women once he had the prizes? She wouldn't put it past him. What did he have to lose? The FBI already suspected him for one murder. But, she knew, they had very little evidence against Fitch. She might be able to use that knowledge as a bargaining chip.

Marcus stepped in close behind her, in case a neighbor or passing car caught a glimpse, and nudged her toward her pickup truck.

"You're driving. Your place, as I'm sure you know."

Her eyes darted back and forth, looking for anything

that might help. She could hit the panic button on her key fob, but there wasn't a soul in sight on the quiet lane, no one to question or react. She opened her door and climbed into the driver's seat. No point in trying to drive away fast—he would simply go back in the house and kill her daughter as a lesson. He wasn't going to let them go until he had the boxes in his greedy hands.

She remembered her cell phone in her pants front pocket, but Fitch was inside the truck in under two seconds, and the gun was pointing directly at her gut. She started the truck.

"Fasten your seatbelt," she told him.

"How kind of you to care about my safety, but I'm not taking my eyes off you."

"Fine." She sent a smug look toward him.

He seemed to realize she could cause trouble with the truck, so he switched the gun to his left hand for a moment and stretched the belt into position. While he did so, Sam made a production about fastening her own belt. The last number she'd dialed on her phone had been Beau's; if she could only get it to redial … She fussed with the seat belt and touched the button on the phone as she clicked her belt in place.

Now, to feed enough clues to her husband. She prayed. If this call went to voicemail she and her daughter were most likely doomed.

She talked loudly and used Marcus's name, until he shouted at her to shut up. By the time they reached the ranch house he was agitated and twitchy. Ranger and Nellie saw Sam's truck and ran forward to greet her, stopping when they saw the stranger whose scent bothered them. Hair bristling and teeth bared they started to circle.

Fitch aimed the pistol at the border collie first.

"No! I'll get them under control," Sam pleaded.

He kept the pistol in place. "You got one chance."

She grabbed Nellie's collar. Was this a mistake? The two dogs might jump him, take him down. But she couldn't let them take the chance. Not against a gun.

She got Ranger's collar and led the two dogs into the kitchen, firmly closing the door.

"The box," Fitch said with a nervous glance toward the scratching sounds at the kitchen door. "Get it."

Sam looked around. "Let me see … I can't remember where I left it."

"Your friend Isobel said something about keeping it locked in a safe."

"Uh, well, I take it out and use it for my jewelry a lot of the time. I'm pretty sure I left it upstairs in the bathroom."

He followed her up the stairs. At the top she was tempted to spin around and kick the gun from his hand, but he'd gained on her and the barrel was again pressed into her ribcage.

"You'd be dumb to try anything," he said. "Don't forget I know where your daughter is and she's sitting there helpless at the moment."

"Just hold on. I'll find the stupid box. You can have it." She went through the motions of checking the bathroom vanity and a dresser in the bedroom.

"No reaching into any drawers," he said, more impatiently than ever.

"I might have left it in the living room." She headed back down the stairs, taking her time. *Please, Beau, get here and have the whole squad with you.* She scanned the living room windows for any sign of his cruiser, actually debated making a run for the front door for one crazy moment.

"Find that damned thing *now!*" Fitch yelled.

She desperately didn't want to reveal the safe. Standing in the narrow coat closet, she would be pinned, with no way to escape his bullet once she'd taken the box from its hiding place. At that point he would have nothing to lose by killing her.

The dogs were yipping now, scratching the kitchen door as if they would take it down.

In a corner of the front window, Sam caught a glimpse of a khaki uniform.

Fitch caught the movement too. He yanked Sam's shirt tail and flung her toward the couch. "Sit there!" he hissed as he tucked himself behind the front door.

Slowly the handle turned and the door swung inward on silent hinges. Beau led with his pistol held in a firm shooter's stance. His eyes sent Sam a questioning glance when he spotted her on the couch. She tried to tilt her head toward Fitch but he saw the motion.

In a blur, Fitch grabbed the door and yanked it inward. Shots rang from both weapons, a deafening explosion. Sam's hands went to her ears, her eyes blinking against the horrific noise and smell of gunpowder.

When she opened them and looked, Fitch was on the run toward the woods. Beau lay on the floor. She raced to his side. A plate-sized blood stain had already filled the center of his shirt.

Chapter 43

Evan Richards was the first of the deputies to run into the house. His boots screeched a little on the wood floor when he saw Beau. Sam had grabbed a wool blanket from the sofa, folded it into a thick square, and was holding it against the wound.

"This is serious," she said, pressing Beau's chest as hard as she could. "Get us the fastest ride to the hospital that you can."

He reached for his shoulder mike and gave the code for a law officer down.

Rico's cruiser roared into the driveway and Evan ran out to meet him. "Keep vehicles out of the way," he shouted. "We need space for medical help."

Rico took his vehicle closer to the barn, ran back to the house, and began directing others. "Where's the suspect?"

Sam didn't look up. "It's Marcus Fitch again. He ran toward the woods, but it's probably been a couple minutes or more. You might catch him on the county road."

Rico ran back outside and sent one of the other cruisers in pursuit.

"Helicopter's on the way in," Evan announced. "Beau, if you can hear me, just hang in there."

No response.

The whopping sound of the rotor blades reached Sam. She talked quietly to Beau, assuring him. Still no response. And in one minute, it was all out of her hands.

"They said it was a chest wound," said a breathless EMT who rushed to take over. Another wheeled a gurney across the porch and they slid a board under Beau. They cut away his clothing and pressed an oxygen mask to his face.

Evan stepped over to Sam and helped her to her feet, holding her close against his chest.

"We gotta get him to the trauma center in Albuquerque," she heard the EMT say. "Taos hospital can't handle something like—" He glanced at her and quit talking.

"I'm coming with you," she said.

As they wheeled Beau to the waiting helicopter, she grabbed her bag from the truck. "Evan—can you take care of the dogs and post a guard on the house? What Fitch wants is still here. And—" The thought hit her suddenly. "Go by Kelly's and take care of her. She can explain."

Explain the completely surreal turn all their lives had taken this morning? How?

Chapter 44

Marcus thanked his lucky stars for the foresight to do all that jogging in the past few weeks, although he had to admit the air here at seven thousand feet was a lot thinner. He had a terrible stitch in his side, and by the time he'd covered the half mile to the county road he felt almost ready to pass out. He gripped the painful spot, gasping, and his hand came away with blood. Not much, and it didn't show on his black shirt. He heard a vehicle.

Not law enforcement, he saw with relief. Some kind of old farm pickup truck that had once been white but now wore a coating of brown mud spatter. He turned his wounded side away and stuck out his thumb.

"What's a matter?" asked the old guy behind the wheel.

"Aw, stupid me. I started out jogging and didn't realize what a hot day it was. Can you give me a lift? I live near the gas station, the one by the intersection at 64."

"Ya oughta carry water, you know. Middle of summer, not smart to get all dried out."

Marcus gritted his teeth and climbed in the passenger side of the truck. He wished the old man would just shut up and drive but he didn't dare show the pistol he'd tucked into the back of his pants or reveal his wound. Even though his shirt tail covered it, leaning back against the inflexible bench seat made the gun dig into his back.

Two Taos County Sheriff's Department vehicles roared by in the opposite direction, lights and sirens going full bore, and the old man pulled off the side of the road to let them have plenty of clearance. Marcus pretended interest in a big tree out the side window.

Damn that Samantha Sweet. Somehow, she'd managed to get that sheriff husband of hers out to the house in the time she'd stalled him over getting the box out of the safe. And why'd the sheriff have to come walking in like that? If he'd stayed back and shouted through a bullhorn or something … well, he wouldn't have needed to get shot.

Don't be an ass, Marcus. The sheriff didn't ask for it. You did it. You killed a lawman. He knuckled the side of his head to get the voice out of there.

"Here, this is close enough," he said to the pickup driver.

"It's just the convenience store and gas station. No houses around here."

"Yeah, well, my neighbor works there. He'll give me a ride home when he gets off in, uh, half an hour." Marcus opened his door and was halfway out.

The old guy looked at him a little strangely. "Okay, you say so."

Marcus went inside the store and bought a roadmap. At

this point he just needed to get back to Colorado Springs and the private plane that would fly him to the coast, but he wasn't sure what his options were. He sneaked a peek at his wound, relieved to see it wasn't bleeding heavily. It stung like crazy though. He looked out toward the gas pumps.

Two people were gassing up—one a hefty twenty-something guy in a muscle shirt and baggy shorts. The other was a petite girl probably still in high school. She was chewing gum and studying the instructions on the pump. As the big guy finished and got into his truck, Marcus approached the girl.

"Need some help?" He flashed a smile.

"My mom didn't give me her card today, so I guess it says here I gotta go inside and pay with cash before this thing will start up."

"Um, yeah, that's probably right. If you want to go in, I can start it pumping the gas as soon as the attendant turns it on," he said, noticing she'd left her keys in the ignition.

"Oh! Okay, cool. Thanks." She started for the building, tottering on platform shoes that nearly unbalanced her.

The moment she entered the building, Marcus hopped behind the wheel of her car, jammed it in gear, and roared out onto Highway 64. It was the main drag through Taos, and he could only hope he didn't get caught up in traffic before he got to Kelly Sweet's house. Or before this tub ran out of gas, he thought as he noticed the gauge. Sure, the girl could report it stolen, but that would take a while and by his guess local law enforcement was just a little bit busy right now.

He felt his temper rise again. Another way Samantha Sweet had screwed him. She'd locked her truck when they arrived at her house, with the box he'd taken from her daughter's place inside. He'd debated smashing a window, but the sirens in the distance, so soon after he'd fired at that sheriff ... he'd been too flustered to think straight. One extra minute and he would have had it. Was there *nothing* that could go his way today?

Okay, Fitch, he lectured himself. Stay cool and think ahead. At least get back to the rental car. You just need the backpack with that Facinor box—well, and the cash. That's step one. Step two—find the quickest way to Colorado Springs, preferably on a route where there won't be a lot of cops looking for you.

The stolen car ran out of gas a block from Kelly's house. But that was fine. They'd chalk it up to him being a joyrider and at least no one would track him down on that little offense.

He practically tiptoed up the driveway where his rental still sat, watching her windows, although he'd tied her up solidly enough she wouldn't be getting up off the floor anytime soon. He backed carefully out and left the short lane where she lived, making a right turn on Kit Carson Road.

He needed to pull over somewhere and study the map or check to see if his phone app actually got a signal out here in the sticks, but he sure wasn't going to do it until that cop car behind him went somewhere else. When it turned onto the same lane he'd just left, he counted his blessings. Close, but not close enough, copper!

Chapter 45

Kelly felt new energy surge through her as she bit through the edge of the plastic strip around her ankle. Thank goodness for flexibility from all those yoga classes, she thought wryly, and for having handled the box this morning. But the smile died on her lips. Her mother was out there and her life was in the hands of Marcus Fitch.

The man was certifiably insane. The crazed look in his eye when he'd burst in earlier and spotted the carved box, Manichee, on her table told it all.

She got to her feet and managed to pull the heavy wingback chair into the kitchen. A knife would be a much quicker way to remove the remaining ties. Still, working a knife with her teeth until she freed one hand wasn't a fast process. And the whole time she was thinking, *what next?*

She discarded the idea of calling Sam—if Fitch was

still with her, a ringing phone could set him off. The smart thing would be to call Beau, get the sheriff's department out to the ranch house to arrest him. She sawed away until the last of the ties came off. Her wrists were puffy and red, but at least she was free.

She peered out the kitchen window and froze when she saw the plain white car Fitch had arrived in. Of course—he'd forced Sam to drive her truck. He would either need Sam to give him a ride back here, or he had simply ditched this car. She should convince Beau to send a deputy here to wait for Fitch to come back. She dialed the department.

"Dixie, it's Kelly Sweet, um, Porter. I really need to talk to Beau."

"Oh, honey …" The dispatcher's voice cracked. "You haven't heard."

The news sent Kelly to the floor, her knees folding, her back grazing the kitchen cupboards as she sank. Beau, shot? She couldn't believe it.

"Where's my mom?" Sobs broke up her words.

"Let me find out for you, honey." Dixie didn't even bother to put the phone on hold while she radioed.

Kelly caught words here and there but not enough to make sense of the conversation, which was completely unreal to her.

"Kelly? Deputy Rico says Deputy Evan just left for your house. Stay there and he can fill you in. He'll be there real soon, okay?"

"Dixie! Don't hang up. Is my mom hurt too? Did that guy kill them both? Please tell me."

"Nobody's been killed," Dixie said. "But Beau's hurt real bad and is on the way to the trauma center in Albuquerque. I think your mom's with him. Deputy Evan was there. He can tell you all about it. Give him about fifteen minutes."

A tornado of emotion whirled through her as she set the phone down. Her head felt stuffed with cotton and her ears echoed with a tunnel-like hollowness. She thought she heard a car on the gravel driveway but didn't have the energy to look up. Evan would be here in a while. She trusted him. He was Riki's fiancé, a good man.

But she needed to be held and loved. She dialed Scott and blurted out the skimpy details she knew.

"I'm on my way home," he said immediately.

She felt drained by the whole day's experience, and it wasn't over yet. When Scott and Evan both arrived at the same time, she got up to let them in. That's when she realized the white sedan was no longer in her driveway.

Chapter 46

An hour after arrival at UNM Hospital, Sam felt her brain unraveling. She half-remembered giving Evan orders to take care of things at home and to inform Kelly, telling Rico about Marcus Fitch and the direction he'd taken when he ran.

But had she really acted with such clarity? Had she only imagined her reactions, which now seemed fuzzy in her memory?

The entire day seemed like a blur now, from the landing of the helicopter on the hospital roof, to the trauma team rushing out to get Beau and whisk him away, to the nurses and orderlies who physically had to hold her back from chasing his gurney down the hall and into the surgical suite. She sat on a stiff chair in the waiting area, fiddling with the strap on her purse, unable to think of anything but the horrible wounds she'd barely glimpsed on Beau's body.

Kelly had called. Sam couldn't even remember what they'd said to each other, but she had the impression Kelly and Scott were on their way.

"Mrs. Cardwell?" A blonde nurse in scrubs stood near her chair.

"Oh, god …"

"There's no news. The doctor just sent me out here to let you know your husband is still in surgery." She lowered her voice and sat in the empty chair next to Sam. "The worst of the wounds is near the heart. We're doing everything we can to repair the damage, but it's a very tricky area. The other shot went through his shoulder, badly grazing the bone."

"Will he …?"

"I can't sugar-coat this. He's in very critical condition."

Sam felt as if she was hearing the pronouncement through a thick pillow. The sound came through but the meaning didn't seem clear at all.

The nurse rose again. "I'm going back in there and I'll come back as soon as there's anything to report. I know it seems like it's taking forever—just know that there is an expert team with him." She squeezed Sam's shoulder before she walked away.

It only made Sam feel marginally better. She could only imagine what was going on behind those closed doors. Her mind shut down when she thought of medical television shows and how the patient was a cloth-draped hunk of meat and organs, with instruments and masses of gauze protruding from his body. She couldn't go there. Couldn't think of the specifics of what they might be doing to her beloved Beau.

There was a window at the far end of the waiting area, and Sam focused on the tips of a leafy tree in a wide expanse of blue, unbroken by even a single cloud. The green leaves shimmered in the heat. At least if there had been a cloud or two she could occupy her mind by watching them form familiar shapes.

Movement near the elevators caught her attention and before she knew it Kelly rushed into her arms.

"I'm so glad you're okay, Mom," Kelly sobbed against Sam's neck.

I'm so far from okay … you have no idea.

She looked up. Scott had a somber look on his face. He tried to send her a brave smile, but it didn't quite work.

"How's Beau? They said he was in surgery?"

Sam nodded. "It's taking a long time. The nurse came out—" She glanced at the clock on the wall. Had it actually been two hours ago? Other people who had been sitting in the room had left without her noticing. "It's critical, they say."

Kelly stepped back and swabbed at her eyes with a wad of tissues.

"How did it—it was Fitch, wasn't it?"

Sam could only nod. "He took Beau by surprise. I … I did so many things wrong. Why didn't I leave the dogs free to attack him? He threatened to kill Ranger and Nellie and I locked them up."

"Mom, you couldn't have—"

"I should have just handed over the box. In light of all this, it's just *not that important.*" She raked her fingers through her hair. "I can't believe I called Beau out there. I wanted him to come and capture Fitch, but I've led him to his—" She couldn't think the word *death*, much less say it.

"No … Mom! Don't start blaming yourself. It's just what happened."

"Sam, a lawman's life involves danger. We all know that," Scott said.

A new thought hit Sam hard. Knowing he would be in danger, why hadn't Beau been wearing his Kevlar vest? Was he lying in that operating room now, his life in the balance, because he'd simply skipped such a crucial step? She realized she might never know the answer.

She sank back onto the uncomfortable chair with her head in her hands.

Her phone lay on an adjacent chair. When it rang, Kelly looked at the screen. "It's coming from the bakery."

"Can you …?"

Kelly picked it up and walked toward the big window. "Jen, hey." The girls had been friends since fifth grade. "We don't know anything yet. Surgery. Yeah … Okay … I'll tell her."

She turned to tell Sam that the bakery crew sent their love and would take care of everything back home; she was not to worry about business. But then she spotted the doctor standing in the doorway, looking toward their little group.

Chapter 47

He tried to take the winding roads at a reasonable speed, but everything in Marcus Fitch's body told him to hurry. He needed to get to that plane and get as far away from New Mexico as possible before the word got out. As he passed by little mountain towns with colorful names like Angel Fire and Eagle Nest, he forced himself to watch the speedometer and keep an eye on the posted speed limits.

His white sedan with Colorado plates shouldn't be a particular standout here, but he had no way of knowing what that daughter had witnessed or whether her neighbors might be on the ball enough to write down the number from an unfamiliar car.

He turned on the radio and tuned to a station from Taos. Word of the shooting was out, but the details were being kept minimal. A confrontation, a shooting, a lawman wounded. If the sheriff had died, wouldn't they be saying so? Maybe not. Maybe they knew he was listening and wanted him to become complacent.

He caught himself. *They* knew he was listening? Seriously?

But most certainly his description had been sent out to law enforcement in the area by now. He tried to think what to do. There could be roadblocks—almost certainly *would* be roadblocks or checkpoints at the state border. He picked up his phone but was in a dead spot on a road that ran alongside a creek in the bottom of a deep canyon.

If he could reach his pilot, the plane might be able to come get him at one of these little regional airports—if there was one. Marcus had no idea and no internet signal. Or, what if he could reach the OSM offices? Um. Not good. Under questioning he'd have to admit that he'd not only failed to get the box from Samantha Sweet and the other one from her daughter—feats he'd bragged he could do—but if the board found out he'd become involved in a shooting that brought attention to the organization they would, as the saying went, disavow all knowledge of him.

Okay, so that option was out. The nagging pain in his side worsened.

What was the best thing he could do—right now—to help his situation? He debated for a few more miles until he noticed there were a number of campgrounds and fishing spots along this road. He watched for the next one and pulled into it. A number of vehicles, mostly RVs and trailers, were parked in designated slots for camping. If he could switch the plates on his car, that would throw anyone off the scent who might have his number on their watch list.

Then he got a better idea.

One end of the rambling campground seemed to be set aside for long-term camping. Here, he noticed most of the trailers had their curtains drawn, and there was a definite lack of removable items such as folding chairs, grills, and coolers in these camp sites. He remembered a friend from his teen years in Pennsylvania whose parents took their camper to the mountains and left it parked at some campground for the summer, then the family would drive up from the city in their car, camp out for the weekend, drive home Sunday afternoons to be back for the work week.

Hiding out for a week or two ought to give the story time to die down in importance. He circled the car through the rest of the area and back out to the highway. A quarter mile farther along was one of the day-fishing areas. Signs warned that a fee was required even to stop and picnic. Fine. He inserted money into the little machine, got the day permit sticker in return, and placed it as the instructions indicated on his windshield.

Taking up his backpack containing the box Facinor, he hiked back to the long-term campers. He was careful to keep to the woods as much as possible, and he saw no one the whole way. Feeling like a customer on an RV dealer lot, he began shopping until he found the right one. Lots of dust indicated the owners hadn't been back in a while, and the older-model camper had a lock a four-year-old could bypass.

After dark, he would make his way back to the rental car and find another vehicle to switch license tags with. Meanwhile, he would get familiar with his new hideout.

Chapter 48

The doctor's expression seemed grave. Sam felt despair welling up inside.

"He came through the surgery alive," the man, who reminded her of Mark Harmon, said.

Expressions of relief all around.

"His condition, however, is still very critical. The chest wound, of course, being the worst. We repaired the damage as best we could. I'm afraid bullet wounds can be very, very damaging. The shoulder was less serious, but there may be impaired movement in that arm."

Sam wished he would quit saying 'very' about everything.

"He'll be unconscious for a while. In fact, we've induced a coma to keep him still."

"I need to see him," Sam said. "And this is my daughter

and son-in-law. Can they come too?"

"One at a time is best right now. We'll see about later."

He showed her to the nurses' station and then to the glass-fronted room nearby where Beau lay, unmoving, while monitors and machines ticked all around him. A pump-like thing breathed for him through an uncomfortable-looking apparatus taped to his mouth, and strands of tubing ran from IV bags on a tall stand and disappeared beneath the edge of the thin cotton gown.

Sam's breath caught and tears sprang to her eyes. She'd never considered what her final sight of her husband could be, but she would hate for this to be it. She nodded to the doctor, wanting him to go away.

As soon as they were alone, she took Beau's free hand and began talking to him, keeping the tears out of her voice. Trying to think of positive things to say was the challenge. There seemed nothing positive at all about this day's events.

"I wish I could change everything about this morning," she said. "You need to wake up and get well so I can tell you all the things I left unsaid. Please do it, Beau. Please wake up."

Her allotted ten minutes vanished in a blur, and the nurse was telling her it was time to go.

"I'm not leaving the hospital."

"We'll set up a cot and some blankets for you." The woman's eyes were kind. She saw the pain in families all the time, Sam realized. "You'll be right there in the room with him. Unless you'd prefer a real bed. There's a family room one floor down."

"No—here, please."

Kelly was practically dancing on the balls of her feet when Sam returned to the waiting area. Sam told them about the arrangement for her to stay the night.

"Mom, open your bag. I want you to take this." She pulled open her own tote-sized purse to reveal that she was carrying the box, Manichee. "Maybe it will help."

Sam's heart lifted. "Thanks. You're so smart, my brilliant daughter." She slipped the box into her backpack purse.

Scott returned from the vending machines with a bottled water. "There's not much in the way of food in those things," he said with a tilt of his head. "But I'd be happy to bring you something."

"I'm not hungry."

"It's after ten p.m. and you haven't eaten anything all day," he reminded.

"Not now. Not the diet I'd choose, but maybe I'll lose a few pounds this week," she said in a feeble attempt at humor.

"I got us a room at a hotel down the road," he told the women. "Sam, anytime you want a shower, a better bed, real food … just say so."

She'd given no thought to how she must look or smell, she realized. "I'm fine for now. I'm going back in there."

She swore Kelly sent her a subtle wink.

Chapter 49

Marcus explored the camper in the last of the fading daylight. There was an old flashlight in the glove compartment, but the batteries barely lit the bulb to a dull glow. He switched it off. The tiny galley revealed plastic bins with a few food items left behind. He devoured a whole pack of cheese crackers before he noticed they were stale, almost to the point of being rancid.

One bin held canned goods—three cans of green beans and two of tomato sauce. A box of Triscuits in an overhead cupboard had been chewed into by mice. He shoved it back in place. A drawer beneath a small clothing locker was jammed full of miscellanea—a pink barrette for a little girl, a screwdriver, a roll of electrical tape, a wrapped packet of fish hooks, two C-cell batteries, four clothespins, and a piece of thin cord about two feet long. He compared the batteries to the flashlight he'd found, but they were the wrong size. It required D-cells. He kept looking.

The clothing consisted of two cheap windbreakers and a pair of ladies rain boots, circa 1970. In fact the entire camper seemed to come from that era, probably owned by some old couple who never aspired to anything nicer. He reminded himself to feel at least a little speck of gratitude; they were, after all, providing him with a temporary hideout.

He looked at the wound, knowing he should tend to it, but he'd uncovered no first aid supplies in the RV. Maybe it would just scab over, on its own.

He took his phone from his pocket and looked at it. Still no signal, and the battery was now down to twenty percent. There was one electrical outlet in the camper, but when he pulled his charger cord from his backpack and plugged it in, there was no response. Probably needed to run a generator or some such thing to use the vehicle's electrical system, and he didn't dare make that much noise. He drummed his fingers on the cheap dinette table, deciding what to do.

"Okay," he said to the empty space. "The plan was to wait until dark—that's what I'll do."

The light inside was nearly gone, so he quickly gathered the few useful items. He placed strips of black electrical tape over the lens of the flashlight so its beam, although not bright, would be directed in a narrow strip toward the ground. The screwdriver would come in very handy.

He peered out the edge of one of the window shades, but a couple was walking a big black dog along the paved lane that separated the campsites. He let the shade fall back in place, hoping he hadn't left footprints in the dust around the entrance to his lair. But they were talking and gesturing and didn't even glance in his direction.

An hour later it was fully dark outside. He felt edgy and out of touch without his phone, but he allowed another hour for people to get tired of sitting out in the chilly air, to go inside their RVs and settle in with television or playing cards or whatever people did in these places to avoid being bored to death.

Finally, around ten p.m. he stepped quietly out of the camper, flashlight in hand, screwdriver in a front pocket. The temperature must have dropped twenty degrees since this afternoon. His pistol was tucked into the waistband of his pants and his backpack was securely in place. No way he was going anywhere and leaving it behind. He made his way to another unoccupied RV, four spaces away, and quickly removed the license plate from it. The reflective material glared alarmingly in the dark, and he quickly shoved it into his pack, next to the wooden box.

Backtracking his way through the woods to the pullout where he'd left the rental car was no easy feat, and the stupid flashlight began to flicker shortly into the journey. He switched to his cell phone light, and it, too, was down to a dim glow by the time he spotted the car. Everyone else who'd parked there during the day was gone now, and he realized his would be obvious to any forest ranger or cop who cruised by. Plus, he was chilled to the bone and needed supplies.

He wondered how much farther until he could get out of this canyon and receive a phone signal. Would there be a police roadblock along the way?

Screw it. He quickly switched the car's license plate for the one he'd taken from the RV, burying the incriminating one under a couple of inches of dirt and pine needles. He tossed his pack on the passenger seat and climbed in, starting the car and turning the heater controls all the way to the hottest setting. How could it be so freaking cold in the middle of the summer, for chrissakes?

His phone charger came with a cigarette plug adapter, which he put to use immediately once the car was running. No doubt he could fully charge the phone and be on his way out of here if he could make it to Colorado Springs, but that was still a good four hours away and he didn't dare get on the interstate. For sure, there would be cops looking for him along the major highways. His plan to hide out of sight was still a good one. At least a week, he guessed.

So far, only two vehicles had come along—one from each direction—and neither slowed or paid him the slightest attention. He put the car in gear and started rolling, heading in the same direction he'd been going, away from Taos.

Ten miles later he came to a little fork-in-the-road town of sorts, indicated by a reduced-speed sign and the name of the place: Ute Park, Elevation 7,413. Holy crap—he might as well be in the Alps! No wonder it was cold here. A combination gas station and convenience store sat back from the road, and ahead he caught a glimpse of a reflective sign with the US Postal Service logo.

Two vehicles sat near the log building housing the convenience store. One had two flat tires and both were coated so thickly in dust they obviously hadn't been driven recently. He pulled off the road, hoping that if anyone was observing they would think he was looking to pump some gas. Dumb city guy who thought things stayed open 24/7 everywhere, right? If they noticed him at all, they certainly wouldn't make themselves known.

He rolled slowly through the station, saw no activity, and cut his headlights. With a quick glance around, he steered to the back of the building and made sure he was out of sight of the road.

Yes! a phone signal. He quickly tapped the number he'd been given for the charter pilot. Three rings and voicemail. Of course. Had he really thought the guy would wait up until all hours? He left a message: "I've been delayed but still coming. Don't leave without me. I'll touch base again when I get closer to your location."

There. Hopefully he could string the guy along several days by saying he was nearly there. If he'd admitted that he didn't plan to show up for a week, his ride would abandon him. Still might. Marcus's one regret was that he'd left his large suitcase with all his clothes on the plane. Dammit. He should have been done with Taos forever and back to the plane in under twelve hours. He was already sick of the stink of these bloody clothes.

With a glance toward the back of the convenience store, he sized it up. Okay—one chance to stock up. He got out, picked up the pistol, and locked the car. A wimpy yellow bug bulb near the store's back door provided the only light.

He tried the door with no luck—even this far out in the sticks, people weren't *that* trusting. Beside the door was a window about two feet wide by three feet high. He reached up and whacked it with the butt of his pistol, working quickly to break out enough of the glass to pass through without slicing himself, then did the same to the yellow light bulb.

By the light from the refrigerated cases that held mostly beer and sodas, Marcus did a quick shopping trip. He filled two of the store's plastic bags—bandages, adhesive tape, antibiotic ointment, aspirin, batteries for the flashlight, tuna in pull-top cans, crackers, fried pies (he'd always been a sucker for those), a fistful of breakfast burritos, and a TV dinner type box of chicken (fully cooked, just heat and eat!). He didn't care; he could eat it cold at this point. From a rack of touristy T-shirts, he grabbed several.

Debating the wisdom of it, he made two limping trips out to the car, stashing a case of bottled water and two six-packs of beer in the trunk. Luckily, the only vehicle that passed down the road didn't even pause.

He stood beside the car, listening to the eerily quiet night. He honestly couldn't recall ever having been anyplace where the only sound was the occasional swish of bird wings and the faraway call of a coyote. When he was absolutely certain there was no moving vehicle within miles, he started his car and headed back toward the campgrounds down the road.

His earlier adrenaline rush gone, he found his eyes drooping. The pain in his side throbbed and he felt feverish. He'd been awake more than twenty-four hours, he realized, as he pulled his car into the woods. Less than twelve hours ago, he'd killed a sheriff. He'd really believed he'd never sleep again, but now he felt it was inevitable. He tried to focus on his plan: get to San Francisco, buy a ticket. He'd long dreamed of Bali—perhaps too obvious a choice. Singapore—no tolerance for criminals. Indonesia—there were thousands of tiny islands there, perfect little hiding places.

He held to those thoughts while he dragged his aching body toward the RV park. He barely made it inside before he drifted off.

Chapter 50

Sam had thought she would never sleep until Beau opened his eyes, until she knew he was safe, but it all caught up with her in a crushing blow about midnight.

Fifteen minutes, she promised herself. I'll take a fifteen-minute nap and then go back to his side. She weaved her way to the quasi bed the nurses had rigged up, something that looked like it had come out of coach class on an airplane but could be stashed upright against the wall on a moment's notice in case—she didn't *even* want to think about that worst-case scenario. They had left her a small pillow and a thin blanket, and in her present condition these small comforts were welcome. She kicked off her shoes and lay on her side with the blanket pulled up to her neck.

She clasped Manichee against her, hoping prolonged contact would help. After Kelly handed the box to her earlier in the evening, Sam had tried her usual approach—laying her hands gently on top of it—but this box failed to react in the same manner Virtu did. No golden tint to the wood, and of course this one didn't have stones on it, another indicator Sam often used in order to know when the box's power was at its greatest.

And yet she knew this one had power, too. She had witnessed firsthand when Kelly touched it. She had become impatient, disgruntled with the few attempts she'd made—limited to sporadic times when medical personnel weren't interrupting. Cuddled against the box now, she closed her eyes and imagined it warming, sending waves of healing power into her although it didn't change its appearance at all. *Just fifteen minutes ...*

She awoke with a start. It was 4:13 a.m. when she peeked at her phone. Four hours!

She threw back the blanket and padded to Beau's side. He lay so very still. Tears stung her eyes again. The numbers on the monitors said he was breathing and his heart was beating. They were her only assurance. The bandages and tubes were sterile reminders of the hideous injuries beneath, of the horrible things that madman had done to the love of her life.

Her hands felt warm—from holding the box so long?—and she placed them on Beau. First, his head, cupping the sides of his face, sending waves of love to him. She moved to his shoulders, avoiding the bandages while trying to make contact with as much of his exposed skin as possible. Down the arms to his hands—the left one was taped up with a plastic contraption that allowed fluids from the bags hanging on a rack to drain into him—but she ran her fingertips gently over his skin where she could.

She squeezed his right hand.

No response.

She watched his face. No response at all.

The box sat benignly on her makeshift bed, sending no signal or assurance her way. Maybe if the box touched Beau directly. She looked out the wide window toward the nurses' station. Doubtful they would think it a good idea to put their patient in contact with anything so potentially germ-laden. But Sam knew better. At least she thought she did. She'd seen amazing things from these old artifacts.

She picked up Manichee and carried it to the bed, slipping it under the sheet to rest against Beau's bare hip. The skin prickled, as if chilled. But the faint shimmer of goosebumps went away immediately, and Beau's expression didn't change at all.

A nurse slipped into the room, so quietly on her rubber-soled shoes that she startled Sam.

"Just need to take a peek here," she whispered. For some reason it seemed normal to speak aloud in daylight but nighttime required whispers.

Sam pressed against the bedside where the box lay hidden, holding her breath slightly, but the nurse only looked at the clear plastic bags on the rack and checked something about the connection where the fluids entered the tube on Beau's hand. Then she left.

The bedside chair where she'd sat half the night was still in place. Sam sat again, took Beau's hand, and laid her head on the bed beside him.

"Oh, Beau. Talk to me, squeeze my hand, blink … something. I need you to give me some little sign you'll be okay. Please be okay …"

Nothing moved or twitched.

She stroked his hand, ran her fingertips up the arm to his shoulder. Her other hand encountered the wooden box, still hidden beneath the sheeting. She should put it in her pack, out of sight in case the nurses came back to check his wounds or change the dressings.

As she set the box down and zipped her pack, something Kelly had told her came back. Bobul's prediction that Sam might find herself alone. She swallowed hard and choked back the tears that rose when she gripped his hand again.

"I can't do this without you, honey. I can't. You're my rock. You are the one who gets me through. I've taken on too much—I know it. I'm going to figure out a better way. Just let me know you'll be here for me to come home to. That you'll always be there."

Did she imagine that the beeping heart monitor quickened? She stared at it. But the numbers were all the same. Not the faintest movement crossed his handsome face.

* * *

Kelly came in the morning, about the time the head nurse informed Sam that it was time for them to change Beau's dressings and she would need to leave the room.

"Come on, Mom. You have to get some breakfast," Kelly said.

"I can't leave the hospital," Sam insisted. "He could need me."

"Fine. The cafeteria is only down one floor." Kelly sent the nurse a look to explain Sam's near frantic demeanor.

The attempt to get Sam to sit down to a meal barely happened. From the cafeteria's buffet line, she took a small scoop of scrambled egg, one strip of bacon, and a single slice of dry toast. The only thing she treated herself to was an extra-large coffee. The food was gone in a half-dozen bites and she was insistent on getting back up to the ICU.

"I called Grandma and Grampa," Kelly said. "She wanted to hop in the car and drive right out here."

Sam's eyes widened. "Oh god, I hope—"

"I talked them out of it. Told them no one's allowed in except you, and there wouldn't be anything they could do."

"Thanks." Sam pictured her mother's take-charge personality. Her own stress level rose at the thought.

"You should call them," Kelly said as they left the cafeteria. "I don't know how long my influence will hold them back." She gave a lopsided grin.

Sam squeezed her hand and said she would check in with her parents in a day or so. In the elevator she told Kelly what she had tried during the night with the carved box. "Yours didn't work for me, Kel. I need you to try it this morning. Maybe each of us has come to possess the box we have for a reason. If you hold Manichee, I feel sure it's *your* healing touch that will work on Beau."

"Tell me what to do and I will," Kelly said.

Back in Beau's room, the fresh bandages gave a sense of new hope, but fundamentally nothing had changed. When Kelly picked up the box and laid her palms against it, the wood began to lighten and warm.

"Look! It's working," she exclaimed.

Sam was standing guard at the door. "When it feels really warm, almost hot, you can set it down. Then go over and touch Beau. Try touching his hands and arms, then his face."

"Are you sure it will be okay?" Kelly's hands were

becoming very warm now. When she could barely touch the box's surface anymore, she put it aside. "Whoa—that's amazing."

She did as instructed, warming Beau's cool fingertips and forearms.

"Try laying your hands flat against the bandages. Right on the wounds," Sam suggested.

Beau's eyes moved behind his eyelids, and the heartbeat on the monitor went up a few beats.

"Maybe I'd better quit," Kelly whispered. "What if it's too much for him?"

"But he's reacting."

Kelly raised her hands and backed away from the bed. "Let's see what happens before I do any more. Don't forget, the doctor said they've induced this coma state. Maybe they don't want him to wake up just yet."

Sam's face slumped. "I know. You're probably right." She paced to the window and back to the bed. "I just want him to wake up." Her voice went shaky and fragile at that last part.

A shadow crossed the doorway. Doctor Albertson, the surgeon. How much had he heard?

"We know you're eager, Mrs. Cardwell," he said. He held a chart in his hands.

Kelly had quickly carried the box to Sam's cot and was zipping it inside her pack.

"Is he improving, doctor?" Sam asked.

The doctor looked different today, without his surgical scrubs and the cloth cap covering his hair. Today, in dark pleated slacks, a blue button-down shirt and a white coat he looked like he'd walked off the set of some medical TV show. He took time to lift the metal cover on the clipboard chart.

"The wounds seem to be healing well, considering we operated less than twenty-four hours ago. The biggest danger is infection, and we have him on some fairly heavy-duty antibiotics to keep that at bay. We'll begin withdrawing some of the sleep medication by the end of today and hope to see a positive response." He held the chart to his chest. "There's been a lot of trauma to his body. To be truthful, he's not out of danger yet, and it may be a long haul."

He looked as if he'd be willing to answer questions, but Sam couldn't think of what to ask. Her brain seemed to stick on the phrase 'he's not out of danger.' Dr. Albertson gave an awkward pat to her shoulder before he left. Clearly, he was better with the patients than the families.

A young nurse with long, dark hair bustled in and proceeded to take a vial of blood by connecting a tube to the device on Beau's forearm. She gave a ready smile and asked if there was anything she could do for Sam. "An orange juice might do you good," she suggested.

Kelly, meanwhile, had slung her purse over her shoulder. "Scott and I are going to drive home, and we'll bring your truck and some fresh clothes for you. I know you're sick of these," she said, reminding Sam she'd been wearing the bakery clothes she'd dressed in two days ago. "And I'll bring *that book* I wanted you to read. We'll be back by five or so, and I think it would be a good idea for you to come to the hotel for a shower and let us take you out for some dinner."

The nurse had finished with the blood draw and some little process where she flushed out the line. "For sure, Sam. Everyone needs a change of scenery after they've been here a day or so."

Sam wanted to snap at both of them, to say they should quit telling her what to do, quit planning her life, but she couldn't. Kelly's offer came purely from love, and all the nurses had been so kind. She nodded silently, then turned back to keep watch over Beau.

Chapter 51

True to her word, Kelly phoned a little before five o'clock. "We're down in the parking garage, Mom. Found a primo parking spot for your truck. Do you want to meet us and head out for a quick clean-up and dinner?"

Sam hesitated. Beau hadn't moved a muscle or flickered an eyelid all day. "I really shouldn't leave him."

"We thought you might say that. Scott's on his way up. He'll stay with Beau the whole time, and he promises to call you if there's any change at all."

Before Sam could formulate an argument, her son-in-law showed up at the ICU door.

"Kelly's worried about you, Sam. If nothing else, do this to humor her." He repeated what Kelly had told her, that the hotel was only ten minutes away and he would call if there was the slightest change to report.

She picked up her bag and stuffed her phone inside. With a lingering look toward Beau, she left his side for the first time in nearly seventy-two hours.

The late afternoon sun blasted her eyes as Kelly pulled out into traffic. Light, noise, motion—Sam hadn't realized how insulated she'd felt in the separate little universe of the hospital. Once there, small bits of the outside world had existed only through tinted windows. She lifted the neck edge of her shirt and sniffed.

"Ugh, you're so right. I really do need a shower."

Kelly laughed. "I didn't actually mean anything by it when I suggested this." She pulled into the lot at the hotel, parked, and retrieved a suitcase she'd quickly packed.

Sam followed along. "This all feels so otherworldly."

"I know, Mom. We'll just take a step at a time." She set the suitcase on one of the queen-sized beds. "Here's your stuff, there's the bathroom. I shall go back out and procure us some dinner. What sounds good?"

Sam couldn't remember when she had last eaten, but she didn't feel the least bit hungry. "Nothing."

"Mom … you won't be helping yourself or Beau if you become rundown. Give me a hint or you'll get whatever I happen to find. Burgers? Pizza? Salad?"

Sam shrugged. "Something with protein?"

"Good idea. You need your strength." Kelly left the room and Sam unzipped the suitcase.

The otherworldly feeling persisted, but she knew she was doing the right things. Cleanliness and food would help immensely. By the time Kelly returned, carrying two large chef salads, Sam was feeling somewhat better already.

"I would have insisted on taking you to the restaurant to get you out into some fresh air," Kelly said, "but while we're alone and without Scott wondering what we're up to, I wanted to tell you about the book."

They set out their meal on the small table in the room and concentrated on the food at first. Sam didn't want to admit it, but she did feel better with each bite. Everything Kelly had said about keeping up her own strength was so true—she would need the energy to go into the next phase, once Beau came home.

Tell Miss Sam she might end up alone ...

Sam shut out Bobul's words. It was foolish to put too much stock in something he'd said weeks ago and in another country. *Beau will be home. I will be strong and energetic for him.* She speared a slice of turkey and one of cheese from the salad and munched them down.

"Remember, I told you I was able to read the book after handling the box?" Kelly set her fork down and opened the leather-bound book to a random page. "Well, the ability only lasts a short while. Right now, it looks like gibberish to me again."

Sam had a sinking feeling. "What was I thinking? I should have given you the combination to our safe and had you bring the other box. I could be using it to help Beau now."

Kelly's eyes widened. "No! We have to be really careful when we bring them together. That's what I wanted to tell you. What I read in the book talks about the power of the three boxes. If all three boxes come together at once, there's a strong chance that their power will go to the evil side. Yours, Virtu, causes good things to happen. Mine, Manichee, is neutral—it picks up the intention of the user. The third one, Facinor, which we believe Marcus Fitch has right now, is evil. Bobul told me that, and the book confirms it. If Facinor and Manichee come together, they'll both go to the evil side and their power will overcome that of Virtu."

Sam felt the dizziness return. "Are you sure about all this? I've never experienced—"

"It's what the book says. I don't think we can dare take the chance, especially not with Beau in critical condition."

"I need to get back to the hospital," Sam said, placing the lid on her salad container and standing.

"In a few minutes. There's something I want to try first." Kelly finished her salad and wiped her hands. "You have the box with you, Mom? Get it from your bag."

Sam did so.

"Okay, run your hands over it and give it a chance."

"But, it didn't—"

After a couple of minutes Kelly reached for the box and held it. In her hands the wood began to warm and glow.

"Okay, Mom, open the book and see if you can read it."

Sam felt skeptical but she complied. She stared at the page—words appeared in English. "My god."

"Tell me what it says."

Sam sent her daughter a puzzled look, but she read the first few lines.

"Good." Kelly seemed relieved. "There was a passage I read earlier that made me wonder if we would see the same things. We do."

"I wonder why I can handle this box and read the book, but I wasn't able to help Beau with it."

Kelly shrugged. "I have a feeling there are many things we don't yet know about these boxes."

Wasn't that the truth? Sam thought.

"Take the book with you to the hospital," Kelly suggested, "and the box. You need something to take your mind off staring at those monitors endlessly, and maybe you'll find something in here that can help—both with Beau's situation and for the long term."

Long term. Sam couldn't think beyond the moment when Beau would open those beautiful blue eyes of his and give her one of the smiles that had first melted her heart. He had to. He simply had to. And if she could find help in this book—anything—she'd take it. Afterward—the long term—that remained to be seen. It was tempting to consider destroying the two boxes, burning the book, whatever it took to get Marcus Fitch and that OSM group to leave her alone. And the sooner that could happen, the better.

"Okay, you're getting antsy, Mom. I'll take you back." Kelly placed the box and book in Sam's backpack purse, and they briefly discussed which items to take to the hospital and which to leave in the hotel room. Sam settled on her makeup bag and one fresh shirt.

On the way out to Kelly's car, she said "On less urgent matters, I got Riki to watch Ranger and Nellie at her place, until you get home. They were both really happy with that solution; they love her."

"I'm sure they were. I can picture the way those dogs get all waggy and excited."

"Oh, no, they actually told me." Kelly grinned over the roof of the car. "I looked Ranger in the eyes and he said, quote 'I love Riki' unquote."

Sam knew Kelly wanted to cheer her up, so fine. She gave the smile her daughter wanted to see. By the time they returned to the hospital Sam was eager to get to the ICU and check on Beau. Kelly insisted she take a moment to show Sam where her truck was parked, even though Sam swore she wouldn't be going anywhere.

"Jen wants to give you a call sometime," Kelly said as they rode the elevator. "She says everything's fine at the bakery and chocolate factory. She just wants to hear your voice and check on you. I thought that was really sweet."

"It *is* nice. I'll give her a call tonight."

But the higher the elevator carried her, the more remote her everyday life seemed. This was her world now. It almost felt as if she'd traveled to a foreign country where they spoke a different language, and she had lost all touch with home. But that was how it would be until Beau could leave here.

She emerged from the elevator to be met by a handsome man in a dark suit.

"Rick Gonzales, FBI. Is there somewhere we can talk?"

Chapter 52

Marcus struggled to wakefulness through a veil of pain. When he raised his arm to get a look at his watch, a bolt of hot lightning shot into his side. The watch said 7:28. Was it morning or night? The dim light inside the camper provided not much clue.

Unless he'd slept twenty-four hours it must be evening. There'd been a convenience store, a broken window, an excruciating walk, all remembered as a blur. Mind-boggling pain as he doused his wound in alcohol and taped on a bandage. The handful of aspirin must have permitted the long sleep. He rolled toward the edge of the too-narrow couch bed and nearly fell off, his breath catching in a small, girly shriek.

He was dying to pee, but it took a good five minutes to get himself standing and to shuffle to the back of the camper and the phone-booth-sized bathroom. He relieved himself, holding his breath against the growing stench. Too bad he couldn't risk the use of the water pump to flush the thing. If he could get back to his car he should bring back extra bottled water for the purpose.

Thinking of the car reminded him that he likely had received a ticket for failing to pay another park fee in the new area where he'd left it. He hoped he could remember where that was. He used a thin terry cloth towel and wiped sweat from his face and neck.

On the table sat the stolen first aid supplies and his remaining half bottle of drinking water. He tipped a handful of aspirin into his hand and swallowed them. Now he had about a quarter cup of water. Yeah, he had to get back to the car—and soon. But he had to wait until the campground activity settled for the evening. Three more hours or so.

He let out a ragged breath and sat on the edge of the couch-bed, noticing his wound had oozed during his sleep, and the tan plaid upholstery had a circle of red on it. He looked down at his side.

The bullet had entered a couple of inches below his ribcage and exited straight through the back. He supposed he should be thankful it wasn't inside him, but even the relatively clean wound was already showing the violent red and puffiness of infection. If he could get into a pharmacy he might be able to make off with some antibiotics … but those places had much better security and locks than the rinky-dink place last night. Better if he could get to the OSM airplane and have them fly him back to the big, anonymous city where no one was looking for him.

A new thought occurred. He could make it back to

his car, drive far enough to get a cell signal, and call the pilot. He'd seemed like a regular guy, helpful. If he said the right things and offered enough cash, someone could drive down here, pick him up and drive him through the checkpoints, or at least the pilot could fly the plane to a closer airport. The plan comforted him and the aspirin seemed to be taking the edge off the pain. He leaned into the cushions and drifted back into an uneasy sleep.

When he woke, it was pitch dark. He struggled to sit and then stubbed his toe when he began fumbling around to find the flashlight. By its narrow beam he could see that his wound was bleeding worse. Maybe the aspirin hadn't been such a great idea.

He gritted his teeth while he ripped off the bloody bandages and replaced them with clean. He hoped that sheriff really was dead. It would be a pisser to go through this and find out the guy's Kevlar vest had taken the shots. At least he could take a little pride in having gotten off the first shot. There was no lawman who would have missed Marcus's heart by this far unless he'd been knocked off balance first.

Water. More bandages. Stronger pain killers. The plane. His life depended on his getting out of here. He started for the camper door. Wait—he told himself he wasn't thinking straight. Where was the flashlight? Oh yeah. And his jacket to cover the massive red place on his shirt, and his gun, just in case. Oh, and he'd be nowhere without his phone and car key.

Marcus staggered out of the small RV, wishing he believed in a God who would save him, the way his cousin Maurilio did. Unfortunately, in the real world outside the Vatican, a man had to look out for himself.

Chapter 53

Rick Gonzales was one of the good guys. Beau had talked about him. He had honest eyes and a sympathetic manner as he sat across from Sam in an empty waiting room they'd found on the surgical floor. Kelly had gone along to the ICU, where she would try another session with the box and a hands-on treatment for Beau's wounds.

Rick asked first about Sam, how she was coping, and she gave the answer he wanted to hear. She would be okay, Beau would be fine.

"We're on the trail of this Marcus Fitch," he told her. "We know he's wounded. There were blood drops leading away from your house. Every hospital and medical facility in the area has been notified and he hasn't shown up."

Sam felt a small measure of pride that at least one of Beau's shots had hit the mark. She would have been happy to hear Gonzales say that Fitch had been found dead nearby. Something stopped her from voicing it aloud.

"When we traced his movements, he didn't show on any commercial flight manifest. The last charge on any of his credit card accounts was for a rental car in Colorado Springs. We got the car information and there's a BOLO on it."

"How—?"

"Private jet. We checked the general aviation facilities at COS—Colorado Springs—and learned a Learjet registered to an organization called OSM had landed there, stayed overnight, but left again this morning. The flight plan said it was going to San Francisco. Do you have any ideas about that?"

"Not really. I'm aware of this OSM group, but Marcus Fitch is the only member of it I've had any firsthand contact with. I understand they have offices in Washington, DC."

"That's our understanding, but it's really low key and doesn't seem to be a part of the US government or any lobbying group that we've been able to trace."

"No, it isn't. From what I've been told, it's some kind of group with an interest in artifacts." Sam paused, choosing carefully what to reveal. "There's another organization, a non-profit called The Vongraf Foundation, in Alexandria, Virginia. Isobel St. Clair is the director, and she can tell you more about OSM, probably even give you the names of OSM's leaders."

"I think we've already gotten that far. The director is an older man, Elias Swift, and our agents have spoken to him. On the surface he seems to be somewhat cooperative. Claims Fitch has 'gone rogue' and is not following any OSM orders."

It was the second time Sam had heard the term and the

second time OSM had denied knowing of Fitch's actions. Could it be true? Or was it just the official line, in order to keep scrutiny away from the organization itself?

She found that she didn't care. As long as Beau's life hung in the balance, her attention would be fully on him. She felt herself becoming itchy to go back to his side, and the FBI man picked up on it. He wished her well and said he would be back in touch.

Kelly was standing at Beau's bedside when Sam walked in.

"Any change?" Sam knew her voice almost sounded desperate.

Kelly shook her head. "The, um—" she glanced up to be sure none of the medical staff was near. "The box worked as before. My hands are warm." She touched Sam's arm to demonstrate. "But he still doesn't respond. I don't know what else to do."

Sam hugged her daughter and felt a soothing warmth settle into her own body. She'd needed that. "You go back to Scott. I've got some phone calls to make, and I'm going to try to actually sleep tonight. The shower and fresh clothes were a good idea, Kel. Thanks."

She walked Kelly to the door and watched as she said good night to the nurses at their desk. A glance at the time told her it wasn't too late on the east coast. She dialed Isobel St. Clair's personal number and recapped briefly what Rick Gonzales had said.

"He called this morning and I tried to be helpful," Isobel said, "without giving away too much. He asked about the motive for Marcus Fitch to come out west and why he would be tracking you down. I just said OSM was interested in some old artifacts and believed you had one of them."

"Thanks for that. I've been trying to avoid specifics. Hard to explain magic to a straight-up agent like that. It's not the kind of thing law enforcement puts much stock in."

"Right. Anyway, he has the name of the OSM director and has talked to him. I got the distinct feeling Mr. Gonzales was willing to listen to Elias Swift's disclaimers, but that he still doesn't fully trust anyone there."

"Neither do I," Sam said.

"You *should* be skeptical. Apparently Swift's story is that they simply want to talk to you about purchasing this old box you own and Fitch was originally sent to negotiate that. The others claim to know nothing about the lengths he's going to."

And none of them knew Kelly had the second box yet. Sam would see to it that secret was kept safe. What she said to Isobel was, "I don't care how much they offer—with my husband lying here at death's door, I'm not parting with it."

It was the first time she'd said it aloud, the acknowledgement that Beau really could die. She barely got through saying goodbye to Isobel.

There were other calls to make but she needed to get herself together first. She stashed the wooden box out of sight in her bag and walked to the nurses' station. The night nurse looked up in sympathy.

"You look tired, Mrs. Cardwell. Can I get you anything?"

"Is there some place to get a cup of tea without having to go down to the cafeteria? I've already been away too long."

The young nurse looked as if she wanted to deliver a little lecture on caring for oneself, but all she did was smile. "I'll take care of it for you. Go, give your husband a hug. I'll be right back."

Behind one of the anonymous doors on the ward there must be an employee lounge, Sam guessed, because the nurse returned less than five minutes later with a tall cup of hot water and two tea bags on a tray. "I wasn't sure if you'd want regular or chamomile." She handed over the small tray and gave Sam's shoulder a pat.

Sam dunked the chamomile bag into the cup. Although she would have loved the caffeine hit from the black tea, she knew everyone was right. She really did need to sleep tonight. She took Beau's hand, staring at his face and then the monitors. Nothing had changed. She spoke softly to him, assuring him of her love and the good wishes of all their friends. Not a flicker behind the eyelids, but she felt in her heart—she knew—he surely must be able to hear her.

Kelly said Jen had asked about them. Everyone at the bakery was worried. Sam picked up her phone and dialed. She sipped her tea while Jen went through a list of assurances that all was going along all right at the bakery.

"I also talked to Benjie this afternoon," Jen said, "and he's got it all under control at the chocolate factory. They sent a big shipment out today for Book It Travel's charter jet clients."

"Thanks. I appreciate your checking on everything for me."

"Sam, you know if there is anything, *anything* at all … You have so many friends in this town, and everyone wants to help if they can."

Sam nodded, tears blurring her vision again. "I know. I can't think what to ask for. Just prayers, I suppose."

"*Everyone* is doing that," Jen said with a small chuckle. "They're even writing them down and bringing them to the shop. You have quite a collection of good wishes and cards already."

"Thank you. Tell everyone …" Her mind went black. What *would* she tell everyone? "Just tell them thanks."

Jen's words and descriptions ran through her mind after she hung up, but Sam had a hard time putting herself back into the world of the bakery. Right now, the universe revolved around this tiny glassed-in room and the man who was the center of her life.

Chapter 54

Marcus gritted his teeth against the pain as he limped to his car, where he'd left it deep in the forest. It had rained during the afternoon, and he hoped the vehicle wouldn't become mired in mud. He hadn't dared to leave it parked on any of the paved or graveled roadways. His wound was leaking again, despite the new bandages he'd applied just before leaving the camper tonight.

A jolt of pain shot through him as he edged into the driver's seat. He started the car to give his cell phone battery a charge while he took a few minutes to catch his breath. Dammit, dammit, *dammit!*

He concentrated on breathing and brought the pain slightly under control. He *must* get to that airplane! He put the car in gear and backed up, thick bushes scraping the side of the car. Couldn't *anything* go in his favor? He drove the same route he'd taken two nights ago, bypassing the convenience store where surely his little midnight raid had been discovered. The place didn't seem to be swarming with cops, but no doubt it was on their watch list now.

A couple miles farther along he spotted a Forest Service office on the left. No lights, no vehicles, but there were a couple of buildings. He could get out of sight behind them while he made his calls.

The pilot's number rang four times and Marcus was sure it would go to voicemail when a grumpy sounding voice answered. He explained that he'd been delayed.

"So, can I get you to fly into another airport? The map shows one just outside Raton, New Mexico." He couldn't very well say he didn't dare get on the interstate and head for Colorado.

"You're kidding, right?" said the pilot. "You didn't show and we got another call. Took off early yesterday morning. The aircraft is in San Jose right now, and we're scheduled for Omaha in the morning."

"Wait a minute—I had you booked." Marcus's head was beginning to throb.

"Yeah, three days ago. An airplane on the ground ain't earning any money, bub."

"Hey! Show some respect. OSM pays you very well. You need to get back here and pick me up."

"Too freaking bad. The head office called and rescheduled us. I don't know what you did to piss them off, but you aren't my client anymore, and I don't like being waked up in the middle of the night." The line went dead.

The organization will disavow any knowledge of you …

A cold sweat broke out on his forehead. Where could he turn?

He thought of Maurilio. They were blood—surely

Maury wouldn't let him down. It had to be mid-morning in Europe by now. He tapped the private number of his cousin's Vatican office.

"Maury, I'm in trouble in New Mexico."

"Marcus—what are you—?"

"Wait, just listen. That wooden box you gave me … I needed to get the others … I just wanted to talk with the lady that has one. But then the sheriff of Taos—" He realized he wasn't making sense, but his fevered mind couldn't think straight. He began to sob. "Maury, can you come get me?"

"Marcus. Listen to yourself. How would I just 'come get you'? I'm in Vatican City. The Holy Father has an appearance before a huge crowd in just a few hours. I couldn't come if I wanted to."

If he *wanted* to? "But we're cousins. Blood means more than—"

"It used to, Marcus. It used to. But you've used me too many times. This last time, switching passports with you, giving you something that rightfully belongs in the archives here—you've pushed it too far. I have to answer to God for those things, and you need to beg His mercy and get some help."

Marcus's eyes widened in disbelief. This was *not* the Maury of their childhood. Where was the fun-loving kid who readily switched places in school to fool the nuns?

"Good luck to you, my son. I shall keep you in my prayers." The call disconnected.

My son? What kind of pompous ass had Maury turned into? Marcus flung his phone away but it only bounced off the inside of the windshield, hit the passenger front seat, and fell into the darkness below. He reached for it and saw bright specks in front of his eyes as fresh pain ripped through his gut.

Chapter 55

Sam dozed on the makeshift bed until movement caught her attention. She snapped to and sat up. Beau had been awake and speaking, in her dream. But when she started for the bed, she saw that his eyes were closed and the machine was breathing for him. A new nurse stood beside the monitor, checking something.

"Sorry—didn't mean to wake you," she whispered. "Everything's okay." She smiled and left the room.

Nothing is okay. Nothing will be okay until he smiles at me and I can tell him how much I love him.

She reached into her pack and picked up the box Kelly had left with her. *Manichee, help me to help Beau. Please* … But the box remained dark, her hands cold. She cradled the box in her arms and leaned sideways to lie down, but sleep eluded her.

The room felt chilly. She got up and pulled an additional blanket over Beau, then found one for herself and wrapped it around her shoulders. The nights were so *long* here. But the days were no better.

Remembering something, she pulled the leather-bound book from her pack. Would the words make sense now or were they only readable when Kelly was present? She curled her legs up onto the bed and cuddled pillows around herself for the slight bit of comfort they provided. She opened the book to the first page. At first the letters appeared to be runes. Then, gradually, the words appeared to her in English and she began to read.

She skimmed the sections Kelly had already told her about, the revelation that the three boxes together would likely turn toward the side of evil because of the influence of Facinor. There was a chapter detailing the good things the box Virtu was capable of—Sam smiled because she had experienced many of them, along with a few things the book didn't talk about. Together, Virtu and Manichee provided even stronger positive forces, said one chapter.

She began to notice small details about the book itself. The pages were not all of the same paper. In fact, some sections appeared to be much older than others, although they were all connected together into the same binding, all within the sturdy leather cover. The hand-lettered wording was different throughout the book, as well, not only in calligraphic style, but in word usage. It seemed the book had multiple authors.

Most likely it was a collection of knowledge from several sources, which someone had gathered together and bound as a book—that was the most likely explanation. Sam had been flipping through the pages randomly, admiring the thick paper and handmade quality of the book, when a heading jumped out at her.

Destroy Facinor

Maria Obrenivici gives the spell which will destroy the box Facinor.

Sam blinked. Could the writer be the witch Bobul had spoken of? It seemed way beyond coincidence that a Romanian name would be linked with the name of the bad one of the three boxes. In the dim light of the hospital room she read on. *Fire cannot destroy it*, she'd written. Bobul had told Sam as much, soon after she'd met him. *The box cannot be crushed. It cannot be thrown from a cliff or drowned in the sea.* Whether or not any of it was true, it seemed this Maria woman believed she had discovered a way to rid the world of what she, at least, considered one of the worst of the true evils. And the method she described in detail had not existed until fairly recent history.

Sam turned the book over and looked inside both front and back covers, wondering exactly *when* this volume had been written.

Chapter 56

Sam's cell phone rang before she was fully awake. She was tempted to ignore it but it could be Evan or Rico with news. She threw her blanket aside and picked it up. The number on the ID was Stan Bookman's. She wondered if the man ever slept, but odds were he was in some other country where it was already midday.

"Sam—great news. I hope I didn't catch you at a bad time," he said.

A cynical laugh caught in her throat. There hadn't been a good time for days now. "Stan, I—No, it isn't a good time. I'm at the hospital with my husband."

"Oh, gosh. I hope nothing serious." Before she could explain, he went on. "I wanted to let you know Cruceros Privados is thrilled with the latest samples they received, and they're ready to roll. They need to know how soon they might add your chocolates to their High Tea menu."

"Stan, I don't know. Beau's in critical condition and I can't think beyond that right now."

"Oh. Sam, I didn't know. I'm so sorry. If there's anything I can do, a service I can provide …"

"I appreciate that, Stan. I can't think right now, and I'm sorry I don't have an answer for the cruise people. Can they delay this decision for a little longer?"

"We'll work out something. You take care."

She could hear the disappointment in his voice. He was a man who liked to solve a business problem and move on. She slipped her shoes on and checked on Beau, then fluffed her hair, took advantage of the sink in the room to brush her teeth, and wandered toward the nurses' station.

"Coffee, Sam?" asked the head nurse, getting a nod in return. "You can go on in our break room. You're practically family."

The woman gave a warm smile and indicated an unmarked door to her left. Sam walked in to the scent of fresh coffee—a better brand than that sold in the cafeteria, she could tell. The young nurse who always came for the lab draws was pouring herself a cup and offered to do the same for Sam. An orderly sat on a long couch, working his phone with both thumbs while he kept an eye on a wall-mounted TV tuned to a news channel.

Sam glanced up at it. She hadn't seen any news for a week now. The story was apparently about the pope delivering a message to a crowd of people in Vatican City. The camera zoomed in close and caught the man's kindly face as he repeated whatever he'd just said, this time in Italian. But what caught Sam's attention was the man standing on the balcony directly behind the church's leader.

It was Marcus Fitch.

He wore the red robes of a cardinal and stood with his hands folded at his waist, his eyes directed toward the man speaking. Sam pulled her phone from her pocket and quickly located Rick Gonzales's number.

"Fitch is in Italy," she blurted out. "He's on television right now."

The nurse and orderly stared at her, and the nurse set the full Styrofoam cup down.

"Which channel? Okay, I've got it. Wow. How could he—?" There were voices in the background. "Okay. Sam? We're checking it out. I'll let you know what happens."

Sam paced the length of the break room, then picked up her coffee and went back to Beau's room. Still no change, she noted as she automatically looked at the monitors.

"Honey, we're close to catching Marcus Fitch," she said to him. Nothing changed on his face.

She drank too quickly from the coffee cup and flinched at the burn. How had Marcus escaped the country with so many lawmen looking for him? He was surely on so many wanted lists that he couldn't have boarded a plane. Plus, she remembered Gonzales telling her their suspect was wounded. She was about to call Evan—surely the Taos County Sheriff's Office would get news quickly, and she knew she would be higher on Evan's priority list than that of the FBI—then Doctor Albertson walked in.

"Well, our patient is responding remarkably well," he said. "I've never seen this extensive a wound heal so quickly."

Sam knew the reason for that. "But you said you withdrew whatever medication was keeping him asleep. Why doesn't he wake up?"

Albertson shrugged and gave a rueful smile. "In many ways, coma patients are still a mystery to us. Sometimes we know the reasons, sometimes we don't. I had one patient who remained in a coma for more than a month, then one day woke up seeming rested and refreshed."

"So, what happens next?"

"We'll remove the breathing tube this morning. There's no need for it now, and some of the other monitoring devices can go. He's ready to move to a regular room, in my opinion."

Sam felt a moment of panic. "Doctor, don't forget this is a lawman who was shot on duty. The man responsible is still at large." Although having seen Fitch on TV this morning was somewhat reassuring, the fact remained that the man would not rest until he'd taken the prize he wanted.

"I'll speak to APD and see if a guard can be posted at his door."

See *if?* Sam vowed she would go further than that. The moment the doctor left the room, she dialed Rick Gonzales.

"Sam, I was about to call you. Sorry to report, the man on TV isn't Marcus Fitch."

"So he could still be in New Mexico."

"It's possible. I've got a call coming in—I'll get back to you as soon as I know anything else."

Okay … she didn't get the chance to tell Gonzales about needing a guard for Beau, but maybe his own department could get the message through to the right people. If nothing else, she'd bet that Evan or Rico would drive down here and sit outside the room himself. She dialed the sheriff's office and asked for Evan.

"Sam! Great timing. I just got a call from Colfax County. They have Marcus Fitch in custody. Rico and I are driving over to Raton to arrest him."

Sam tempered her relief with caution. What if this was another false sighting?

Chapter 57

A hundred questions raced through Sam's mind. She stood by as the nurses came into the room and removed Beau's breathing apparatus and made little adjustments to all the various tubes connected to him.

Was Fitch really under arrest? Could it be true?

"All right, Sheriff Cardwell," said the head nurse, addressing Beau and patting his hand. "You're getting a change of scenery."

The woman's voice was so perky and cheerful Sam hoped Beau really could hear what was going on around him.

"You can take the time to gather your things, Sam, and then come along whenever you're ready. We're going down one floor in the elevator, and he'll be in room 306."

Sam didn't need any prep time. All she'd brought

was her backpack purse, which contained the box and the book, along with bare necessities for the overnight stays. At Kelly's insistence, she'd been back to the hotel once each day for a shower and fresh clothes, while Kelly had come to the hospital to *treat* the wounds. And it had worked! Despite the fact that Beau hadn't yet opened his eyes or spoken to her, she felt the first hint of optimism. She followed his wheeled bed as the staff rolled him along the hallways.

Evan called a couple of hours later, just about the time Sam was already bored with the new room. No guard had been posted near the door, but she supposed the danger might be past. At least that's what she hoped Evan would say.

"Sam, it's definitely Fitch and we've placed him under arrest. It was a lucky turn for us."

She tapped the speaker button on her phone and set it where she hoped Beau would hear.

"Tell us everything," she begged. "Where was he caught. He didn't injure anyone else, did he?"

"It's a little complicated, but no one else was hurt. He's in the hospital in Raton. Some hikers found him in the forest outside Ute Park, passed out on his face, with a pretty ugly wound in his side."

The rest of the story had been pieced together. The hikers had put Fitch in their SUV and driven him to the hospital, figuring it would take too long to call 911 and get a response that far out. Draped around one shoulder was a backpack so they'd brought that along, too, and it contained Fitch's ID and passport. Once the doctors in the ER determined the injury was a bullet wound, someone remembered law enforcement was looking for this guy and a quick-thinking orderly strapped his arms to the metal bed rails.

"Good thing," Evan said. "He started to come around and was madder than a hornet. He would have tried to make a dash for it. But doc says he wouldn't have gotten far. He's got a nasty infection in the wound, so he'll be confined for a while. He's under arrest, so a Colfax County deputy is stationed there to keep watch. We'll be bringing him back to Taos once he can travel, but I think the FBI has an interest here, too."

As if by telepathy, Sam's phone rang with a second call and she saw it was Rick Gonzales. She let it go to voicemail. She was getting more information from Evan.

"How did Fitch get so far from Taos? He must have had a car."

"Right. And we think we have that, as well. A sharp park ranger spotted a sedan in one of the little day-camping areas. Said it had been there more than three days, so he took a look. It had the wrong type of license plate, one that began with RV, meaning it could only be registered to a recreational vehicle. We're guessing Fitch knew we had the BOLO out for the car with Colorado rental tags, and he must have thought it smart to switch it for a New Mexico one. He just didn't know how easily that one would have stood out if he'd been pulled over."

"Was there a box among his things?" Sam asked, half dreading the answer.

"Yeah, come to think of it. We did log in something like that. Why?"

"I can't tell you much at this point, but just be sure you lock that box away someplace safe. Keep it in the evidence locker and don't turn it over to any other agency, okay?"

"It has something to do with one of these shootings?"

What could she say? "Indirectly." A new idea was forming in her mind. "I'll talk to you about it when I'm back in Taos."

Sam watched Beau's face for signs that he could hear Evan's voice. There was no reaction, and her mood dipped a little. She thanked Evan for the call and told him to thank the hospital staff who'd recognized Fitch and detained him. Then she turned to Beau.

"Honey, it's coming together. They caught the guy. Everything's going to be okay." At least she hoped it would. He still hadn't responded. She squeezed his hand then dialed Rick Gonzales.

"Hi Sam, I wanted to thank you for the tip about the Marcus Fitch you thought you spotted in Italy. Turns out the guy at the Vatican is Fitch's first cousin. With an inter-departmental link, we were able to interview him by video chat. Name's Maurilio Fitch. It's uncanny how much alike they seem, although this Maurilio spilled everything once he found out how serious the charges were. He claims all he did was switch places with Marcus for a flight from DC to Rome, then the two of them met up in Ireland for a couple days."

"So that blows Marcus's alibi for the day of the shooting, when we thought there was no way he could have been in New Mexico," Sam said. "He was the one who killed Tony Robards." She didn't voice the idea that either Isobel St. Clair or Sam herself had really been Fitch's intended victim.

"When I asked the reason behind the trips and why they met in Ireland, Maurilio really didn't want to answer. But when we pushed, he admitted he'd taken a really old artifact from some deep, dark place in the Vatican archives, at Marcus's insistence, of course. The trip to Shannon was to deliver this box."

The box Evan had now confiscated.

Gonzales was still talking. "Based on his cousin's testimony we got a warrant to search Fitch's Georgetown condo and I'm happy to say that our agents found a Tikka T3 assault rifle under the floorboards of the bedroom closet. Ballistics tests are being run on it now."

When the call ended Sam felt as if her insides were buzzing.

Chapter 58

With mixed feelings, Sam agreed to leave the hospital and spend a night at the hotel with Kelly. Scott had needed to return to his university job in Taos, and Kelly insisted Sam could use a better night's sleep than she could possibly get with the makeshift arrangement in the hospital.

They ordered room service and sat on the beds in their pajamas.

"This reminds me of middle school," Kelly said. "You and me, pizza and sleeping bags on the living room floor. I'd put on some tunes and get you to dance with me."

Sam smiled. "Those were fun times. I wonder, at what point in my life did I stop being a fun person?"

"Deep down inside, you still are. It's just been an intense month."

"I think I started getting intense about everything

much further back than that."

She thought of the added responsibilities of the past couple of years. Going back, she'd begun to take life much more seriously about the time she was given the carved box, when she met Beau. Well, there comes a time when we all need to grow up.

Grow up, but don't become a drudge.

Sam flipped through the book of magic, reading only a phrase here and there, wondering if something would inspire her. And then it did.

"Kel, I've been thinking of something. I want to take Beau home."

"Mom … he's not conscious. What would you do? How would you care for him? How would you even get him there?"

"That last question is the easiest. Stan Bookman called me yesterday and offered to help. He's asked a lot of me in recent months—I think it's fine to ask something of him. We could arrange a plane to fly Beau to Taos."

"But then … what's next?"

"We've been using your box, Manichee, because I didn't have the other one here. You were able to heal his body—the doctor was frankly amazed at how rapidly the wounds have healed. With the power of Virtu, I believe I can heal his spirit. The book talks about that—healing the body as separate from healing the spirit. Do you think that's possible?"

"Mom, I think *anything* is possible."

A sensation of lightness filled the room. "Thank you."

The following morning Sam broached the subject with Doctor Albertson, minus the parts about magic. She had checked their insurance coverage. A home nursing service would be covered. And Sam could learn how to monitor and change the feeding and hydration bags. A proper bed could be rented and set up in the spare downstairs bedroom.

"I can't recommend such a drastic action," he said immediately.

"My husband will be better off at home," she insisted. "You've already told me there isn't much more you can do for him medically. He'll wake up from the coma when he's ready, and I can't imagine that he *must* be in this building for it to happen."

"I can't let you do this."

She gave him a level stare. *Watch me.*

He turned his back and walked away. Sam called Zoë, who knew a skilled nurse practitioner.

"Sam, you have two businesses to run. How will you handle all this?" were Zoë's first words.

"Better than I'm handling it from Albuquerque," Sam replied. "I need to be back in Taos. Beau needs to be back there. Can you contact your nurse friend, or at least give me her number?"

Within two days, Sam had the details arranged for the Taos end of the new setup—bed, nurse, medical supplies. The doctors in Albuquerque all tried to talk her out of making the move, and Albertson ended up writing "Patient checked out against medical advice" in large letters across the form. The ICU nurses wished them well. An ambulance service made the transfer to the waiting airplane, Sam rode at Beau's side, and Kelly drove Sam's truck home.

The visiting nurse insisted on staying at her patient's side through the first night, to monitor all vital signs and be sure the trip had not harmed him. It was after ten p.m.

when Sam sneaked the carved box out of the closet safe and carried it upstairs where she held it close and concentrated on pulling its healing energy into her hands.

She left the box upstairs and went down to her husband's side.

"I need a few minutes alone with him," she told the nurse. "The kettle on the kitchen stove is hot. Help yourself to something if you'd like."

Alone, Sam cupped her hands on each side of Beau's face and kissed him tenderly. If she'd been expecting a Sleeping Beauty wake-up scenario, it didn't happen. She continued to touch him, running her hands down his neck, across his shoulders and down the arms. Still no change. His chest and shoulder still showed angry red scars from the wounds. She placed a hand over each area and let the warmth seep into his skin. Nothing happened. Disappointment surged over her. She'd felt so certain about this.

She lowered herself onto the bedside chair and watched. Sitting beside his bed in the spare bedroom was only a slight improvement over sitting by a similar bed in the hospital. The reminders were still there, the prognosis still so uncertain. When the nurse returned, Sam bade her goodnight and went upstairs.

It would probably take more than one session, she told herself as she brushed her teeth. When Kelly touched the wounds it had taken several treatments. She repeated the thought like a mantra, then climbed into Beau's side of the king-sized bed, wanting to warm it for him.

Please, please, please … she whispered. Please let him be back in this bed beside me very soon.

Chapter 59

He did just great through the night," the nurse said the next morning as Sam poured two bowls of cereal in the kitchen. "From this point on, it's your choice how often to have me here. Of course, I'll at least come by twice a day to check on things, to replenish his hydration and nutrient bags."

Sam had gone to Beau's side immediately after she woke up, hoping to see a sign that he was aware of his surroundings, but nothing had changed. He lay on his back, peacefully sleeping, not a muscle moving.

"Can you stay for an hour or two this morning?" Sam asked. "I need to run a couple of errands and stock up on groceries."

"Certainly. I'd be happy to."

Among the errands was a stop at Puppy Chic, Riki's

grooming shop, where Ranger and Nellie would be waiting to come home. Maybe the presence of the dogs would be part of the magic formula to awaken Beau. Sam knew she was grasping at straws, but was willing to try whatever might work. Plus, Kelly was back on the job today and Sam wanted to run an idea past her.

"I'm coming with you," Kelly said. "This isn't something you should tackle on your own."

"We'll be back for the dogs soon," Sam told Riki after thanking her profusely for giving Kelly so much extra time off.

The sheriff's department felt different in subtle ways without Beau there. His private office stood dark and silent. It made Sam sad and glad at the same time. At least they expected Beau to return, had not replaced him. Although when she heard Dixie, the dispatcher, tell someone on the phone that she would put them through to 'acting sheriff Evan Richards' it sent a pang through her heart. If Beau didn't wake up and come back soon, the county would be forced to appoint someone else in his place.

She and Kelly walked into the squad room. Rico spotted them immediately and jumped up from his chair. Evan was on the phone but waved from his desk across the room.

"Sam, is anything changed?" Rico asked, his young face so hopeful it made Sam want to hug him.

She shook her head. "But we're hopeful. We just have to see how it goes now with him at home." She took his arm and led him toward Beau's office door. "I understand you caught the man who shot him."

Rico nodded.

"I want to see his personal effects."

The deputy wanted to ask why, she could tell, but his

natural respect for Beau's position kept the questions at bay. "Everything's in the evidence locker, as instructed."

Evan Richards had finished his phone call and he walked over. Sam repeated the request, and he signaled Rico to retrieve the box of evidence. He had the key to Beau's office, so he opened the door and switched on the lights.

"Mind if I ask what you're looking for?" he asked.

Sam was saved from an immediate answer when Rico showed up and placed the box on Beau's desk. Each item was bagged separately, she noticed, as was standard procedure. There was a navy and black daypack, which had probably been new a few weeks ago. Now it was stained with dark blotches of what might be blood and covered with a thick dusting of mountain dirt. A cell phone, a roll of gauze bandage, a lightweight windbreaker jacket, a nearly empty bottle of aspirin, a watch and a ring. The pistol—she couldn't look at it; her thoughts would run rampant.

And the box.

She stared at the carved object, so similar to hers but so different. The wood was nearly pure black and the stones shone with a dull glint. It was difficult to see their colors, although she suspected they would be the same red, green and blue she already knew. She wondered what happened to the artifact when it was touched—both by a person of good intent and by someone with bad wishes. She picked it up gingerly. Kelly drew in a sharp breath and took a step back.

"That was inside the backpack," Rico said. "Just an empty box. We can't figure out what he had it for."

Sam's fingers grew cold, as even through the plastic the

box exerted an influence.

"We have to get rid of this," she whispered. "It's too close to him."

"Ma'am, it's part of the evidence found on the suspect," Rico said. He also took a step back, she noticed.

Sam turned to Evan. "Is this box actually connected to the crime?"

He fidgeted from one foot to the other. "Well, not that we know. I mean there's no blood or trace evidence on it. Lisa checked it briefly, but she didn't seem to want to touch it much."

"And you have enough to take Fitch to trial without this box?"

"Oh, definitely. The rifle the Feds found is a match for the Robards killing, and this .45, well, it's a match for Beau—" Evan cleared his throat. "Marcus Fitch is going away forever, Sam."

"So the box was just a personal item that happened to be in Fitch's possession when you arrested him." Sam didn't break eye contact.

"What are you saying, Sam? You want to take it?"

"It's best if we have this conversation alone," she said, giving Rico the eye. The younger deputy took the hint and backed out of the room.

Sam's fingers were freezing now and she set the box down on the desk. "Evan, you'll have to trust me on this. If this box does not provide some direct evidence to the shooting, I need to take it with me."

"But—"

"I know about chain of evidence and all that. I also know that you are only the acting sheriff and this puts a burden on you. If there's a way to make it disappear from the list of Fitch's personal items, maybe you can make that happen. Or if you want to turn your back and later make a note that one item went missing from the box … that might be the way it goes."

Kelly tapped Sam's wrist. "Mom … there's the other thing … about the *method*."

Sam stopped. Kelly was right—they would need help with this.

The old witch's description in the book had said the boxes could only be destroyed by the same method they were created—a direct strike of lightning. She had brooded over this for days now. How would she manage, even if she carried the box into a thunderstorm, to assure lightning would strike the box and destroy it?

She turned to Evan again. "Do you happen to have a way to create an explosion?"

Chapter 60

They drove out into the desert at midnight, Evan's low headlights cutting through the black landscape. Appropriately, it was the night of the new moon. Starlight sparkled above but did not give off enough illumination for anyone to witness their mission

The property belonged to a rancher Evan had known, twenty miles west of Taos, covered in sagebrush with only two narrow tracks leading off the county road. It was one of those wannabe dreams, land that would one day become a sheep ranch—only it never had. The old rancher had died years ago, before building a single structure, and it seemed his heirs would never come claim the place. It was ideal for their purpose tonight.

Sam was, frankly, surprised she'd convinced Evan to help. It must have been something in the fact that she'd handled Virtu this morning, giving Beau another dose of its healing power. Maybe Evan had responded with kindness for the same reason. She didn't know. She only knew that he'd quietly brought out a brown paper bag to hold the box, and she had carried it out of the department without questions from anyone.

She had stashed the package in a locked cupboard at the Victorian chocolate factory, hoping—praying—the evil box would not somehow find a way out. She didn't dare take it home. Beau's condition was too fragile and her own abilities to deal with the bad side of magic too new. A half hour ago she had retrieved Facinor from the cupboard and gingerly carried it as she and Kelly met Evan for their mission.

Evan brought his black Jeep Wrangler to a stop. "This should be a good place," he said.

He'd dressed in military camouflage and the weapon he brought from the back of the Jeep made both Sam and Kelly stare wide-eyed. He hadn't directly answered her question about explosives. His silent nod was the only answer.

Using whispers and a flashlight with a red lens, he and Sam carried the evil box twenty-five yards farther down the dirt track.

"Take it out of the bag and set it there on the ground," he said.

She did as ordered, wadding up the paper sack and plastic evidence bag together.

"Go back to the Jeep."

For a moment Sam wondered what she'd got herself into, but Evan's confidence allayed her worries. He took a stance, aimed the grenade launcher, switched on a red beam trained on the box, and fired. The explosion seemed deafening in the quiet night, but it was gone in seconds. They waited in total darkness for two full minutes, but no sign appeared that anyone had noticed.

All three of them walked to the spot where the box had stood. A blackened smudge about three feet in diameter marked the dirt. Tiny shards of wood had landed in some of the sagebrush, and when Evan shone a light around Sam saw they were scattered over a wide area. Some of the pieces flamed for a few seconds before they died.

While Evan kicked dirt over the blackened earth, Sam felt relief wash over her. Facinor, the artifact whose powers had haunted her and enabled a killer, no longer existed.

Chapter 61

The drive back to town passed in silence, and Sam knew none of the three would speak of this again. Evan delivered the ladies to the driveway at the Victorian, where they had left their vehicles scarcely an hour earlier.

"It feels surreal, doesn't it?" Kelly said after Evan drove away. "A month ago, I didn't know about any of this. Tonight, I feel like we did something that will change the world."

Sam nodded. There was no way to explain it differently, although she still believed there was more to her mission. First, she had to get Beau back. She'd just reached into her pocket for her truck key when she sensed movement beyond the portico.

"Miss Sam. Miss Kelly." The voice was unmistakable.

"Bobul!" Kelly rushed forward, almost taking him into

a hug. His reserved demeanor stopped her a step short of physical contact.

"Bobul, how did you get here?" Sam asked. Silly, she realized. He never explained himself.

"Bobul bring a friend to meet you." He turned, and an old woman stepped from behind him. She was so tiny that his bulk had completely concealed her. "Bertha Martinez," he said.

"Bertha—?" Sam's thoughts flew back to the old woman who'd given her the box. But she had died that day.

The little woman in front of them laughed. "Yes, I'm Bertha Martinez, but the one you are thinking of was my aunt."

"Miss Bertha bring you a message," said Bobul.

Sam wasn't certain who he meant, since he kept looking at Kelly.

"It's about the boxes," Bertha said. "I suppose I should explain a little. I only knew my aunt for a brief time when I was a little girl. She had a legacy as a healer, a *curandera*, here in this area, and she wanted to pass that along to me. Unfortunately, my parents had careers and moved our family back east so I never got to know my namesake aunt very well. But from the time we spent together, I knew a little about the powers of the carved box."

Sam's smile froze. Was this Bertha here to reclaim the box? She thought of Beau—she still needed the box.

Bertha seemed to read her mind. "I am not here to take it. Nor yours," she said, facing Kelly.

Of course. Bobul would have told her about Kelly's find in England.

"From the time I was small I was enchanted with the story about the box. I combed libraries everywhere—my parents moved us around a lot—and I found small tidbits of information. I made it my lifelong hobby to learn what I could, and I eventually put together the story about there being three boxes. But I knew one was not good. That box gave men of evil intent the power to carry out their deeds."

Sam nodded. She knew all this by now, too.

"The bad one is gone now." Bertha said it without question. "I cannot say how I know this—it is just a feeling. The box was near here somewhere, and now it's gone."

Sam sent Kelly a warning glance. They still did not really know this woman.

"What I came to tell you—what Bobul brought me here for—is to let you know that the future of good magic rests with you now. Samantha and Kelly—together you will do great things."

"My husband … he's been gravely hurt …"

"All will be different now," Bertha said. "But it will turn out well. My aunt passed the box to you for a reason. I do not know what that reason is, but I trust her instinct in choosing you."

Sam remembered the day. She'd been breaking into houses back then, and coming upon the dying old woman in a supposedly empty house had been purely a fluke. Hadn't it?

"Virtu and Manichee are yours and Kelly's now, beyond a doubt. They are your destiny. Use them well. Practice using their power to achieve good things. And one day you will find another person to whom you will pass along each of the boxes. The answers will come to you, each in good time. Always remember, two are more powerful than one."

Bertha stepped aside, looping her thin arm through Bobul's. He patted her hand then raised two fingers to the brim of the wooly looking hat he always wore.

"Goodbye, Miss Samantha." He turned to face Kelly.

"Goodbye, Miss. You take care both."

Sam had been fiddling with her keyring and now it dropped to the ground. When she picked it up, Bobul and the mysterious Bertha were gone. Kelly had a curious smile on her face.

"I never quite get everything Bobul says. What did he mean by 'take care both'?" Sam asked.

Even in the dim circle of light from the Victorian's porch lamp, she could tell Kelly was blushing.

"I meant to save the news for after Beau wakes up. There's just been too much happening in recent weeks."

"Yes?" Definitely.

"Mom, I'm pregnant."

Sam grabbed her daughter in a hug. "No wonder Bertha said things will be different. Wow."

Kelly stood at arm's length. "She also said the power of the two of us is stronger than either alone. Don't you realize what that means?"

Sam was still trying to grasp the idea of becoming a grandmother.

"It means we both need to get to Beau's side." She spun toward her car, parked behind Sam's truck. "Now. Manichee is locked in the trunk. We're going to your house!"

Chapter 62

The night nurse was dozing on the cushy recliner chair in the corner of Beau's room when Sam and Kelly arrived home. Ranger and Nellie had settled at her feet, as if they felt they needed to be near Beau, as well.

"We don't dare use the boxes in front of her," Sam whispered in the living room. "We have no idea how this will go. She might witness something and the gossip around town could happen instantly.

"Right." Kelly had carried Manichee inside. "We could pretend we're just back from a night on the town and send her home."

Sam almost giggled at the idea. The last time she'd come in from a party she was home by ten. It was nearly two a.m. now. But she didn't want to wait until daylight to see if Bertha Martinez's advice would work.

"I'll never fall asleep anyway," she said. "I'll tell her."

The woman seemed a little peeved until Sam assured her she'd be paid for the full eight-hour shift. She gathered her things and said she would see Sam the next evening.

Let's hope not, Sam thought as she watched the nurse's car drive away.

Kelly was sitting on the sofa with the box on her lap. "Do you suppose there's some little ceremony we should do? Light some candles or incense or something?"

Sam emerged from the closet where she'd taken Virtu from the safe. "I have no idea. I haven't used them before. Of course, I've never blended the power of this box with another. And I don't think anyone else has stayed so stubbornly asleep as Beau."

"Well, let's just give it a go without props," Kelly said. "I say we take the boxes into his room and then maybe we touch them at the same time or something."

Sam felt a nervous flutter, some combination of fear and excitement, as she carried Virtu into the bedroom. Kelly carried Manichee. They closed the door, ordering the dogs to the living room, and took positions on each side of the bed. Beau lay quietly on his back, breathing evenly. Other than the tubes connected to him, he might have been simply enjoying a good night's sleep.

Both boxes were now glowing softly, golden. The stones on Virtu had become brilliant red, green, and blue. Sam's and Kelly's eyes met across the space above Beau's chest.

"Do we dare let them touch?" Sam whispered.

Kelly nodded. "According to the book, yes. I think that's when the power is greatest."

Leaning forward slowly, each woman held the box out toward the other. They were directly above the spot where Beau's most severe wound had been when the boxes touched.

A vibration began. Sam felt startled but kept her grip on the box. Now, a hum.

From the size of Kelly's eyes, she guessed her daughter was experiencing the same effect.

The humming sound rose in pitch, like a steaming tea kettle, then higher yet, until they could no longer hear it but knew it was practically screaming. The dogs, closed out on the other side of the door, were making frantic little sounds.

When do we let go? The thought flashed through Sam's mind, but the need to keep the boxes together was compelling.

A second later a light flashed and both women felt a jolt. The boxes dropped, repelled from each other by some unseen force, as if they were saying, *Now—it's done!*

Sam looked down. The boxes had landed on Beau's chest and tumbled away. They were lying at his sides now. But the real miracle was when she looked at his face. His eyes were open, blinking, and a beautiful smile came over his face.

"Beau! Beau, can you hear me?" Sam took his hand and looked into his ocean blue eyes.

"Sam—what's going on?" His gaze darted back and forth. "Kelly?"

"Oh my god, Beau—you're back," Kelly said.

Chapter 63

Inexplicably, Sam burst out crying. All the worry, the tension, the fear of the past weeks came to a head and then left her body. Beau reached for her hand but the confusion of the attached tubing drew his attention. Kelly circled the bed to Sam's side.

"Mom—we did it! Can you believe it!"

And with that, Sam was laughing and crying at the same time. They raised the head of the bed so Beau could see his surroundings.

Kelly wiped the moisture from her own eyes. "Look, I'm going to leave you guys alone. You have a lot to talk about, and I'm sure Scott didn't expect me to stay out all night."

She opened the bedroom door and both dogs rushed in, ecstatic to see Beau sitting up. He reached over the edge to pet them, speaking their names. Sam felt another rush of relief. The doctors had left her with the frightening idea that Beau might not recover his memory, that there could be permanent brain damage. So far, he had recognized everyone.

Kelly blew kisses to Sam and Beau before calling Scott to say she was on the way home. When Sam heard the front door close, she turned to Beau.

"Kelly and Scott are married," he said. He paused a moment, thinking. "The wedding was in the forest."

"Is that the last thing you remember?"

He shook his head slowly. "There was a murder case. We were working a murder …"

"Do you remember the name Marcus Fitch?"

His expression hardened.

She decided to skip the parts about Fitch coming after her and only briefly touched on the connections to OSM and The Vongraf Foundation, and the fact the FBI had been brought in and helped with the arrest.

"The good news is that Marcus Fitch is in jail. His attorney is pushing to move the venue, since the story has been front page throughout northern New Mexico for a while now. Evan and Rico have done a great job putting the evidence together for the attorney general's office and it looks pretty solid. Fitch won't be getting out."

"Okay," he said. "that's good."

Sam watched his face carefully. The indifferent response wasn't like the old Beau.

"You're tired," she said, "and I don't want to wear you out with too much detail at once."

She lowered the head of the bed a bit. "I'm going to stretch out in the recliner right over there. You just make a little sound if you need anything."

"I love you, Sam." His smile seemed a bit faded, but it was genuine.

She kissed his mouth gently. "I love you, too. Welcome back."

* * *

The day nurse came at nine, her tap on the door waking Sam from the first solid sleep she'd had in a long time. The woman exclaimed and fussed, and wanted to call in the news of Beau's improvement to her supervisor and report it to the doctors in Albuquerque.

"One thing at a time," Sam said. "Can you at least take out all those tubes and things? He wants to get up."

Cautions were issued about how weak his muscles would be and how he should take it easy with solid food and a dozen other things; Sam merely filed it all away. The phone had already begun to ring, starting about the moment Kelly would have arrived to work at Puppy Chic. Riki, Jen and the bakery staff, Evan and Rico. The outpouring of love was amazing, but Sam had to remain firm, especially with the deputies, that Beau wasn't quite up to taking phone calls yet.

When she saw the next call was from Stan Bookman, she preempted what he was about to say by thanking him profusely for the use of his plane in bringing Beau home.

"I'm happy to hear it has turned out so well," said Stan. "Such a relief. I hadn't wanted to bring it up, Sam, but the cruise line is still waiting for some answers …"

Sam felt a flash of irritation. Seriously? She had only got Beau back a few hours ago, and already it was business, business, business. She answered with a short "I'll have to get back to you on that" and hung up. She owed Stan a debt of gratitude, definitely, but she'd begun to see the relationship in a different light. The question was, how would she handle this?

She left her phone on the table and walked into the kitchen. While the coffee maker burbled and hissed, she fed the dogs and performed a few other automatic tasks. But her mind was focused on the bigger picture.

During the entire time of Beau's hospitalization and recovery, she had done a lot of soul searching, bargaining with the powers that be. If she got Beau back, she would reevaluate her life's priorities. Now a grandchild would be in the picture, and she knew changes were in order. The bakery and chocolate factory required a huge commitment of her time, and the latter would only become more demanding as time went on. Stan Bookman's call just now was a vivid reminder. And yet, she had signed a contract. How could she get out of it without serious legal and financial penalties?

She poured a mug of coffee for herself and one for the nurse. She carried them to the bedroom where the nurse was stowing equipment.

"Look at me," Beau said with a smile. "Free of wires."

"That looks awfully good to me," Sam told him.

"Looks like a miracle to me," said the nurse. "I've treated several coma patients over the years, but haven't seen one yet who talked about wanting to get up right away."

Beau sniffed the air. "Can I have some of that coffee?"

Sam looked toward the nurse.

"Try a sip and make sure it'll stay down."

Sam handed one mug to the nurse and gave her own to Beau. "You heard what she said. While you give it a try, I've got a phone call to make."

She went back to her phone and looked up a number. It would be late afternoon in Switzerland, but she hoped to get an old acquaintance, Wilhelm Schott, on the line right away. Her chocolate dilemma might have been solved.

Chapter 64

Six months later ...

Kelly looked as if she had a beach ball under her shirt as she directed placement of Valentine decorations in the front entry. Sam and Riki continued to twist strands of greenery laced with hearts along the stair railings and across the balcony. Jen was placing red, pink, and white flower arrangements along the center of the dining table. Zoë was in the kitchen, making certain there were enough napkins and place settings.

"Can we get that beautiful red and pink pendant thingy attached to the chandelier?" Kelly asked.

Beau steadied the ladder while Scott climbed it and aimed the hook toward a link between crystal pendants. The Valentine's Day wedding would take place in the grand entry hall of the Victorian. White chairs had been rented for the guests; Riki would come down the staircase to join Evan under the chandelier; a long table in the dining room would accommodate twenty-four friends in style. The caterers could take advantage of the professional-grade appliances that remained from the chocolate factory days.

Sam thought back. When she'd called Wilhelm Schott, president of the major Swiss chocolate company, *Qualitätsschokolade,* he was thrilled to purchase the Sweet's Traditional Handmade Chocolates brand, given that a huge contract came with it. His company had the facilities to produce the quantities the cruise line wanted, without hardly blinking an eye. Schott had purchased the brand name, the logos, recipes and techniques—including a supply of Sam's secret ingredient—and the contracts with Cruceros Privados and Book It Travel, all for an obscene amount of money. It didn't make sense to ship basic ingredients such as chocolate and sugar to Switzerland, nor the packing boxes and shipping supplies. *Qualitätsschokolade* had all that, so it was largely a matter of transferring title and paperwork.

In September Sam had spent a week at the big candy factory just outside Lucerne. It was a bittersweet experience, bidding her little business goodbye, but at the same time a huge relief. Beau's recovery from the coma had been steady, but slower than she had hoped. And his change of attitude toward his law enforcement career was another surprise. He'd watched the news of Marcus Fitch's trial during the winter months, but seemed detached as to the outcome.

He would remain on leave from his county job for a while longer. Evan Richards had assumed the role of acting sheriff. Both he and the county would decide, as it got closer to election time, whether Evan would run for the office officially. Much depended on whether Beau wanted to go back to work by then. With the money she'd received for the chocolate business, early retirement was definitely an option.

Scott came down the ladder and stepped back to appraise the decorations, draping an arm across Kelly's shoulders. They smiled at each other. Their new pet, a calico cat named Eliza, sauntered through the foyer, giving Kelly a knowing look. Cats were different communicators, she was discovering. Dogs told her, straight out, what was on their minds. The cat was far more subtle—and highly intelligent. She had showed up on the front porch the night they moved into the Victorian.

"Glad we bought the house?" she asked Scott.

"*So* glad." He turned her toward him and kissed her, as if the Valentine pendant above their heads were mistletoe.

"I love your change in career, too," she said.

"Temporary, so far," he reminded. "But let's hope it works into a permanent gig."

At the semester break in December, Scott had put in for a sabbatical from university teaching—the purpose was twofold: be home with Kelly when the baby came, and have several months to write. With all the research he'd done in and around Bury St. Edmunds and Cambridge, he had enough material for a book on the reclusive author, Eliza Nalespar, who'd grown up in the Victorian house. With the dead author's fame and the local connection to New Mexico, he'd been offered contracts from both US and UK publishers. The advance had been banked away to cover living expenses.

Already, Scott had ideas for other books, especially now that they had lived in the Victorian for a few months.

The creaky sounds from the old house gave him the idea for a series of children's books featuring a reclusive writer who lives in a haunted house and solves mysteries. When he'd run the idea past his agent, she raved, "That idea will probably earn you more than the book on the history of the old place."

Jen came in, slipping her arms into the sleeves of her coat. "Table is set—beautifully, I might add—and I'm off to pick up my dress for tomorrow from the seamstress. Becky says the cake is done, and she'll bring it when they come for the ceremony."

Zoë was close behind. "Darryl's home wondering what's for dinner," she said with a laugh. "He'd better watch out. He'll be having a bologna sandwich if he's not careful. I'll be back tomorrow early enough to watch over the caterer."

"Thanks, everyone," Riki called out from the balcony above. "See you tomorrow." To Sam, she said, "I'm going home for a nice long evening of mani-pedi and a facial. The guys can do the bachelor party thing if they want, but I shall be radiant tomorrow."

Sam kissed her cheek. "You're always radiant, you and that gorgeous English skin of yours."

Soon, it was the four of them—Sam, Beau, Kelly, and Scott—and they settled around the small kitchen table for a light supper. Beau had opted out of going along with Evan and the younger deputies for a night on the town. Sam watched him carefully, as she had for months now. Although he was as loving and attentive as ever with her, he'd lost some of the old spark and hadn't rebounded from the shooting as quickly as she'd hoped. These days he seemed content to tend to the animals and putter about the ranch, and he hadn't said anything about resuming his office as sheriff. But perhaps time would tell.

"I'm glad you chose salads for tonight's meal, Mom," Kelly said. "I can hardly eat anything these days without heartburn killing me."

"Two more weeks," Sam said with a smile. She faced Kelly's mid-section. "Are you ready for your appearance in this world, Miss Anastasia Sweet Porter?"

"Ow. Careful about talking to her—she answers with kicks."

Beau chuckled whenever Kelly said things like that. He helped Sam clear the dishes and then the men retired to the room Kelly had insisted Scott set up as his man cave, to watch football on the big screen TV. Sam cleaned up the kitchen while she heated water for tea.

"I wonder what the future holds," Kelly said. "The baby, Scott's writing career, so many things."

"The magic. I can't help thinking about Bobul's last visit, along with Bertha—niece of older Bertha. She said the two of us should embrace the magic, use the power we have together for good purposes. I'm trying to imagine how that will go."

Kelly laid both hands against her belly. "I'm beginning to wonder if it really will be the two of us. This one—she's showing some unusual signs …"

Sam stared at her daughter.

Kelly read her thoughts. "Nah. It's just me, my puffy ankles and sore ribs and too much time to think about things."

But it was true, Kelly had already been pregnant when she first encountered the power of the boxes. Could it be? Would Anastasia be born knowing things, with abilities they could only imagine? Sam found that her heart welled with hope and joy at the thought of that unknown future.

Thank you for taking the time to read *Sweet Magic*.
If you enjoyed it, please consider telling your friends or
posting a short review. Word of mouth is an author's best
friend and is much appreciated.
Thank you,
Connie Shelton

**Sign up for Connie Shelton's free mystery
newsletter at <u>connieshelton.com</u>
and receive advance information about new
books, along with a chance at prizes, discounts and
other mystery news!**

**Contact by email: connie@connieshelton.com
Follow Connie Shelton on Twitter, Pinterest,
Instagram and Facebook**

Connie Shelton is the *USA Today* bestselling author of more than 30 novels, and three non-fiction books. She teaches writing courses and was a contributor to *Chicken Soup For the Writer's Soul.* She lives in northern New Mexico with her husband and two dogs.

53695390R00204

Made in the
USA
Lexington, KY